A COLLECTION OF ⌐⌐⌐⌐
FROM THE WITCH WALKER WORLD

TALES
FROM
TIRESSIA

CHARISSA
WEAKS

Tales from Tiressia

FIRST EDITION

Cover and Title Art by Krafigs Design

For the readers who live on the spicier side of life.
These tales are for you

ALSO BY CHARISSA WEAKS

Recommended Reading Before Enjoying Tales from Tiressia

The Witch Collector

City of Ruin

The Wolf and the Witch

A NOTE ABOUT CONTENT

If you would like to know if this book contains any content or story elements that might be of concern to you, please visit the book's webpage.

Thank you and happy reading!

FROM THE AUTHOR

Hello little rebel,

The following stories will take you deeper into the Witch Walker world and our beloved characters' histories. While some scenes are alternate versions of their original counterparts, others are new tales that occurred long before Raina met Alexus on that fateful Collecting Day. If you've not read books one through three, I recommend doing so before reading this collection. I do include the opening pages from reimagined scenes to refresh your memory.

Though these Patreon nominated scenes were never meant to be canon, I sprinkled connections to the overall plot with each installment. However, A Winter's Wish, Paramour, Alexus's Dream, and To Kiss a Prince reveal important details from Colden, Alexus, Nephele, and the Prince of the East's pasts. Some even wed nicely to books four and five.

Also, please note that these scenes are very explicit, especially A Winter's Wish, which reveals much about Alexus and Colden's lives together prior to Raina. If you're game, sit back and let me tell you their stories.

~ Charissa

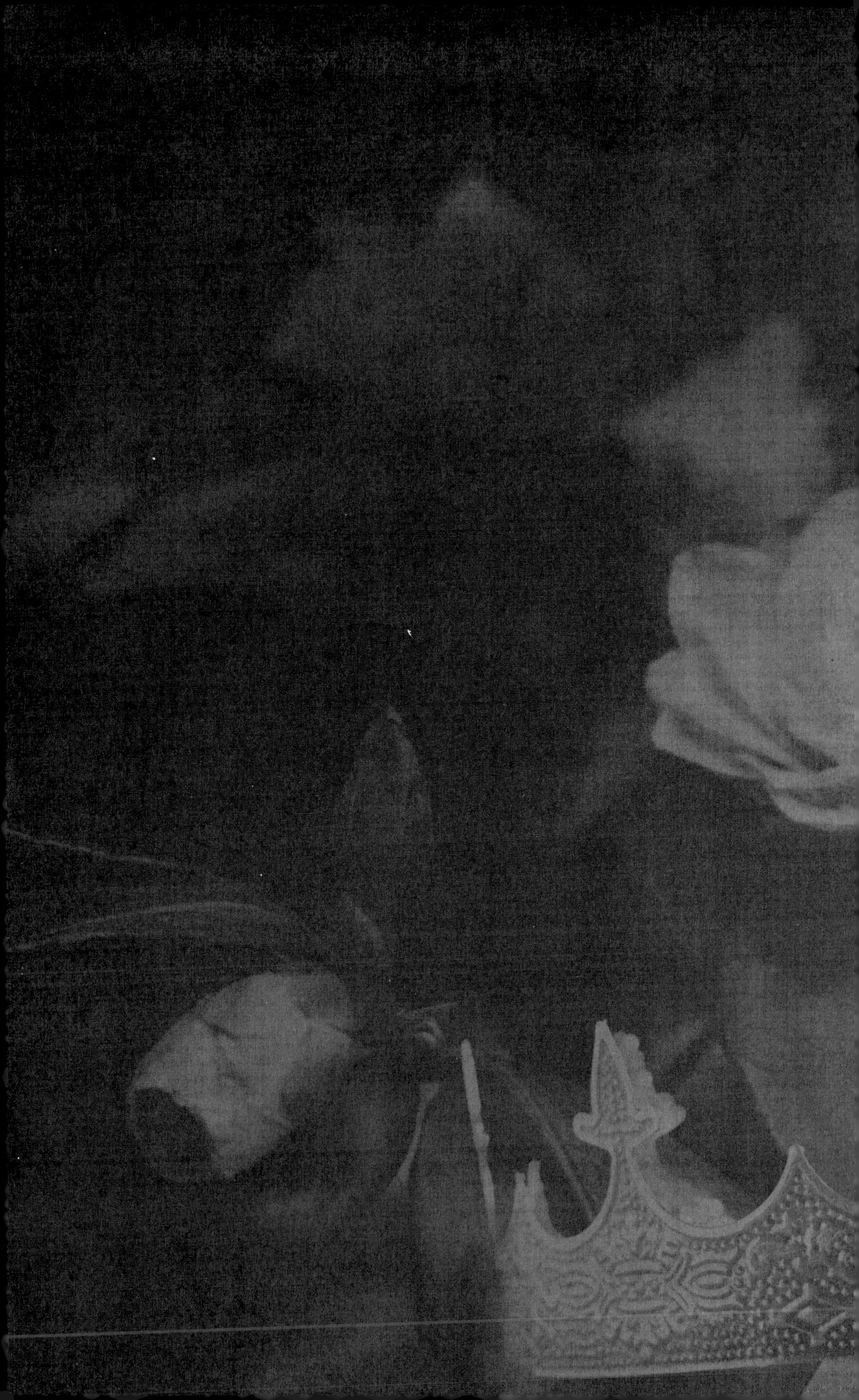

THE REFUGE SCENE
(UNINTERRUPTED)

From The Witch Collector

❧

A Reimagining of Chapter 23
Alexus & Raina

RAINA

"**G**ods' death, Raina. I could kiss you right now."

Alexus sits on the other side of the fire, half-hidden by soft swirls of gray smoke as he gnaws on a roasted crow's wing. Even from here, I can see those full lips, shiny from the fat of dark meat. He drinks from a moonberry root and looks at me over the dancing embers.

"For killing the bird," he adds.

"Of course," I sign. *"For killing the bird."*

My cheeks warm—and not from the flames flickering between us. I know full well he's only relieved to have a bite to eat, a blazing fire, and a place to rest our weary bones. I'm not sure why part of me wishes it was something more.

Curled up inside his cloak, I tip back a moonberry root and empty it before placing its husk in a pile with the others I've drained. I'm thankful for the nourishing liquid that quenches my thirst, but also for the roots, fleshy with thick skin. If we clean out the pulp, they'll make excellent storage for the berries, providing protection against the cold. Maybe, along with the berries, they'll keep us from starving, which I'm sure was Nephele's intent.

I lean against the log at my back and let out the longest, deepest sigh. The God Knife lies buried under a tuft of moss beside me, and Mother's bowl sits on a rock near the fire, handfuls of snow melting inside. They're the two things that symbolize what's been digging at me ever since we sat down to eat. I want to check on the Eastlanders and the Prince, and on Helena, too. But now, I even feel brave enough to look for Finn. I need the closure of knowing what happened to him, especially after everything I went through with Hel.

As for the God Knife, I can't let go of the niggle in my mind that perhaps I should tell Alexus it exists. That level of honesty with him should feel so foreign to me, but it doesn't anymore. Instead, I'm left wondering if maybe he knows something about such things. Maybe he can provide insight.

Or maybe telling him will complicate things further.

I'm so tired—too tired to get into that tonight. It's a kind of tiredness my body has never experienced but that I have no right to complain about. Before we got the fire going, I healed the frostnip on our fingers, and after Alexus prepared the crow and set it to roasting, we washed our hands and faces and even took turns cleaning up a bit more intimately behind a tree. When that was done, he minded the bird while I healed my feet and the horses' minor cuts and ice-shod hooves. Even those small acts of healing made me tired.

Though I feel rejuvenated now, it's hard to feel at ease. Here I lie with food in my stomach, stretched out on warm grass that has no right to exist inside this frozen forest, while a band of Witch Walkers works tirelessly to keep this construct intact, lest the remaining East-landers invade their home like they did the village. Then there's Helena, trapped like an animal and suffering the terrors of a demon alone in the cold. The heat in her body had to have come from the wraith, so she's most likely safe from freezing, but I still worry.

I can't help Hel or Winterhold's witches unless I'm whole, so I try my hardest to shut out the guilt I feel for these hours of reprieve.

Dropping my head back, I close my eyes and focus on how wonderful the heat of the fire feels, the way it chased away all the numbness and replaced it with life. But a white wolf howls, and I open them immediately and sit up, the muscles along the back of my neck tight.

I can't stop worrying about seeing the Prince of the East again, or being flooded with memories of our burning, dying village, or images of Helena fighting her demon, or dead men buried under ice and snow. I'm not sure I'll ever be able to sleep again.

"Helena is out in the open," I sign when Alexus looks up at me from cleaning his hands. *"There are wolves."*

"She's fine, I swear." His eyes are ever the anchor, calming the flutter of worry inside my chest. "Her scent alone is enough to send a pack of wolves in the other direction. But also, my scent is all over her. It's the only reason the wolves haven't bothered us. They know to keep their distance. She'll be safe. And *we're* safe." He stands and gestures to the ground beside me. "May I?"

I nod, and he sits with his back against the log, long legs bent at the knee.

"You should sleep. You barely slept while we were traveling." He motions toward the fire where the gambeson hangs on two sticks. "It'll be dry now and so warm. It makes a right bed, if you remember."

How can I do anything but grin at him like a fool? There's so much to think about, and yet he's worried about me sleeping and having a 'right' bed.

"I remember," I sign.

It would be impossible to forget.

Before, I wondered how Nephele could be friends with Alexus, but now it isn't hard to imagine. I can't say I understand it, why he takes people from the vale and why they don't hate him for it, but I can't seem to hate him either, much as I wanted to before all of this happened.

I reach across the small space between us and take his hand in mine. There's a bone-deep knowing when it comes to him, and so I'm not surprised when the lines crossing his palm call to me. I'm sure they're not calling to me the way palms called to Mena, but the need to see them closer is real.

I trace Alexus's lines into memory, reveling when he shivers at my touch. I've no idea what they mean, but I wonder.

"Do you read palms?" he asks. "We've a lady at Winterhold, from Penrith, who does."

"No," I sign. *"Not a clue."*

"Minds?"

I laugh and press another *no* into his palm.

He winks and smiles, then lets his head fall back as I tickle his skin. "That's probably a good thing. Though I bet you could if you tried."

Funny how he worries about me knowing what he's feeling and thinking. First, he asked if I read people's emotions, and now this.

I wish I *could* read him—his emotions, his mind, his palms. Mena always said the lines of the hands define who we are. She labeled me well enough, calling me an idealist with volatile tendencies and someone who struggles with a mundane existence. She called me impulsive, impatient, and imaginative, a restless being who needs freedom to flourish and love to thrive.

I think she was right, but I fear those last two requirements for peace might be impossible anymore.

Alexus exhales and relaxes, as though my touch is all he needs to unwind. Though we've been pressed against one another for days, I would be lying if I said it didn't feel good to touch him outside the mode of sheer survival, just like it felt good when we touched at the stream. His hands are big and calloused, scarred in the way of a swordsman, strong and warm in ways I shouldn't be thinking about.

Delirium. It must be.

But maybe it isn't. Because ever since his words before we left Helena, I can't stop ruminating about how much I *do* trust Alexus, how I knew that I trusted him the moment he asked me to as we stood in the snow. Trust is earned, and though he hasn't had very much time to do so, he's only proven himself as unfailing. If I had to imagine what his palm would tell me, it would be that.

Unfailing.

When I'm grieving, he provides comfort. When I'm angry, he lets me rage but tempers my fury. When I'm frightened, he's right there beside me, facing whatever comes my way. And sometimes tossing pebbles to scare me.

I stifle a smile. My mind is in tangles over him.

Shaking my head, I snap out of the spell and rest his hand in my lap. He still has a little frostbite in places and blisters from the reins, so I set to healing him.

He winces and flinches and even hisses a time or two as I weave the tattered threads of his flesh back together. Eventually, he settles, watching my hands as I sing and work. Such a mystery, this man, though he also feels like an open book. Perhaps there are pages and lines I simply haven't had the time to read yet, chapters to lose myself inside. And perhaps I shouldn't want to.

But gods, I do.

Once the strands of his injuries are entwined, I ask, *"Any more wounds?"*

He twists his mouth up to one side as though considering if he should tell me something.

"No shame, just show me. Is it your feet?"

He barks out a laugh, as if what I said were funny, but I meant it. My toes looked horrendous, black-tipped and covered in blisters from too-small shoes. Feet are bad enough without all that damage.

"Frostbite?" I spell out, stifling a laugh myself. *"On your toes?"*

"No," he laughs again. "Somehow, my shameful feet are fine. But this—" he hooks his thumb in the hem of his tunic and tugs the fabric up his long torso "—is another story."

I swallow hard. Not just because awful scrapes zigzag from navel to collarbone, but because I did not need to see this much of him right now. Sometimes I wish my face wasn't so expressive.

This is one of those times.

"When did this happen?" I ask, distracting myself from the dark dusting of hair on his chest and the even darker trail that disappears inside his britches. But I remember when he had to receive these marks, and he sees the recollection on my face.

"Damn thing dragged me a good ways. Rocks and roots and sticks and gods know what else lay beneath the snow and upturned soil. It'll heal fine on its own, though. No need for you to exhaust yourself even more for a few scratches."

I shove my stirring feelings aside and shift to my knees. More than scratches. Some are deep, probably painful.

"It should be easy," I tell him, which isn't a lie. They're not complex wounds, but they've been there for days now, and they don't look good. Even though I feel like I could sleep for a week, eating and drinking have replenished much of my strength, so I begin my work.

His strands are becoming so familiar, and each time I tinker with healing him, the tiny darkness of his stolen death hums and churns and sparks, a little lightning storm inside my heart. It's strange, that connection, that reaching out of energies, but I find I like it, feeling attached to someone other than myself.

It doesn't take long to heal his scrapes. I decide to heal the cut still marring his lip too—the wound I gave him. When it's over, I relax and open my eyes.

A yawn awaits, but my mind shuts it down, instead opting to send my hand straight to Alexus's body before I can think to rein myself in.

I dance my fingertips lightly up his healed skin, where a shallow cut traveled over his rippled stomach to the bottom of his chest only moments ago. There are scars I couldn't see before. Strange markings that remind me of runes, raised and rough like someone carved into him with a hot knife.

His midsection flinches at my touch, and he shifts his hips. "Raina."

I freeze at the sound of his husky voice, stopping my inspection over his pounding heart.

Only it wasn't an inspection. It was an exploration. My hand caressing, not analyzing.

When I look up at him, my pulse throbs so hard it's all I hear. Those green eyes stare back at me, dark and promising, and I can no longer make myself care that he's the Witch Collector. All I can see is the man who's been with me for days now, the man who carried me from a fiery village, who washed blood from my hands, who thought of me and me alone when he woke from near-death, a man who kept me warm while he froze.

I see a man. Nothing more and nothing less.

And I want something from him, though I can't tell if I only crave the comfort of closeness or if I'm searching for something more.

He trails his fingertips along my jaw. "It would be best if you didn't look at me like that."

I lean closer and lick my lips. *"Like what?"* I sign.

He gives me a piercing look. "Like you want me to kiss you. Because I will."

Softly, I rub my thumb over his healed lip. He slides his hand into my hair, fisting the roots, a pleasant invitation shining in his eyes.

Desire tumbles down my spine and pools low in my belly when he tightens his grip. I don't move. I just hold his stare, a challenge that I hope I'm up for.

I'm fully aware I'm testing any resolve either of us might've erected concerning one another, but the barriers I've assembled in defense of hatred no longer seem necessary when it comes to Alexus Thibault. I know what I want, even if I shouldn't want it. Even if I'll regret it later. And right now, I want his mouth on mine—delirious from exhaustion or not.

I want to forget. To find some sort of peace—even if only for a little while.

Alexus slides his hand down my side to the back of my knee. In one swift movement, he drags me onto him, my legs straddling his hips. He removes the dagger and belt from my thigh, tossing them aside, and tips the hood of his cloak from my head, untying the laces at my throat. His fingertips forge a fiery path across my collarbone, over my shoulder.

When the cloak falls away, leaving me sitting in leathers and the remains of my dress, a chill courses over me. The air is a mixture of the surrounding cold, the blazing heat of our fire, and the warm comfort of a meadow. It makes my skin feel alive and sensitive, hyper-aware of his every subtle touch.

With his torso still bared to my eye and his hands resting on my hips, Alexus stares up at me like I'm some kind of enchantment. Hesitation dances in his gaze, too, and I'm not sure why.

"You are so tempting," he says. "But you need to know something." He takes my hand. Presses it to his chest. "There is darkness inside me, Raina. Darkness you will not like."

I trail my palm over the curve of thick muscle, across his hard nipple, and down his stomach, making him flinch again.

"There is darkness inside me too," I sign. *"Perhaps our darknesses can be friends."*

He does have darkness. I've seen it, like I'm seeing it now, moving like a phantom behind his eyes. I heard the wraith, too. I know Alexus has secrets.

And I don't care. More than anything, I want him to touch me, and when he finally does—when he runs those deadly hands up my thighs to my waist, traveling along my ribs to my breasts—the pressure of his grip sends burning desire tearing through my blood.

Alexus folds his arm around me and draws me down, wrapping his fist in my hair again. I plant my hands on the log behind him, but he tugs me closer, until there's no space between us. I can feel every rigid inch of him, and he feels divine. It's a heady moment, making me long for so much more than a kiss.

He brushes his mouth against mine, a whisper-kiss, the contact so gentle yet so painfully forbidden, if only by me. Still, I quiver down to my toes when his lips ghost across mine, like he's savoring every curve, preparing to devour.

He meets my eyes again, another flash of hesitance, of too much thought, but the battle waged in his mind ends, and he truly kisses me.

I don't expect the raw hunger that ignites at the sweet taste of him, but in the time it takes my heart to flutter, I sink my hands into his dark hair, and it's *me* who's devouring. I can't think around anything other than this yearning inside me, this rush, the way his heat and hardness tempt me beyond all rationalization, the way his tongue sliding against mine makes me gasp.

I was supposed to kidnap him, not kiss him. Not want him so badly I can barely breathe.

We become a tangle of roaming hands and kisses, any indecision about the situation gone. I tug Alexus's shirt over his head and marvel at the sight of him. Those broad, round shoulders and arms that could hold a woman for days. Then I dip my mouth to his chest, dragging my teeth over his firm, scarred flesh in a soft bite. He groans, a sound of ecstasy that sets fire to my senses.

I've hated being helpless these last days, feeling powerless. But right now, I feel like a god.

Skillfully, he unthreads the laces at my back, one by one, kissing me all the while until the garment loosens. I sit up, strip free of the bodice and my thin undergarment, and toss them both aside. My witch's marks glow in the firelight, shades of gold, crimson, violet, and silver.

Alexus rests his hands at my waist, stopping me from returning to him. He skims his warm palms over my naked skin, admiring my marks, my curves, every dip and hollow. My body responds, tender parts of me tightening, aching, throbbing, so keenly aware of his eyes on me, his hands learning what takes my breath.

He's breathing so hard, his lips slightly swollen, his hair mussed. It's a lovely sight that I tell myself only makes me swoon because I need relief only he can give. This has nothing to do with anything more than that. Nothing to do with my heart.

Nothing at all.

"Gods, Raina." He closes his hand over my breast in a possessive grasp. "I want you."

I don't intend to make him wait.

It's been a long time since I've been with a man—been with Finn—but instinct becomes my guiding light. I lean down, pressing my naked body against Alexus's bare chest, and trail my tongue along the column of his throat. In response, he whispers my name, a choked, desperate sound, like he can't take much more when we've only just begun.

I love the way my name sounds falling from his lips. I want to make him say it a hundred times more. I want him to beg me to kiss him, beg me to take him, beg me to never stop.

He grazes his rough palms over my shoulders, curves those long fingers around my ribs, and I arch against him, my skin tingling when his touch slides down my back and over my hips. Digging his fingers into my backside, he presses all that hardness between my legs, making me shiver, making me want.

This is desperation. Desire so enthralling that I roll my hips over and over, demanding and greedy, feeling like I might die if I don't feel him inside me soon.

He slips his hand between us, tugging at the ties of my trousers. Breaking our kiss, I lift my hips for him, and he slides his hand inside the leathers.

I close my eyes on a gasp, letting him touch me where I want more of him. He's deft with that hand, and in seconds, I'm climbing toward the point of no return.

This shouldn't be happening. It shouldn't be the Witch Collector drawing such damp heat from my body, making my mind numb to anything but the ache he's stoking like a fire. That thought evaporates as he presses his teeth into my shoulder, returning my soft bite from earlier, and dips his hungry mouth to my breast. I move against his touch, chasing the promise that lives in the feverish swirl of his tongue, the rough tip of his finger.

He drags his teeth from my breast and kisses a scorching path to my ear.

"Don't stop. Take what you need." His lips move hot at my throat, and then close over my mouth, swallowing my sighs.

That feels like a dangerous invitation. What I need isn't his hand, as good as it feels.

I stop and take a breath, gathering myself enough to think beyond the desire clouding my mind. We might not live through these next days—this refuge won't last forever. This could be my last time to feel this sort of pleasure.

His touch falls still. "What's wrong?"

I pull his hand from my leathers.

"Did I do someth—" I lean down and kiss him, temporarily silencing him as I reach between us and unlace his britches. "Raina..." My name drifts in the form of a warm breath across my lips. "This isn't—" I slip my hand inside his pants and touch his silky, hard length. "Fuck, yes," he groans, pushing his cock into my touch.

His breathing hitches, but in all truth, when I slide my hand down a little more, it's me who falters.

Alexus Thibault is not an average man—*in any way*. Part of me shivers with nerves at the thought of being with him intimately while another part thrills at the idea of having all this throbbing hardness inside me.

He cups my face and stares into my eyes. "Tell me what you want. I'll do my damnedest to give it to you."

I hesitate, only because I'm a little intimidated. Lust and intrigue win out, however, as I close my fingers around his cock and squeeze.

His eyes flutter, half-closing in bliss before he blinks them open and takes a deep inhale. Again, he looks at me, sliding his hand down to encircle my throat with a gentle, yet promising touch. "Are you telling me you want me to fuck you?"

My heart beats so fast, slamming against my chest, and hearing him talk like that only makes it pound harder.

After the mustering of a little bravery, I nod and trail my fingers up his shaft. A drop of slickness has pearled at his tip, and when I run my thumb over him, smoothing the wetness over his swollen head, he flinches, and his cock twitches in my hand.

"Gods' death, you are torture on a man's resolve." He draws me down for another mind-bending kiss before pulling away to speak. "If we do this, you have to swear that you won't hate me afterward. For any reason."

I cross my heart and stroke him again, eliciting a groan. And finally, I see it: the decision in his eyes, and the hunger in his gaze.

I'm forced to let go of him and brace myself as he runs his hand up my side and captures my breast in his grip again. Kneading and squeezing, he rubs my nipple between his fingers until the sweetest sensation zings through my body, straight to my clit.

When I gasp, he smiles with one side of his lovely mouth. "I like taking your breath. I'm going to do it so many times tonight. Are you ready for that?"

I'm not. Yet I am.

I'm terrified. Yet I cannot wait.

"So ready," I sign.

Alexus slides his hands down my back and into my leathers, pushing the fabric over my ass, his smile brightening, something I would've never believed could light up my world, and yet I can't stop looking at him.

"Let's get you naked," he whispers.

ALEXUS

Two thoughts are running through my mind as I look at Raina Bloodgood lying back on her elbows, naked on the gambeson, legs bent and spread just enough that I can glimpse her soft brown curls and that delicious pink slit, her witch's marks shimmering under the firelight.

Those two thoughts are that, for one, I could fuck her for days if she'd let me. Every single thing about her makes my cock so hard it aches for release. There's just one problem, and that's the second thing running rampant through my mind. As excited as I was moments before, I now feel apprehensive, because it's going to take everything in me to suffocate Neri long enough that he has no part in this.

I swear I can hear the bastard laughing at me, but I tighten my magick around his spirit, clenched like a fist, and drag him to the deepest, darkest part of me, until he is completely, utterly silenced.

"You're certain," I ask Raina, needing her assurance one more godsdamn time.

I stand at the foot of the gambeson, gripping one side of my unlaced britches. She said she's taken birthbane, and I trust her. That isn't the issue. The issue is that I need to know that she won't despise me once the truth about my darkness is revealed.

I expect her to sign or nod. What I don't expect is for her to spread her legs a little wider and slip her hand down between them. She opens herself for me, her slit glistening and ready as she fingers her clit.

Mouth watering, I exhale a shuddering breath, because fuck all. With that one simple move, I am done for.

Quickly, I shuck my leathers and brais and kneel between her legs, my hands on her knees. I don't miss the way her throat moves on a swallow as she glances at my cock. I know it's a little intimidating. Having lived for three centuries, I've seen that look before. But I know how to use my body for a woman's pleasure, or how to *let* it be used, how to be careful until she's ready for me to be punishing.

I push her knees further apart for a better view, and she begins to withdraw her hand.

I *tsk* and shake my head. "Don't stop. Let me watch."

There's a delicate timidness to her, though it hides beneath her fire. If she feels any insecurity or hesitance as she begins working her pussy, it's now buried under lust and determination. She wants this, so much, and with that look on her face, that mask of sheer need, I couldn't deny her if I wanted to.

I sit back on my heels and just watch, stroking my hands up and down her sleek thighs as she dips her fingers inside herself, her mouth open as she pants softly.

"Such a good girl," I tell her, just as I slide my finger inside, too, the both of us moving in and out.

She gasps, and I smile. She's so tight. So wet. So perfect.

But then reality hits me in the face. She said she had a special someone in the valley, and she's a grown woman, but that doesn't mean she's ever slept with someone.

"Have you taken a man before?" I ask, moving my finger more tenderly.

Her breathing picks up as she nods. She fixes her gaze on my hand, biting her lip, and then she looks into my eyes with hunger in her stare. I don't even need her to sign. Somehow I know that look and what it means. Like I've seen it staring back at me for centuries.

She wants more.

I insert a second finger. "Does that feel good?"

Her hand falls away to let me take control, and she signs a simple *Yes*. But it's the silent whimpering look on her face that tells me just how good it feels.

Testing her limits, I push a third finger inside her and rub her clit with my thumb, my cock throbbing all the while. With her chest rising and falling fast, she grinds against my hand, which sends a bolt of delight and longing through me.

"There you go," I tell her as she fucks my fingers. "That's a little closer to what my cock is going to feel like."

Her dark blue eyes storm over, and she signs, *"I want you."* Then she pushes up on her hands and stares at my mouth like she needs to kiss me.

Gripping her hips, I drag her onto my lap. I want her close tonight. I want as much intimacy as I can get with this woman. I tell myself that I'll let her set the pace. That I'll give her control. She isn't used to me, and I need to let her acclimate. But gods if I don't want to bend her over and ravage her with all the ferocity I possess right now.

As I tamp down my desire, she wraps her arms around my neck and buries her hands in my hair. I kiss her like she wants. A divine kiss. A kiss that awakens my soul.

I would swear I've felt this mouth before tonight. That I've already claimed it as my own. It's too easy, my lips and tongue too sure. There's no clumsiness. No needing to learn her mouth.

I already know it.

I know the softness of her tongue against mine. The plumpness of her lips between my teeth. I know her taste and the way she arches against me when I kiss her deeper. It's like she's been mine all my life. Forever and an age.

Breathing hard, I pull away, keeping one hand in her hair. "I want you to take me inside you, as much as you can. Sitting just like this. Then I'll move us into the perfect position."

Her eyes search mine for a moment—*nervousness*—but then she's straddling me, and all that perfect softness begins to envelop my cock.

As her body closes over my throbbing head, I lean down and take her nipple into my mouth, sucking, biting, and flicking my tongue as she lowers onto me, inch by inch. I can hardly stand it, the feel of her working me inside, can hardly keep myself from thrusting up into her. Because that sensation—being wrapped in her tightness, her wet warmth—leaves me breathless with yearning. It's like I've been searching for something and finally found it, as though after all these ages, I'm exactly where I'm supposed to be.

With her.

She tips her head back, luscious lips parted, her hands braced on my shoulders, fingers digging in as she takes the last of me. I watch her for long moments, the way she rocks to feel me deep. It feels so godsdamn good, every tempting rub against the tip of my cock a reminder that I'm going to get to come inside this woman tonight.

I unfold and sit beneath her, legs outstretched, and though she gasps again at the feeling of me moving even deeper, she naturally wraps her legs around my waist. Any distance left between us is gone, my cock fully seated inside her.

She wraps her hands in my hair and draws me close for another kiss, and we begin to move in perfect timing, a gentle writhing. But then she presses one hand to my knee and starts rocking again, pressing her feet into the ground for more leverage, just before her hips change their momentum to a long slide up and down my cock. I lean back on my hands, and we both look down to where we're joined, watching as she works her pussy along my length, my flesh slick with her desire.

"Fuck, Raina. Look at you taking me so well." When I meet her gaze, what I see there makes me feel like a feral animal in a cage.

Instantly, our rhythm changes, again.

Raina folds her arms around my neck, and I wrap my arms around her waist, and together we *fuck*, hard and fast, her hips pumping up and down, my teeth grazing her nipples as she greedily takes all of me she can.

"Stop," I warn her after too many minutes. "Stop or I'm going to come." I was not as prepared for this as I would've liked to have believed.

She *does* stop and, after flashing a sexy, demure smile, captures my mouth with hers, too pleased with herself for having so easily driven me to the point of no return.

When I can think again, I lean into her, until she drops back on both hands. I mirror her position, and the blissful torture of being with her begins anew.

With our gazes locked, I angle my cock just right and push into her awaiting heat. Her long hair is a dark cascade around her shoulders, a couple tendrils falling over her beautiful breasts as they move with my every thrust, her pink nipples peaked in the cool air. She arches her hips for me, and the sight of my cock moving in and out of her body nearly undoes me again, the need for release throbbing through me.

I close my hand around the back of her neck and draw her near, kissing her like it's impossible to get far enough inside her. But this time, I can't restrain myself any longer. I slide my hands underneath her thighs and rise onto my knees. In one movement, I'm holding her mid-air, her legs around my waist, her arms tight around my neck, her lips on mine as I pound my cock into her welcoming, wet heat, offering what we both need.

Her hands tighten in my hair, her fingernails scraping my scalp, but she rips away from the kiss, gasping for breath as she stares into my eyes. She's so close. My body knows, as though I've taken her before, enough that her climax is a thing I can sense rising inside her.

I lay her down on her back, still buried inside her, watching as her eyelids drift closed, feeling her grow wetter and tighter, her pussy swollen with want. I kiss her throat as I fuck her, dragging my lips to her ear.

"You're going to come for me, aren't you? All over my cock."

She nods, that sweet whimper on her face as she grips my shoulders, and I know—*I know*—that we can come together, and that it will be *everything*.

I push up, bracing myself on my hands, and she wraps her legs tightly around my hips. This angle lets me reach even deeper, and gods, do I ever. With her gaze roving over my body, I drive my cock into her pussy like a man who hasn't fucked in years, because that's exactly what I am.

"Touch your clit," I tell her, putting an edge in my voice.

A command.

She obeys so easily, and that sends a thrill through me that I feel in every muscle. After wanting to kill me days ago, she now wants me in an entirely different way, needs me to destroy the last vestiges of the wall she erected between us. I annihilate that barrier with every thrust, though something else is happening as well, at least for me.

Something inside me thrums with that same, peculiar knowing, something that feels like it's reaching for Raina's soul—and it has *nothing* to do with Neri. My magick has him bound deep, rendered more silent than he's ever been.

No. It's a tender thing, filled with passion but also unity, a connection that feels broken, longing to be mended. It makes my heart ache in a manner it never has before. It even causes tears to prick the backs of my eyes though I choke them down and blink them away. The severity of emotion I feel is unexpected, but it consumes me like a quenching fire.

Leaning down, I kiss the skin over her heart, and then I kiss her mouth, our tongues and lips moving in that same perfect rhythm. My orgasm builds, rising from a heavy ache in my balls to a tingling pressure racing up the shaft of my cock.

Raina clings to my shoulders and tips her head back, that lovely mouth open again in ecstasy. *The things I would love to do to that mouth.* I'm distracted from that thought, however, because a tear slips from the corner of her eye down her temple.

A tear of pleasure. A signal that now is the time.

My claiming is a brutal one. Far more brutal than I'd planned when this began. But she wants it—I see the request in her heated eyes, the longing for more and more and *more*. And I need it, as though my body must bury its presence in her core, a mark that says this woman belongs to Alexus Thibault. Now and forever. If ever anyone was meant to be mine, I know it's her. Even if I can't explain how or why.

I know.

Her name is written on my soul.

When we come, the pleasure is three-fold. There's the divine sensation in my cock as my orgasm pulses through me, each euphoric surge wrenched from me by Raina's pussy fluttering and clenching with her own release. I spill inside her, coming so hard and long I curse and moan into the night.

Then there's the pleasure of the mind, that feeling of floating in endless bliss that comes with climax, that space where nothing else exists but me and her and this moment.

But the last one. The last one is the kind of pleasure I can't remember ever having felt before. It's strange feeling it now with a woman I hardly know, even though she's a woman I feel like I've somehow known for an age. *The pleasure of the heart.* A deep serenity and peace I have no doubt will linger long after the pleasure of the flesh has faded.

Spent and tired and utterly drained, I finally pull out. I have to look at her. Have to open her and memorize the image of my cum spilling slowly from her body. She shivers as I flick my finger over her clit, her teeth dragging over her bottom lip as I meet her gaze.

"You are so fucking beautiful," I tell her, admiring the curves of her body. "And I mean that in every imaginable way."

After cleaning us, I grab the blanket and lie with Raina on the gambeson. She lets me hold her, something I'm not certain I expected. The intimacy of this night was intense for me. But was it as intense for her? Or was this only relief?

When she looks up at me with those heavy eyes and touches my face, running her fingertips through my beard, I think it might've been more than only relief. But this is new for her, I know. *I'm* new. Still a curiosity and an intrigue, though I long to be so much more.

I kiss her, needing her taste on my lips one more time. "Sleep," I eventually whisper. "We've a long road ahead."

She nestles her head against my chest, and for the first time in what feels like forever, I rest soundly.

Because Raina Bloodgood is at my side.

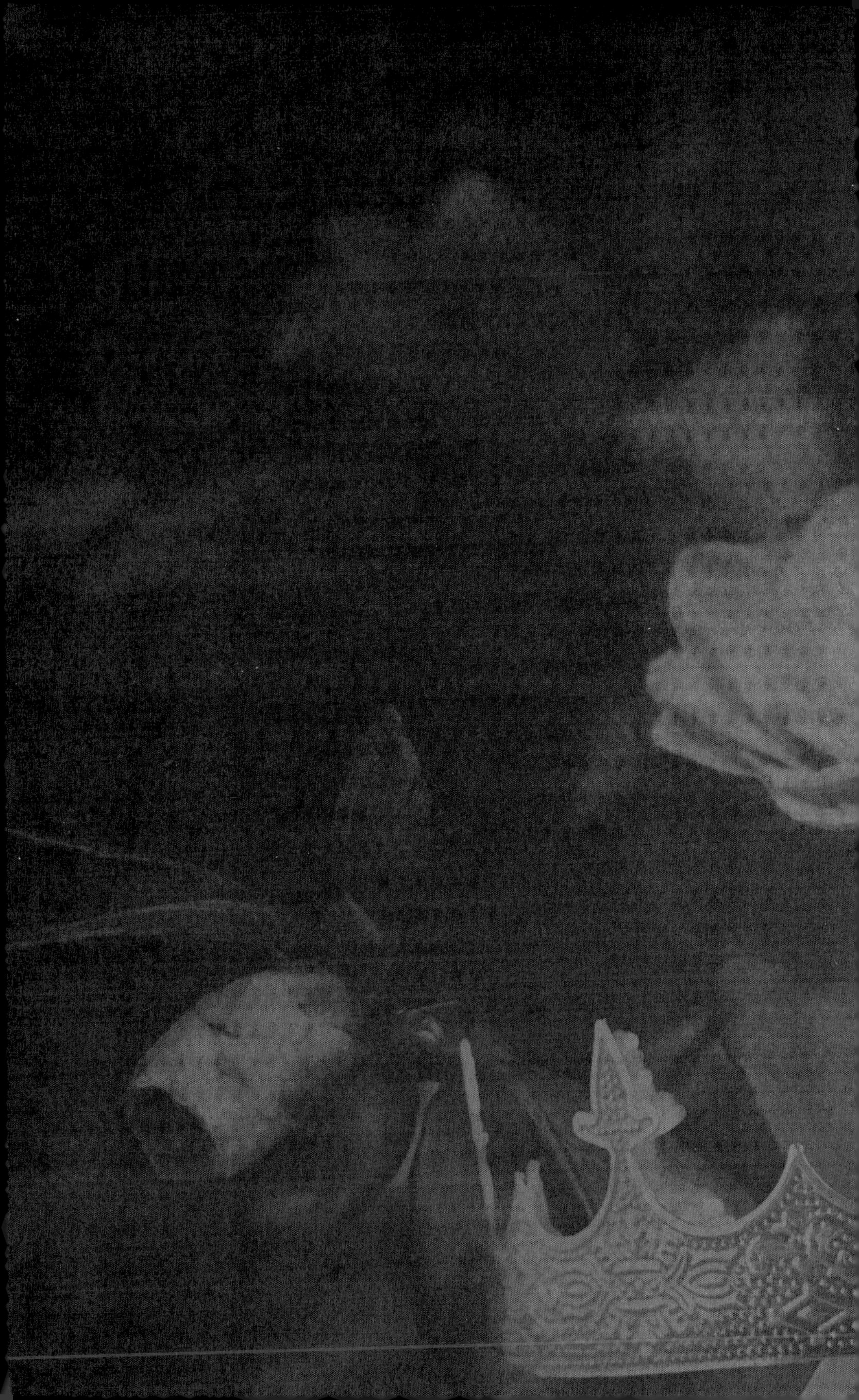

IN THE GARDEN (UNINTERRUPTED)

From City of Ruin

A Reimagining of Chapter 31
Alexus & Raina

𝕴 I 𝕴

RAINA

"W hy did no one tell me this was a formal thing?" Rhonin says as I enter the dining hall.

Everyone's here except for Finn, which stings my heart.

Mari sets a dish on the table, leaning beside Rhonin, quite close. "I think you look handsome, sir," she says with an admiring expression. "I like the shorter hair and the smooth face."

"He does look handsome," Hel counters from my side, her voice stiff and slightly territorial. "Always."

Every head turns toward me and my sisters.

"Perhaps we overdid it a little," Nephele mutters under her breath, because every eye in the room is wide.

Alexus heads straight for me. His eyes grow dark as he skims a gaze over my loose hair and down to my neck where his gift resides. He bought me a simple gold necklace with a single pearl in the center, like my own little moon. It's perfect.

When he reaches me, his eyes fall to my exposed cleavage, then further down to the witch's marks trailing up my leg, visible through the slit in my dress.

He leans close to my ear, sending a rogue chill across my skin. "You look good enough to eat."

My face warms as he leads me to my chair and pulls it out for me before taking his place at my side.

Discreetly, he slips his hand over mine and whispers, "You make that necklace even more beautiful."

I shove away any worry about having eyes on us and kiss his cheek, feeling the slight stubble already growing along his jaw.

His mouth turns up. "Why, thank you."

Grinning like a fool, I turn back to the table. Poor Rhonin, in his plain white day tunic and brown trousers, stands frozen with indecision.

When Hel saunters toward him, she passes Mari on the way and gives her a look from the corner of her eye. But Rhonin's attention is solely on Hel. With her curves on display beneath her clinging emerald gown, he blinks with astonishment, taking her in.

"Why are you gawking?" she asks. "Are you so used to seeing me covered in filth and wielding weapons that you've forgotten that I'm also a lady?"

"Not at all." He shakes his head insistently and moves her chair back from the table. "Okay, maybe a little. But if I forgot, I've certainly been reminded now."

She looks up at him and smiles.

In her silky blue dress that shows off her slender yet strong frame, Nephele stalks toward the last open setting at the table. The one beside Joran. She grabs the back of her chair before he gets a chance.

"I can seat myself. I don't need your help for anything."

He drenches her in a wicked once-over. "Anything? Are you so sure?"

With a look that says she's seconds from gouging his eyes out with a dinner fork, Nephele jerks her chair back. "Positive."

Once we're all set and no one is killing anyone, Mari and Yaz finish bringing the dinner in. The food here has been plentiful, but I haven't felt like devouring a full meal until now. There's a rich, red wine being passed around—not that I need more—and roasted chicken and baked fish swimming in a fragrant yellow sauce, and roasted vegetables and breads and even spiced pies for dessert. My mouth waters and my stomach grumbles at the sight.

Zahira and Yaz stand at the head of the table, arm in arm, wine glasses in hand.

"A toast," Zahira says. "To everyone in this room. May the Ancient Ones show each of you intrepid warriors the truths you need to see and may Loria light your paths with clarity."

We clang our glasses together, and though Zahira's words resonate in each person's expressions, it seems our stomachs resound even louder. We dig in.

It's obvious that everyone tries their best to be reserved and polite, but I'm apparently not the only one whose appetite is returning tonight. Plates are filled, and most of the chatter goes quiet because our mouths are stuffed with food.

As I eat, I can't help but wonder about Finn. If he's all right. If he's eating a hearty meal. Hel said he is well cared for at the Bitter Barrel thanks to Harmon and Zahira's generosity, but I can't help but worry.

Across the table, Rhonin hands Hel a piece of warm raisin loaf which he smothers in butter and honey. "Try it. I bet you'll love it."

The sound that leaves my best friend when she bites into the bready goodness is a deep, unexpected moan that makes Rhonin's mouth fall open.

She eats the whole thing as he watches her lips, then she licks the honey from her fingertips. "Gods, Rhonin. That almost earned you a sticky, wet kiss."

Rhonin closes his mouth and swallows. His face turns three shades of red.

"Maybe next time?" he offers, and I nearly choke on my wine.

Callan laughs under their breath, Keth and Jaega snicker, and Alexus stares at his plate, a wide smile on his lips. Sweet Rhonin. I find myself wondering how many chances he was granted to find love before now, being in the Eastland army and all.

Dinner and too many glasses of wine pass far more quickly than I expected, given that our little band of fighters attacked the spread like they do everything else. As everyone chats, Alexus strokes my leg under the table, causing my overly full stomach to flip. Perhaps eating a large meal and downing nearly an entire bottle of wine before having possibly the best sex of my life wasn't the best decision.

With a grip of my knee, he stands and folds his hands around the back of my chair. "Raina and I are going to graciously dismiss ourselves so we can turn in early. It's been a long day."

"Exhausted," I sign, out of a nervous need to over-explain, and Hel translates with a smile.

Everyone knows we're lying. It's evident on their grinning faces. Except for Joran who, I realize, stopped caring about me and Alexus spending time together weeks ago.

I dismiss the thought and stand as Alexus pulls out my chair and motions for me to lead the way toward the veranda. "I'm right behind you," he says with a wink.

"I bet you are," Zahira says, and the room breaks into laughter. Alexus just smiles and presses his hand to the small of my back.

"Come on. Let's go have some fun."

❧

THE MOMENT HE CLOSES THE CREAKY GARDEN GATE, ALEXUS SWEEPS ME into his arms and carries me down the flagstone path toward the lighthouse. Only he veers left, taking us through a labyrinth of tall hedges into a nook at the garden's edge where the last of the sun's dying rays barely linger. The space is filled with the beginning shadows of nightfall, the briny scent of sea and sand, and the aroma of winter jasmine that grows in a thick, white blanket over the stone wall.

There, beneath the setting sun and rising moon, with waves crashing against the rocks below, Alexus sets me on my feet, tosses my shoes aside on the grass, and presses me against the fragrant blooms. I cling to his strong arms as he kisses me deeply, licking into my mouth, hungrily exploring. His hands are firm and warm on my waist, his grasp sure as he draws me flush against him. He's already so hard that the pressure of his desire makes my heart skip a beat.

"I hope you aren't as tired as you claimed." He traces the shell of my ear with his tongue. "Because it's going to be a very long and eventful night if I have anything to say about it." He holds my chin between his thumb and forefinger and peers into my eyes. "I'm going to make you come on my cock in every position imaginable, Raina Bloodgood. Starting now."

There's no other warning for the delicious warmth of his power as it skims a teasing touch along our bond. I simply feel that familiar sensation, the air sparking alive with electricity, tickling my skin. My body is buzzing from the wine, so I reach for Alexus's threads with my mind, ready to draw his power into me like our night at Winterhold.

"Stop that, you little rebel." A quiet, deep laugh resonates from his throat as he smacks my ass, making me gasp and arch into him. "I told you. Tonight, it's *my* turn." He grips me tight, kneading my flesh as he presses his erection against me again. "Close your eyes," he whispers, "and let me have my way with you."

An insuppressible smile spreads across my mouth, and as though he holds some spell over me, my eyes flutter shut. Before, at Winterhold, I hadn't known what I was doing when it came to tangling our magick, and Alexus's power had been so weak that he'd had no other choice but to let me lead us. And yet, every moment had been divine regardless.

This time, there's no searching for threads at all. No clinging to them with my mind. No novice at the helm, unsure what to look for, unsure what to do. This time, behind my eyelids, the threads of Alexus Thibault's magick shine, limned with golden light, already vining along our bond at a ravenous pace.

My heart beats faster with anticipation, every twist and weave heating my already burning blood. I cannot imagine what it will be like with him in complete control, his power so much stronger now than it was before. How can we bond any closer than what this night holds for us? Bonded not only in body but also through the rune, through the tangling of our magickal threads, and through the sharing of power.

We will be one.

No sooner does that thought travel across my mind, than Alexus's power branches through me. A wave of stunning energy rolls over my skin, setting every nerve ending in my body on fire. That power intertwines with my own magick, sending a trickle of pleasure straight to my core.

"Breathe," he commands, smiling against my mouth.

Obediently, I suck in a deep drink of night air saturated with the honeyed taste of his ancient magick. "Now lift your dress" he says, his voice rough with desire. "And spread those beautiful legs for me."

At his words, my heart thunders with longing, but I hesitate.

"Harmon? The boys?" I sign. They live in the garden house.

"Busy at the stables because I asked them to be," Alexus replies. "I want to lick you and fuck you under the stars if you'll let me. I want you to think of me every single time you walk through a garden or hear the ocean or smell jasmine or feel a godsdamn night breeze on your bare skin. I want tonight to be something you can't possibly ever forget."

That sends a flash of lust through my body that is so desperate I gather my dress around my hips in a hurry and spread my legs.

As I stand there, waiting, I realize that he hasn't asked me how I want him yet. Hard and rough or deep and slow. I don't think it's up for debate tonight. He means to give me everything.

With that hungry look in his eyes, he lowers to one knee and slides his hands up the curves of my thighs. Even that simple touch sends another bolt of pleasure zinging through me.

For a moment, he angles his head in a curious tilt. Then he brushes his fingertips back and forth between my legs. It's hard to focus on anything but the white-hot need raging inside me, but when

a deep and seductive sound rumbles in the back of Alexus's throat—
something torn between a moan and a growl—I blink away the haze
of lust and look down at him.

He's seen the lace.

With a lick of his lips, he meets my stare. His green eyes are bright
as sea glass held to the light of a high-summer sun—and filled with
hunger. He strokes the delicate material again, and I flinch at the
tempting contact.

"I want you in nothing but this and the necklace," he says, something dark and wild hovering at the edge of his voice.

It takes a matter of seconds before my sash is untied and my gown
is gone, reduced to a puddle at my feet. As I stand before him, naked
save for the scraps of red lace Yazmin calls undergarments, ready to
make love against this stone wall if I must, another sound leaves
Alexus.

It's a sound borne of appreciation and desire, escaping his lips as
he admires my bare skin.

He reaches up and brushes his thumb across my nipple. The dark
pink flesh is hard and peeking through the lace. The sensation of that
touch is tenfold what it would be without our power joined along the
bond, making me quiver. I can hardly bear it, yet at the same time, I
must have more.

The leather tie holding his hair falls away as I slide my hands into
his dark locks and clutch him to my breast. In response, he flicks his
tongue over the tip, teasing and biting to the brink of pain, the way he
knows I like.

I still can't wrap my mind around how well he knows me. How
well he's known me since that first night at Winterhold. I never have
to instruct or guide him. He just knows how to touch me, how to take
me, how to please me.

I hold him tighter, fisting my hands at the roots of his hair until
I'm panting. The action seems to drive him because he grips my waist
and his mouth becomes hungrier, his touch rougher, and I find myself

questioning what the tangling of our power does to him. Is he close to exploding like me?

Unexpectedly, he yanks at the lace garment covering my chest, ripping the flimsy top from its silken straps, and throws it aside. I suppose that answers my question.

Alexus slides his palms across my exposed breasts, my waist, and over my ass, where he gathers the lace of my panties in his fist and tugs, putting gentle pressure where I throb for him. I gasp, and a wicked tilt crooks his lips when he grins up at me. He keeps tugging, using rhythmic movements to torture me, knowing exactly what he's doing, all while moving from breast to breast, sucking me into his mouth, rolling his tongue and teeth around my nipples.

Gods, I could climax from this alone, and I half-think I might. But Alexus lets go of the lace and draws back, leaving me pulsing with need.

This night is far from over, so I take my hands from his hair and rest against the soft, crushed flowers at my back, trying my best for patience. With that same rougher touch, Alexus trails his strong hands and warm mouth down my abdomen, skims his broad palms over my hips, and slips his tongue along the edge of the lace.

"Red," he whispers, gripping the back of my thigh. "I love you in red."

He lifts my knee over his shoulder, opening me to him. I can barely remain standing when he leans forward and drags his teeth over me, through the fabric, again and again, until I'm grinding shamelessly in time with his mouth, yearning to feel his tongue buried inside me.

Reading my mind, he hooks a finger in the lace and pulls the material aside. The night wind off the sea is tinged with the slightest cool edge, enough that a chill races over my skin at the exposure.

I drop my head back against the wall and listen as my pulse pounds harder and harder in my ears. I've never been so starved for anything or anyone in my life. Never needed someone so much it hurts.

Again, I thread my fingers into Alexus's hair. His mouth is so close that when I curve my hips, I can feel the damp warmth of his panting breaths. All I can think about is yesterday, straddling his face, his cock in my mouth, the bliss I felt when he came.

"Remember what I said that night at Winterhold?" he asks, looking up at me.

Thoughts ricochet around my mind. He said a lot of things the first night we made love.

"I told you that I was going to kiss you, and that you were going to feel it everywhere. That's about to happen now, but with my power returned and our magick entwined, it will be far stronger. You won't be able to walk out of here. Know that."

I *do* already know this, in a sense, but I feel the warning in his words, the promise that I have no idea what I'm in for.

"You're sure you're ready?"

I nod and arch my hips toward him again in response, all but begging. If being with Alexus Thibault can possibly be any better tonight than all the times before, I welcome the torture.

When he leans in, every muscle in my body tightens expectantly. With a quick hand, he rips my undergarment from my body. That little glimpse of sudden barbaric behavior makes my nipples and clit harden, almost painfully.

Then his mouth is on me, licking a long line of inexplicable pleasure up my center, stopping only to suck that tender nub at my apex while flicking his tongue mercilessly, his magick flowing wild.

A brutal orgasm slams into me, radiating through every muscle, so powerful it robs me of breath. Gasping as stars dot my vision, I thrash against the jasmine wall, wanting *more more more* while simultaneously needing to flee. Because it's too much. His tongue alone could obliterate me like grains of sand scattered on the wind.

I couldn't run if I tried. Alexus uses his shoulders and a firm hand to pin me to the wall, forcing me to endure as he devours. Mindless, I grip my breasts, teasing my taut nipples, the action only increasing the bliss.

Roughly, Alexus pushes two fingers inside me. My body desperately grasps at him in response. "Yes," he rasps, still flicking that gifted tongue as he fucks me deeply. "There's that flutter I love so much. You come for me so beautifully, Raina."

I writhe on his hand as he licks and nibbles, riding out the sudden climax until my vision returns. A handful of starlights light the falling night, illuminating my body so Alexus can see his fill. He holds me open, moving his fingers languorously in and out, laving the soft flesh around my entrance, until it feels more like a lover's soothing caress.

When the ecstasy passes and the world is back to rights, I'm left thoroughly destroyed, and yet still so wanton it's almost inconceivable. Alexus slips his fingers from my body and stands, tall and dark in the dimming twilight.

Not so gently, he leans close and pushes his fingers into my mouth. "Suck," he says against my cheek. "Suck your sweet pussy off my fingers."

A breathy whimper vibrates in my chest as I obey, tasting my release as I waver on trembling legs. He was right. He will have to carry me out of here when he's finally finished with me. If I haven't combusted to ash by then.

Alexus cups my breast and brings his head down to meet it, rolling his tongue and teeth around my nipple with magick-laced attention. His power rolls through me, and somehow, my body reacts again, my clit throbbing with need, my skin rising with goosebumps.

As though sensing the response, he withdraws his fingers from my mouth and presses his lips to mine, his kiss insistent and hungry as he strips free of his jacket and tosses it aside. Greedy, I open for him and suck on his tongue, tasting the honeyed flavor of his magick while I untuck his shirt from his fine trousers and tug it toward his head.

He pulls away just long enough to shed the garment, revealing all that glorious, corded muscle, and I set to unlacing his pants, working quickly, as though we might perish if he isn't inside me in a matter of seconds.

I don't even get his trousers unlaced enough that they'll fall away before he frees his cock and closes my hand around its swollen girth. "Just like that," he says as I stroke the silken skin covering his rigid length. "Fucking just like that."

He presses his forehead to mine, and I slide my hand up and down in a rhythm I've come to know he likes. The shuddering sigh that leaves his chest and the wetness slicking his thick head sends a frisson of lust through me.

I run my thumb through that bead of cum, just as it threatens to fall, and bring it to my mouth instead. Alexus watches as I taste him, and then he buries his hands in my hair and crushes his mouth to mine, the velvet slide of our tongues a heady thing.

It's been a matter of hours since we were together, since I buried him deep in my throat and made him beg for release. But there's a desperation thrumming from both of us that I have never experienced before. A need so great that Alexus spins me around and flattens my hands against the wall.

"Spread your legs," he commands, running his warm, rough palms over the curves of my ass. "Nice and wide."

As I widen my stance, Alexus pulls my cheeks apart, exposing every hidden part of me. A wave of vulnerability and excitement washes over my skin and through my bones, two incongruent feelings at war inside me. There's something about being taken from behind by Alexus, something that makes my heart beat harder with the knowing that, like this, I have no control. Like this, Alexus claims with animalistic need, a knowledge that makes my pulse pound like a drum in my ears.

For an excruciating moment, nothing happens. I can sense the starlights hovering at my hips, and feel their warmth. He likes to see me. Likes to take his time torturing me as he memorizes my body.

One hand leaves my ass while the other wraps itself in my hair, winding my locks around and around like a too-long rein. For a pregnant moment, I wait, thinking I will feel him at my entrance, that he will finally drive his cock into me after these many weeks without him. Instead, the hand in my hair tightens, and a stinging slap races across my backside. Then another, on the opposite side.

Gasping at the delicious pain, I go lightheaded, fists gripping the trellis buried beneath the soft jasmine. Every drop of blood in my body rushes to meet my skin where I'm certain pink handprints will form. Oddly enough, I want them to. I want to see evidence of him on my body, more than just the rune. I want to be so thoroughly marked by Alexus Thibault that anyone in the world could look at me and see him everywhere.

He leans into me, his erection nestled hard and warm against my ass, the soft hair on his chest tickling my shoulder blades as he gently draws my head back, angling my face to look upon his. Little starlights flicker between us, highlighting the golden flecks in his eyes and shadowing the strong planes of his handsome face.

"Mine." He kisses me softly as he caresses my breast. "You know that, yes? You are mine, mon grah."

I nod against his grip, tears dampening my eyes, because it's true. It's the last thing I would've ever imagined when I held the God Knife to his throat while Silver Hollow burned to cinders around us. But now it's the one truth I know as well as I know my name, a truth that resonates so deep within I feel it in my soul.

"Now hold on." He bites at my lip. "Because there's no fucking way I can be gentle tonight."

I stretch my fingers, and then clench the wooden slats covering the wall again, the vines cool and slick with sea mist rolling in off the waves. I brace myself for the assault I know is coming, but there's nothing that could prepare me for the feeling that shatters through me when Alexus Thibault grips my hips and mercifully penetrates to the hilt in a single thrust that drives a bolt of tantalizing magick and relief through my core.

A deep groan leaves him as he tries to push in even deeper, causing a ragged breath to tear from between my lips, like he's telling me *See? No one can reach you here. No one but me.*

You. Are. Mine.

"I could stay just like this for eternity." His voice is husky, the edges dark with desire. "Buried inside you. I fucking swear."

Not that I would mind. He feels so good I can hardly think, so good I'm certain that with a slip of my hand between my legs and a few deep grinds on his engorged tip, I would fracture from bliss. There isn't a part of me he doesn't fill, not a place where my body isn't tested and tempted by his sheer size. I feel stretched, filled to the brim with his throbbing cock—and his magick.

He circles his hips, still planted so deep, and another wave of magickal pleasure chases through my blood. "When I come inside you," he says, the hand in my hair tightening, "you'll feel this cliffside tremor as I roar your name."

Oh, gods. There isn't a single thing I want more than to see him ruined by me again, but the thought of him roaring anything sparks worry. What if someone hears us?

That thought is quickly dissolved as Alexus begins to move in and out of me in long slides, holding onto my naked hip with his free hand. It's only slow for a few moments, just enough time to give my body a chance to prepare for the powerful onslaught that follows.

"Fuck, you're so swollen for me," he groans, grinding and thrusting, the hard slap of our skin resounding through the night as his tempo increases. "So tight and warm and wet I can barely stand it, Raina."

He slows again to temper his orgasm, but I push back against him and pump along his length, hard and fast. He said he couldn't be gentle, but I still feel the ghost of his restraint, and I want him undone. I want this to be utterly destructive for us both. I want to wake up come morning sore and aching and bruised only to see claw marks down his back, crescent moons carved into his biceps.

He curses, over and over, remaining still as I ride him, the bite of pain at my scalp from his grip on my hair driving me to fuck him as brutally as I can.

Again, the heat of the starlights brush over my ass, their warmth then radiating across my sensitive flesh. "I need you to see this," he says, his voice almost pained. "I need you to see how godsdamn beautiful you are."

My stomach clenches, and my core aches. I can only imagine what he's seeing, the view of us united, of my body taking all I can from him. Before I can even form the image in my mind, he pulls out and turns me around, pressing me back against the jasmine. I slide my hands over the curved, thick planes of his chest, over the mass of bulging muscle at his shoulders, and up into his hair. I'm hyper-aware of the chills on his skin, and the way his trousers sit low on his hips, his hard cock twitching between us.

Alexus folds a brawny arm around me and lifts. Instinctively, I wrap my legs around his narrow waist. It isn't until he works one arm under my knee, followed by the other, that I realize what he's doing. Suddenly, I'm being held in the air, my shoulders pressed to the flowers, my legs spread wide open for the ancient sorcerer standing between them.

His starlights twinkle and flutter, gathering into a soft orb of golden light between us. "Put my cock in your pussy," he orders, and I, as ever, obey.

He cups my ass and curves my hips upward as I angle him toward my entrance. The feel of him pushing inside me is overwhelming, our magick and our bond humming with the sweetest vibration through every part of me. But I am wholly unprepared for what seeing him pumping in and out of my body does to me, how the sight of his stiff, unyielding cock, slick with my desire, completely annihilates me.

I move my hand to my clit, tugging upward so he can see as I chase the need building there. Alexus watches with that green gaze pinned to me, but not for long.

"Gods, Raina. I can't…" He lifts his eyes, and I see the plea there.

He's begging for mercy.

His mouth crashes into mine so hard our teeth clash. Neither of us even hesitates. We plunder each other's mouths as he pounds into me almost violently, exactly the way I wanted, hard enough to bruise. In seconds, though, even that is not enough.

"Arms around my neck," he says, just as he'd said our first night here when he carried me from the thermal pool.

I embrace him, and he shifts us so that my back is no longer touching the wall. Instead, his hands cradle my ass as he holds me upright on his cock and carries me into a beam of silver moonlight.

We stand in the middle of the garden, joined as intimately as two people can be joined. I look down upon his beautiful face, and though I say nothing, he somehow knows my thoughts.

"I would walk into the Shadow World for you," he says. "I would fight armies and gods all alone and set fire to their world for you. Don't you ever forget that."

His words rattle something deep inside me, sending a shiver rippling down my spine. The devotion and promise that drenches each syllable is so real and true that it almost hurts my heart. Because I know he would do all those things, and I'm not sure the world would ever recover if he did.

With that, I kiss him once more, letting the delicious taste of him saturate my senses, and we begin moving in a rhythm all our own. He thrusts, delving deep as I ride, pleasure skittering over my skin like a breeze.

But then I feel it, the throbbing orgasm rising inside him, filling the long, thick column of his cock, threatening to erupt. He buries his head in the crook of my shoulder with a groan, his fingers digging into my flesh, his mouth latching onto my throat as I dig my fingernails into the bunched muscles of his wide back.

I'm ready to shatter as well, my breaths coming in pants as Alexus scrapes his teeth across my skin, as though he could devour me whole.

"Mine," he groans again, taking me in long, hard thrusts. "Have you any idea what I feel for you?"

Tears prick my eyes as my release builds in time with his. The earth trembles and the wind off the sea rises over the garden wall as though summoned, rushing like a howling gale. It catches Alexus's cries and the roar of my name and swiftly carries them away across Malgros.

We both fracture and careen through darkness like stars falling from the night sky. Whatever this power is—our magick and our bond together—it envelops us and fills us with the most genuine and pure pleasure, so genuine and pure that I know he feels it too. It's all-consuming, stilling time itself, chasing away everything except what we feel for one another.

At some point, we return to ourselves, ever so slowly, and I find that we're now lying in a naked heap on the grass, limbs tangled and shaking, lungs gasping, hands clutching.

Alexus takes my face in his hand, his eyes soft. "You are where I belong, Raina Bloodgood. Every bit of me. My body. My heart. My soul. I'm yours. Forever. Until the mountains crumble into the sea."

Before he gathers our clothes and sweeps me up to carry me to the lighthouse for a long night together, he kisses me. A lingering kiss. One that has no care for time or place, no worry that someone might happen upon us. No worry for anything.

And I let him. I return that kiss with passion, trying with all that I am to show him that I feel the same.

Because if I'm not mistaken, I think Alexus Thibault just told me that he loves me.

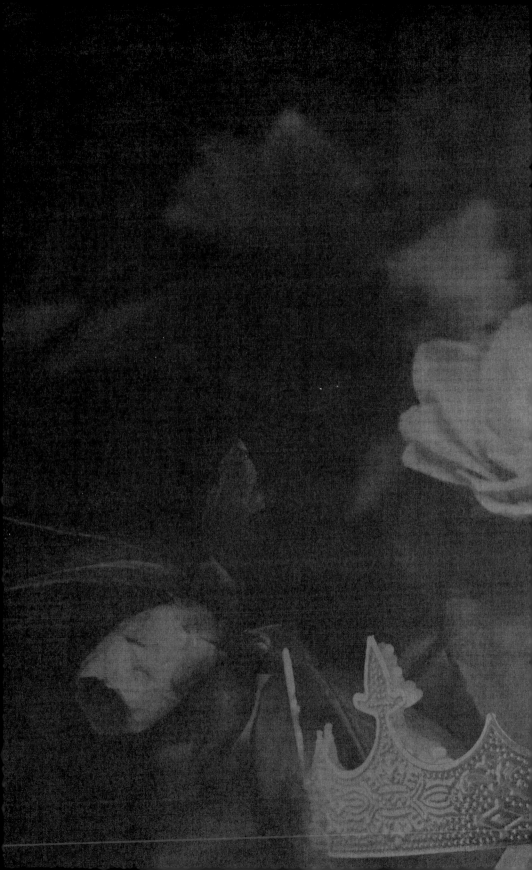

THE JADE RIVER

From City of Ruin

Helena & Rhonin's First Time

I

HELENA

"Of all the things I imagined happening tonight," Rhonin says, "seeing you without a single stitch of clothing wasn't anywhere on the list."

I can't help but smile. "Not even in your dreams?"

He's still waist deep in the water I warmed near the riverbank, his eyes locked on me as I stand in a clearing between two stretches of thick scrub, squeezing water from my hair. It's fucking *cold* in the desert at night, my pebbled skin and nipples proof of that.

Thanks to a little fire magick, we built three fires before we cleaned up, placing them in the shape of a triangle, creating enough heat to surround us after bathing so we could dry out in comfort. The flames burn warm at my back, illuminating the small beach.

And me.

"Oh, I wasn't sure if dreams counted," he says. "You are always unclothed in my dreams. *Always*. But seeing the real thing… Well. It is, by far, superior."

Still smiling, I bend over, reaching for the pack I managed to bring with us through Raina's abyss and retrieve a blanket. Warmth envelopes me as I wrap the wool around my body before facing Rhonin once again.

I should probably feel embarrassed—he's just seen every last inch of me. I've never been one for modesty, though, unlike a certain red-haired gentleman.

Darkness shadows his face too much for me to discern his expression, but if I were a betting woman, I'd say his cheeks just burned through seven shades of red. He'd blushed so brightly when I kissed him at the inn in Itunnan. We'd had a room to ourselves, and I suppose I thought things between us might go further than a first kiss. He was so gentle with me. Almost timid. His touches and kisses had been the tenderest explorations that left me wanting and needing so much more. But when I'd slid my hands downward, he'd stopped me and held me close instead, making me wonder if he really wanted me at all. I swore he did, but I decided he just wasn't ready.

We drifted to sleep that night in one another's arms, overtaken by exhaustion by all that had happened in the city. Though being close like that was nice, and I'd take sleeping anytime over nothing when it comes to Rhonin, I hope tonight doesn't end the same way.

"That water has to be getting cold," I say, eager to have him close to me again. "Do I need to turn around so you can get out and dry off?"

He laughs, though it's a mocking sound, one that makes me giggle. "I just don't want to stun you with my natural beauty," he says. "That's all."

I arch a brow. "I've seen naked men before, you know. While I'm sure your manly bits are lovely, I doubt they're anything new."

"Seen? Or been with?" he asks.

"Both."

He starts walking toward the river's edge, cupping himself, water sluicing off his body as more and more of him comes into view. "You're experienced, then?"

I don't like thinking about Emmitt or the boy before him, a boy I met at market in Penrith. Both are gone forever now.

"Experienced enough. I'm certainly no novice."

As he reaches the beach and shakes water from his hair, I take a few steps back, until I'm standing in the middle of the fires, shielded by walls of heat. Rhonin strides toward me, and I can't look away. He's the most beautiful thing I've ever seen, though I wish he would lower his hands so I could see *all* of him.

He steps into the warm island I've created and stops, leaving a single stride between us, his body glistening in the firelight. I swallow hard at the sight of him, the water running from the strands of his hair over the thick curve of his smooth chest, his hard nipples, the rippled plane of his abdomen. Gods, I'm already aching, and he hasn't even touched me yet.

I'm anything but shy, so I hold open the blanket like wings. "Come here. Let me warm you."

Those bright, innocent cerulean eyes sparkle in the firelight as he looks down, running his gaze over my body. When he meets my stare again, some of the pure innocence that lives inside Rhonin seems to have buried itself away, replaced by desire. I see it in the way he moves with a little more confidence—stepping close and looming over me.

His lip is quivering from the cold, so I fold the blanket around us both, resting my hands behind his neck as I press my body against his, skin to skin. His breath hitches at this first contact. As for me, my breasts suddenly feel so heavy, like they need his touch. His grip. His kiss.

"You can let go of your bits now." I look up at him with a smile. "I can think of far better things you can do with those hands."

He hesitates, like he's uncertain what to do, but finally, he slips his palms over my hips. A shuddering breath leaves him as he grips my flesh. "Gods, you feel so good."

Rising on my tiptoes, I lean close, speaking my words against his mouth. "I bet I can feel even better."

He lifts his hands and cups my face as I press my lips to his, and in a matter of seconds, I'm swept away in Rhonin's kiss. His tongue is the grandest tease, tasting me, moving in ways that make me grow wet with longing. He may seem innocent and inexperienced in some ways, but in this, he is a master.

In Malgros, Rhonin said that one day I would kiss him because I wanted to, not because of a bargain, and he was right. We kissed for a long time that night at the inn, and again the night we went hunting near Elam. Both times, I'd wanted to taste his kisses more than I wanted to breathe. Tonight is no different.

I want his mouth everywhere.

We kiss the way we spar, meeting each other's every movement with the perfect response. I press closer, kissing Rhonin deeper, groaning into his mouth as I feel his erection grow hard against my stomach, though he pulls away before I get the full effect.

"I want you," I whisper. "I want you inside me. Now." I let the blanket fall, our skin blessedly met with warmth from the fires, and begin trailing my hands down his chest, his abdomen, needing to touch more of him. But he grips my wrists, stopping me. Again.

He leans his forehead against mine, breathing hard. "You can't say things like that to me. And you can't touch me like that."

A frown takes over my face. "Why not?"

"Because I want to give you everything you desire, Helena. You have no idea how badly. But I...I've never..."

I pull back and look up into his eyes. "You've never *what?*"

For a moment, thoughts whirl through my mind like leaves chasing each other in the wind, reasons trying to form as to why he can't lay me down right here in the middle of this warm beach and take me for hours. In truth, I can't think of any.

But then, I no longer need to search for answers, because just like with the way we kiss, I've learned Rhonin in other ways, too. That look on his face. That sweet innocence. That tenderness and worry.

I slip my hand up to his cheek. "Rhonin. Have you ever been with someone like this before?"

He exhales, the sound at its edges one of relief. "No. Not like... Not like what *you* want. Other things, yes. Of course. But life in the

Eastern army didn't exactly lend itself to moments of pleasure such as this. There simply wasn't time, and the last thing any of us needed was a child. We don't have birthbane in the East. It simply won't grow. What we *do* have only works some of the time, so sex is a great risk."

Now I'm embarrassed, for not realizing this earlier, because suddenly everything makes sense. Every timid moment. Every nervous smile. Every second of hesitance.

"I'm so sorry for assuming that you had done this. And that you even wanted to do it here, tonight. With m—"

He kisses me, sliding his hands into my hair and drawing me close. His lips are hungrier, as though freed by the truth he didn't know how to speak.

When he pulls back, he says, "I want you, Helena. I want to do everything your mind can conjure. Don't you ever think otherwise. It's just that I want it to be a wonderful experience for you, and I'm worried I just don't know how to make it wonderful."

I press my fist to my heart, feeling it squeeze. "This will be *your* first time, and you're worried about *me?*"

A blush spreads over his cheeks. "Of course, I am. I've done *things*. But I've never done *the* thing. I want to please you. I want to hear and see and feel your pleasure."

I kiss him, long and slow, tangling my hands in his soft, wet hair until we're both panting. "I can show you how," I whisper, my heart pounding. "But first, perhaps I should please *you*. If you'd like that."

A soft smile curves his lips, reaching his sparkling eyes. "I *would* like that. Very much."

To direct the situation, I slip my hand down his body, his skin already warming. Thankfully, this time, he flinches, but he doesn't stop me.

I reach the trail of soft hair below his navel, then my fingertips graze the base of his cock. A small gasp leaves me as I trail my fingertips up, up, *up* his length, and I have to glance down.

Rhonin clears his throat. "That's another thing. My *manly bits* are not like all the others."

Sweet *gods*. Rhonin's cock is enormous. Beautifully made, so engorged it looks painful, and perfectly, wonderfully, deliciously *huge*, much like the rest of him. I take a deep breath, realizing that I stopped breathing for a few moments.

"No one has ever..." I can't even finish my words because my mouth is so godsdamn dry, as though I've been cock-starved until this very moment.

"It's been touched," he says, his voice soft. "Mostly by me. And it's been sucked a few times, until I came. But that's all."

A shiver chases down my spine, not from the cold, but at hearing his honest words, the way they sound when spoken with that deep, gentle voice. I should be jealous. Of all things, I, Helena Owyn, am jealous of anyone touching Rhonin Shawcross except for me. But for some reason, right now, picturing what he just described makes me feel like he has the power to completely unravel me with a few simple utterances.

He leans close, eyes searching mine. "We don't have to do anything. I don't want to hurt you."

My hand trembles a little as I close my fingers around his thick shaft. If any other man said that to me, I would probably roll my eyes. But tonight, I nod in understanding. This is why he'd pulled away from me earlier. So I wouldn't feel his size.

"We'll take it slowly," I whisper, stroking that velvety skin, feeling it slide up and down that promising stiffness beneath. "I never minded a little pain."

His cock twitches in my hand—once, twice—and he utters my name like a plea. As though he can't hold back, he begins shallow thrusts into my grip, even as he pushes my hair behind my ear and stares into my eyes, his gaze glassed over with lust. I glance down again, that throbbing tip beckoning me.

Unable to resist, I drop to my knees. A rush of cold air meets the heat radiating from the fire, causing chills to rise across my fire-warmed skin.

Rhonin sucks in a breath, all but hissing in surprise. "Helena."

I look at him, wanting this, needing this, as I trail my hands up his long, powerful thighs.

Gripping him at the base, I drag my tongue along the underside of his cock, eliciting a groan that sets every part of me on fire. I'll never take him fully like this, so I begin swirling my tongue around his tip as I stroke him with a tight grasp. Again, he slides his hands into my hair, fisting them but then releasing me, ever gentle.

I meet his eyes. "You won't hurt me." I flick my tongue back and forth inside the wet slit at his tip, tasting saltiness there. "Fuck me like this. I like it."

A flicker of shock blinks over his face as he connects what I said to what he's supposed to do. It's almost as though fucking goes against his very nature, but gods' stars, he begins to move his hips.

I can feel him holding back, though, his thrusts far shallower now than before when he was moving in my hand. To encourage him, I take him as deeply as I can and slide my hands up the backs of his thighs, urging him toward me. Harder. Faster.

He reaches down and runs his thumb across my top lip watching closely as I suck him. "Fuck, Helena. This is…" He gasps. "So good."

I keep urging him, running my hands up and down his legs, over his ass, tilting my head so I can take more of him into my throat. Some dark part of me is thriving off this, feeling his control splinter one thin shard at a time, knowing that I will be the one who breaks away that innocent veneer and finds the insatiable lover beneath. I already know he's there. I just have to set him free.

Boldly, I slip one hand between my legs and moan around his cock the second I touch myself. He shudders, breathing hard as I meet his gaze, my fingers working my clit.

"Are you…" He swallows, and the knot in his throat moves. "Are you touching yourself?"

I nod as best I can, moaning again, and when I do, when vibration and realization rock through him, I finally get what I want.

Rhonin Shawcross tilts his head back, tightens his fists in my hair, and let's go.

2

RHONIN

Something inside me snaps.

I'm not sure what the exact cause is. Whether it's the sight of Helena on her knees with my cock stretching her pretty mouth wide, the knowledge that she was playing with herself while sucking my cock, or if it's the absolute life-altering feel of finally being inside this woman in any way. Regardless, she's destroyed a wall inside me, one I didn't even know existed until I began to feel it crumble.

Restraint. Discipline. Control. All bricks in the wall, lessons pounded into me while training for the army during the day and for spying at night. Never let your emotions show. Never give an inch. Never lose the upper hand.

My gods, have I lost it now. All power is held by the woman at my feet. She commands me with a glance. With a touch. With the perfect flick of her tongue. It takes so little, and suddenly, I'm thrusting into her mouth, her throat, taking her far deeper than I should, deep as I know she wants it.

I could've never imagined doing this to her. Not this roughly. But she never makes to pull away, no matter how hard I fuck her, not even when she chokes on me. Instead, her hand pumps harder up and down my cock while the other works faster between her legs. It's enough to make me ready to spill right here, right in her mouth.

That isn't how I want tonight to go, though, so I start to pull away, yet she holds me tight.

"I need to be inside you, Helena," I warn her. "Between your legs. Right fucking now."

Blinking out of her haze of lust, she drags her mouth off me and kisses her way up my body.

She grips my arms to steady herself and laughs a little. "My legs are already shaking."

I didn't know such words could motivate me so thoroughly, but suddenly, that becomes my goal for the night. To make her legs tremble so hard she can't walk.

"How do you want me?" I ask her, letting her guide the night.

"Sitting," she says, jerking her chin at a smooth boulder between two of the fires. "On the blanket. With your back against that rock."

Not what I imagined she'd say, but I'm not arguing. I grab the blanket, toss it over the rock and ground, and sit just as she asked.

When she straddles me, the entire world narrows to nothing but her. She slides her hands over my chest and shoulders and into my hair, leaning in for a kiss. Her full breasts press against my chest, and for the first time, I take them in my hands, kneading her flesh.

She pulls back with a sharp breath, her eyes drifting closed as I touch her. "Don't stop," she pleads.

I wouldn't dare. I've dreamed about these magnificent breasts. Of touching them. Sucking them. Fucking them. Helena is stunning, her curves full and heavy in all the right places. The sight of her bending over earlier tonight had nearly undone me. The way her breasts were silhouetted by firelight, the way her ass swayed when she walked across the beach. I love the bronze and silver witch's marks that dance over her body, her dark nipples, the softness that covers the warrior beneath her brown skin.

Holding her breasts, I take one nipple into my mouth, sucking and biting. I'm unsure at first what she likes, but her smooth breathing suddenly turns to short pants, her spine arching each time I use my teeth.

So I use them more.

"You like it when I bite you?" I ask, and she begins moving her hips, sliding her wet sex along my cock, readying me for the moment we make this happen, when I'll finally slide inside her.

"I fucking love it." Her fingers tighten in my hair. "Bite harder."

Hungrily, I suck her into my mouth and drag my teeth over her nipple before switching to the other breast, teasing her until she's rocking against my cock so hard I know she's about to orgasm.

Gripping her hips, I still her. "I thought we were taking this slowly," I say with a smile.

Struggling to catch her breath, she says, "Yes, well, that was before we started. You might be a virgin, but you certainly aren't a novice at everything."

I slip her midnight-black hair over her lovely shoulder and lean in, kissing her throat, her neck, her ear, feeling goosebumps rise across her skin. "I want to be inside you," I whisper, cupping her ass. "Please. Take this awful virginity plague from me. Put me *inside you*, oh queen."

Her shoulders jerk with laughter as she presses her forehead against mine. "Are you ready?"

I graze my thumb across her cheek and pull back to look her in the eyes. "Yes. I've never been more ready."

After a few moments, she rises on her knees and reaches down between us, positioning my cock at her entrance. I see the bravery in her. The way her want of me conquers all worry.

The moment she sinks onto me, taking the first few inches, her body naturally clenching, I have to fight back the throbbing pulse of my release. "Holy fucking gods."

She remains close to me, trembling a little, her forehead still pressed against mine. "Rhonin, this feels so godsdamn good. You're so big."

"And you're so tight. So warm and wet and soft and..." I drop my head back. "I'm not going to make it through this night. It's impossible."

She kisses the column of my throat, biting playfully, and I feel her smile against my skin. Teasing, she licks a path upward, then sinks onto me even more, her breath hitching when she does.

When that little gasp rushes over my ear, I grip her ass harder and push up into her reflexively, just a little.

"Oh gods, more," she begs, holding onto me, her fingers biting into my skin.

And I oblige, thrusting up into her, harder this time, until she's taking over half of me, her silken heat still gripping me like a fist.

"I'm going to be addicted to this," I promise her. "To you. To seeing how much of me you can take."

"All of you," she whispers against my mouth. "Make me take all of you."

Make me.

All coherent thought leaves my brain for a few moments, but she digs her fingernails into my shoulders, and I shake off the shock that this is happening and do as she asked. Or at least I try, arching up into her again and again, harder and harder until she cries out my name, and I'm finally, blessedly, buried inside her as far as I can go. It's not to the root, but that doesn't matter. *We are perfect.*

"There cannot be anything better than this," I choke out. "You feel like you were made for me, Helena Owyn."

She touches my face, her eyes alight with desire and adoration. "And you for me."

Helena begins moving on me, rocking her hips, the head of my cock being tortured with every rub of the deepest part of her. Her nipples are so hard, her breasts bouncing as she works her pussy on my cock.

I have to taste them.

Sucking her into my mouth, I run my hands over her hips and her ass as she moves, memorizing her rhythm. My release is so torturously close, as though she's summoning it with every motion. She is a witch, and I am indeed under her spell.

Slipping my hands down, I feel for her. *For us.* The moment she senses me touching where we're joined, she pauses, pressing her breast firmly against my mouth and her pussy against my fingers. I run my fingertip around the slick base of my cock, the ring of her flesh stretched around me.

"Yes, don't stop," she says, her voice breaking over the words. "Please, Rhonin."

That plea alone almost takes me over the edge, but I choke back my rising climax, needing to draw this night out for as long as I can.

But everything spirals. Helena kisses me, moaning even as she grinds on me, riding me like her life depends on it. I lift my hips, forcing her to take me even deeper as I lean in and scrape a bite across her pounding pulse, hoping that I leave a mark so that when I wake up in the morning, I know this was real. It feels like every wet dream I've ever had combined into one night. With this woman, I feel like the luckiest man in the world.

"I wanted you the moment I first saw you," I admit, a truth if there ever was one. "I saw the fire inside you, and gods, how I wanted to be burned."

At my words, the fires around us flare, mimicking Helena's rising passion.

"Fire consumes," she warns me, and then she leans in for one more kiss, sucking my tongue into her mouth.

I realize then that I'm filling her. I'm inside her as thoroughly as I can be. That thought and a single clench of her body, and my orgasm rages through me. I thrust up into her, burying my cock as she fists my hair, her body sucking my release out of me without relent.

She rides me through it, clinging to me, her own climax chasing mine until I feel her spasming around me, as though her body demands I give her everything I have.

And I do. I spill all that I am into her, giving over a part of myself I'm certain I'll never get back. A part I don't *want* back.

Because if anyone can guard my heart better than me, it's her.

3

HELENA

"I'd say that has to be the best 'first time' anyone has ever had," Rhonin whispers.

I sit draped over him like a cloak, lifeless and languid. He's still inside me, filling me even as his erection softens.

"I think we need a second time tonight," I reply, feeling absolutely ravaged. "And a third."

I smile against his shoulder and glance up at him, knowing that repeat rounds aren't likely to happen. I'm also a little stunned. I've never felt like this with anyone. Granted, I don't have a long line of lovers, but I never imagined *this*—being so intimate with someone that I ache to be *with* them or *near* them constantly. Love was a distant thing meant for dreamers or people like Finn who wanted a spouse and a home and babies.

Instead of that life, I held dreams of joining the Northland Watch. Of learning to fight and maybe take to guarding the seas. I never imagined anything else, but now I find myself wondering how I could ever leave Rhonin behind. In truth, it worries me a little that I feel this way. That I feel like I need him.

"It's abnormal for me to ask for more," I tell him honestly. "I used to only want the release. Then I was gone."

He brushes the back of his hand across my cheek. "That's a good thing, I think. That you want me. I have a good feeling about you and me."

"It doesn't terrify you?"

He smiles. "That you want me? Should it?"

I shake my head, wondering if I'm broken in some way to think that it could.

We sit there for a while, holding one another, warmed by the fire, listening to the emptiness of the desert beyond. Much to my surprise, Rhonin hardens again, without the slightest provocation.

"Round two?" he asks, and I flash a giddy smile.

As though I would decline.

This time, Rhonin lays me back on the blanket and settles between my legs. I'm already sore, but I want the ache of having been with him. I want him imprinted on my bones.

When he kisses me, it's with a softer edge, his lips warm and lush against my own. "My turn. Are *you* ready?"

I am. Not just for tonight. But for whatever lies ahead for us. Something inside me has always screamed that I was meant for more, and tonight, I feel like a part of that destiny has completed itself, as though Rhonin and I were meant to meet for a reason, as though our unity means something far larger in this world than a night of passion, wonderful as it might be.

"More ready than you can ever know," I answer him.

Even if it scares me a little.

"Good," he whispers. "Because you're in for the ride of your life, Helena Owyn."

Feeling certain that I am, I close my eyes and hold on tight.

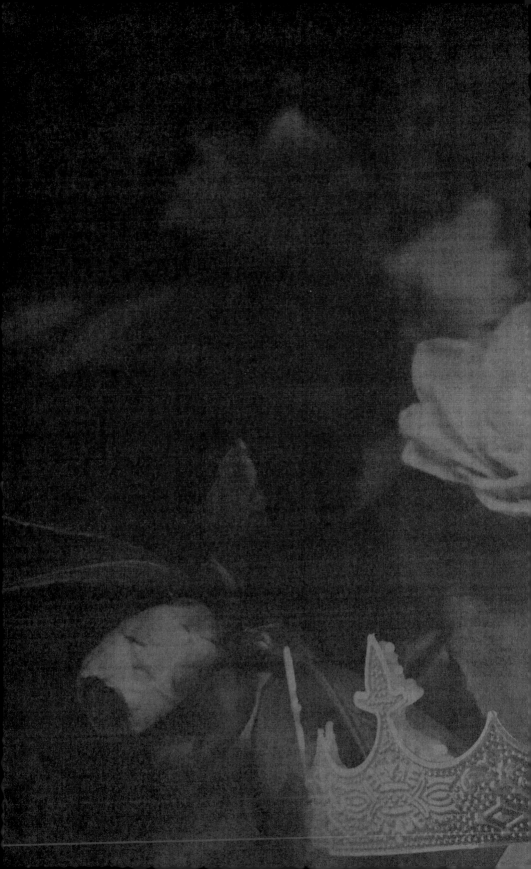

A WINTER'S WISH

*An Old Tale of Friends and Lovers
Told by Petra Anrova*

*Alexus, Colden, & Petra
Thirty-Two Years Before the Attack
on the Northlands*

PETRA

There is no darkness so great as a night sky over the Iceland Plains midwinter.

I decide this as Alexus and Colden guide our horses through the blinding snow toward the faint lights of the village of Nori. Though the cold has turned my bones to ice and muddled my thoughts, I focus long enough to construct a glamour over the marks that rain down my face. Like spilled ink, the birthmark brands me as one of Loria's descended. A curiosity. A rarity.

A commodity.

Near midnight, we reach the main road that cuts through the sleeping village. Nori is a stretch of cramped cottages and shops, a community that's more like a town than the sprawling villages in the valley. It's our last stop before we reach the northernmost village of Reede where I'll make my home, far away from the temptations that torture me at every turn: *the very men at my side.*

Colden leads his horse and mine by the reins while Alexus walks a short pace ahead, clinging to his animal's bridle. His black cloak billows like a dark ghost in the frigid wind, painting him into an ominous figure moving through the snowy landscape.

"I truly wish you would've waited until spring to do this, princess," Colden grumbles up at me for the hundredth time since our journey began a few weeks back, snowflakes clinging to his eyelashes. We've argued many times about my questionable godly royalty, but he won the right to call me princess in a drink-off two years ago, fair and square. "If I lose my balls to the cold," he continues, "and find myself doomed to eternity on this godsforsaken earth without them—"

Before I can laugh at him, a door to one of the tall, crooked buildings swings open, spilling a wedge of golden light across the road. Sounds of soft chatter and faint music drift into the snowy darkness. Drink in hand, a man stumbles across the threshold of what appears to be a tavern. We watch him stagger down the road as we approach, and in minutes, after handing our horses off to a stableman, we're standing inside the warmth of the bar in our rugged clothes, our laden packs dropped at our feet, hearty stale ales in hand.

Colden looks around the tavern from beneath his hood. "I believe we've found the local love shack."

The room is filled with half-drunk people. A few sit alone, but most others are either coupled up at tables or wadded together in darkened corners doing gods know what. There's laughter and murmurs and giggles and grunts to boot.

Eyes are upon us, though, as they've been every stop thus far. We're drifters—travelers—yet thanks to Alexus's shaved face and pulled-back hair, and Colden's drab attire and dirt-smudged cheeks, no one has any inkling that their king, his Collector, and a descendant of Loria are in their midst.

And we want to keep it that way.

"We need rooms for the night," Alexus says to the barkeep, keeping his hood up and his voice down. He leans his big body against the cedar counter and discreetly slips enough silver across its smooth top to buy the woman's silence and nonchalance. "Can you accommodate us without any attention or affair?"

Covering the coin with a meaty hand, she glances at our faces and nods, sweeping the money into her skirt pocket. "I've only one room," she says with a rasp. "The owner's chambers. He's gone on a fishing expedition. It'll be plenty big enough, though 'tis only the one bed."

The three of us share a glance and shrug at the same time. One bed is no matter. We've slept in the same room twice while stopping to rest. There aren't many taverns or inns in these parts to begin with, much less those with lavish rooms waiting to be rented for a night. Sleeping with Colden and Alexus isn't the easiest thing I've ever done —for more than a few reasons. But a bed is a bed, and I'm with my best friends. I won't complain.

"That'll do." Alexus drums his fingers on the bar top. "If you could get the lady settled first, we'll join her shortly."

Again, the barkeep studies our faces, though she pauses when she reaches mine. A knowing smirk tugs the corner of her thin mouth, and her brow flattens. She's either thinking that I'm a whore down to my marrow or that I'm a very, very lucky lady. I cannot discern which, and I truly don't care. I *am* lucky, though not for the reasons she probably thinks. I'm lucky to have these two men in my life, of that much I'm certain.

With a semi-wary look at my friends, I tug my pack over my shoulder, and the woman leads me to the back of the tavern. We climb a narrow set of stairs and stroll down a dimly lit hall to an arched doorway. I think of the dagger hidden beneath my cloak as she jangles a key ring from her pocket. She doesn't look worrisome, but as Alexus has taught me, I watch her closely and keep my guard up regardless.

I can taste magick wafting off her.

She unlocks the door before pushing it open on creaking hinges and gestures for me to enter. I step past her into the cold, empty chambers, shivering in the shadowy darkness. It isn't long before she has a fire crackling in the hearth, candles lit across the room, and a glass of mulled wine poured and waiting for me on a table beside the bed which is far larger than I expected. This place isn't lavish, but it's more comforting than the simple wilderness taverns we've visited before tonight.

The barkeep glances out the single window at the falling snow, then jerks her chin toward the copper soaking tub sitting in the corner of the room. "I'd prepare a bath, milady, but—"

I raise my hand to stop her. "I wouldn't ask you to deal with that tonight. We'll be fine. We just need sleep." What I don't tell her is that I can and will remedy the bathing issue on my own the moment she's gone.

That smirk of hers returns. "I could imagine you'd need a bit more than sleep after traveling with two men such as those downstairs." Her round face flushes scarlet. "I certainly would. We don't see very many people like them in these parts. Handsome lot."

It's my turn to blush. "They are quite lovely. But we're only friends. *Companions.* We'll be snoring within the hour."

She frowns. "And is that what ye want?"

"Of course." I smile uncomfortably, hoping to hide the lie. Having my body pressed between Alexus Thibault's and Colden Moeshka's, sleeping, isn't what I want at all. It hasn't been what I've wanted the two times we've shared a bed on this journey. But I'm not as brazen as Colden or as honest as Alexus, never one to speak my longings aloud. Especially not now that I'm leaving them.

The barkeep gives me an odd look, one of disbelief mixed with disapproval, but also one of doubt, as if she doesn't quite believe my 'of course.'

"That's a pity, milady, but to each her own, I s'pose." She heads to the door and pauses. "But just in case, I'll spin a winter's wish for ye, that the Ancient Ones grant you whatever it is you truly desire."

A winter's wish. What I truly desire. Dangerous combination if wishes really came true.

I thank her, and once I'm alone, I let my glamour fall and face the room, every corner glowing warmly with firelight. I somehow doubt the Ancient Ones care much about my carnal yearnings, or that I would very much like it if Colden and Alexus would grant me one night—just one—in their arms. I know I would be loved. Admired. Adored. I know that every touch would be a pleasure, every moment bliss. I've never felt that with anyone, really. Probably because I trust no one the way I trust my king and the Collector.

And I doubt I ever will again.

I turn to the copper tub. The boys always give me time alone when we stop to rest, a testament to the kind of men they are. They're probably downstairs enjoying their drinks as usual, though I know they're weary and would much rather be stripping away their layers and boots as they relax on the settee by the fire. I consider going down to fetch them, but they've just started on their ale, so I doubt they would come.

Plus, the bath.

In a matter of minutes, I'm sinking into a tub of steaming water. Water magick is a handy gift, and thanks to Alexus's teaching, I know my way around a fire thread or two. Fire magick is so important to him, something he seems to cling to, even though he can't wield it. I've always wondered why, and I've considered attempting to look into his past to find the answer. But a man as private as Alexus Thibault probably hides his secrets for a reason, and my gift isn't meant to pry into my friends' lives. Not unless they want me to. And he never has.

I wash with lavender soaps I found in an amber glass jar, even running some of the lather into my hair and rinsing. I take a deep inhale, then duck beneath the water, relishing the heat soaking into my bones. I linger there, holding my breath.

When I break the surface and wipe the water from my face, I blink my eyes open, only to find Colden and Alexus standing frozen just inside the room.

THEIR EYES ARE WIDE, TAKEN COMPLETELY OFF GUARD.

"Fuck," is all Alexus says, the word hanging on the edge of an exhaled breath, low and deep.

"My sentiments exactly." Colden sets his pack on the floor.

"Pardon our disobedient eyes." He turns and shuts the door behind him, sliding the lock while Alexus, face reddening, clears his throat and slowly gives me his back.

It takes a matter of seconds before it dawns on me that the water isn't covering my breasts.

"Oh, gods. So sorry." I reach for the bath linen and stand, water coursing off my body as I quickly fold the towel around myself and step from the tub. I lean over the still-steaming water and squeeze out my hair. "I didn't think you two would come up so soon."

Colden steals a peek over his shoulder before facing me while Alexus crosses to the dressing table and leans his pack against it, sighing just loudly enough that it reaches my ears like a whisper.

"The barkeep said you decided to forego a bath," Colden informs me. "We knocked. When you didn't answer, we thought you might be sleeping."

"I didn't hear."

That mischievous smile of his unfurls across his lovely face, and one blondish-brown eyebrow arches over a dark eye. "Obviously."

I glance at Alexus's wide back as he sheds his cloak and traveling coat. He's so quiet. I know that seeing me bare-breasted was awkward. We've been careful and lucky on this trip—there've been no other moments like this. Which might be the problem, because a strange tension floats in the air now, radiating from Alexus Thibault like heat. It makes something in the pit of my stomach tighten.

He opens the top drawer of the dressing table and withdraws a black garment. He turns and, after assessing me from crown to foot, walks toward me, handing me the bundled fabric. "The barkeep said to tell you about this. A clean gown."

Clutching the bath linen against my chest with one hand, I hold his gaze and accept the gown. "I'm sorry," I say again, quietly. "I didn't mean to—"

Alexus folds his big hand around my arm and kisses my forehead. "Do not apologize. I'm the one who should be sorry." His thumb strokes my skin, still hot and wet from the bath, as the corners of his mouth lift a little, not enough to call it a smile, though the effort is there. "I suppose that ale was stouter than I believed, because when I saw you, I lost my manners."

I stare up into his green eyes, feeling his warmth so close, his grip gentle on my arm. My nipples harden, and a tender ache builds between my legs. All I can think about is what it would be like to finally kiss him the way I've imagined the last few years. To lay him back on the bed, crawl over him, and ride him while Colden covers our bodies in kisses.

"I think I might take a quick dip in your bath, princess," Colden says, interrupting the moment with his typical, perfect timing.

The heat and magnetism between me and Alexus snaps as we abruptly pull apart, and I try to breathe. Standing by the fireplace, Colden has already stripped free of his cloak, coat, and sweaters. All that's left is his tunic and leather trousers. When he tugs his shirt over his head with one hand, revealing a torso that's just as leanly muscled as I have always imagined, that ache between my legs throbs.

It's just skin, Petra.

Yes. Naked, beautiful, Colden skin. Skin I've longed to touch too many times.

Alexus looks at him too. Their eyes meet for a long moment, the way they so often do. Colden once told me that he and Alexus aren't lovers in the sense I used to believe, that they've only ever shared certain common intimacies, whatever that means. He also told me that Alexus's heart is a mysterious landscape locked behind a wall he keeps erected at all costs. Surely someone must have the key. A part of me has long wished that someone could be me, but somehow I already know that it can't.

Tightening my fist in the gown, I shake my head to clear it. "Enjoy," I say to Colden, trying to ignore the curves of his muscled chest or the deep lines carving his abdomen. "I'm going to dress for bed." I nod toward the dressing screen, a wooden trifold affair with a white, almost gossamer-like material stretched so thinly over the frame I'm certain Colden and Alexus will still be able to see me when

I change. I can't decide if they might want to see me or not. Insight is my gift. Intuition flows thick in my blood. And yet tonight I can't determine what anyone is really thinking except for me.

Alexus steps aside, and I cross to the dressing screen. Behind the thin barrier, I slip into the silken gown which is far prettier and daintier than it should be for a piece of clothing found in the owner's chambers of a northern tavern. It fits perfectly—*if I were trying to seduce the men sharing the room with me.*

There are no sleeves. Only straps. And though the garment comes to my ankles, two slits travel up the sides of my thighs, clean to my hips. The top fits over my ample breasts comfortably, like many of the clothes tailored for me at Winterhold, while the rest is snug in all the right places. It's as though the gown was made by…

Oh, my gods. *Magick.*

The barkeep.

Partly annoyed at the woman, yet also thankful for a clean gown, I take a deep breath and blow it out before stepping from behind the screen. I remind myself that these men have seen plenty of women in far less clothing than what I'm wearing.

As though they're both attempting to keep certain tensions down, neither of them looks at me. Colden is leaned back in the tub, hair wet and slicked back. Beads of water glisten on his skin under the firelight. He's silent, and Colden is never silent, especially in moments ripe for his innuendo-laced remarks. I know he sees me in his periphery, but he keeps his gaze trained on the curved edge of the copper tub.

Alexus sits on the settee in front of the hearth, tunic untied and open, revealing a sliver of scarred and muscled chest. His knees are spread wide, and he has one arm laid across the back of the settee. He cradles a glass of dark liquor in his other hand, the glass at rest on his thigh as he stares into the low flames warming the room.

Quietly, I check the changing table for a robe. Nothing, of course. To end this misery, I could crawl into bed, bury myself beneath the covers, and try to sleep. That would be better than enduring this awkward silence. I'm anything but tired, though. My skin is warm. Flushed even.

And that ache…

Finally, Alexus looks up at me. It's another wide-eyed gaze as he takes me in—crown to foot—slowly. But then his gaze narrows into a dark and lingering look, tracing my curves like a touch. I see hunger and loneliness in him. I've seen loneliness in him before, and it breaks my heart every time. It's as though there's some darkness that haunts him, some great emptiness that can never be filled. But I have still often wanted to try.

"Come sit," he says, and I obey. Alexus has a way about him. When he utters a command in that calm and steady voice, no one denies him.

Still, I'm self-conscious as I move in his direction, and even more so when he doesn't lower his arm from the back of the settee as I sit beside him. I'm glad he doesn't. It's as though he's answering my silent question about whether he wants me near.

Tonight, he does.

He hands me his liquor, like I might need the liquid courage more than him. I'm not sure that's the case, especially when our fingertips touch and his powerful thigh—stretching the leather of his trousers—grazes the bare skin of my exposed leg. I take a healthy drink anyway, enjoying the burning slide down my throat, the way it pools warm in my belly.

Water sloshes in the tub behind us, alerting us that Colden is finished bathing. The air tightens. We've never been together like this. When we've shared a room and slept in the same bed, it's with trousers and sweaters on. The first time, Alexus even took to the floor come midnight. Tonight, however, the atmosphere feels electric, or maybe I'm imagining everything, and my heart is the only one in the room that's racing.

"Gods, I feel like a new man." Colden pads over to the liquor cabinet that stands next to the hearth. He's wearing nothing but a thin, damp bathing linen around his narrow waist.

I take another drink of Alexus's liquor and swallow hard, trying not to stare at my king's body—the way the lines of his back flex as he pours his glass, the way the bath linen stretches across the curves of his ass, the way the material bulges at the front, such a thin barrier between us and what appears to be a very gifted and well-endowed part of his anatomy.

A throb pounds through me, forcing me to squeeze my thighs together to dull the achy need there. It doesn't work.

This is going to be the longest and most miserable night of my life. I'm already in agony.

How I wish it could be different.

"I want to bathe, too," Alexus says out of nowhere.

I snap my head around. My heart all but stops, my hand tightening around the glass. Alexus is looking right at me, though his gaze drifts to my clenched thighs, which I quickly release.

Even Colden turns, stopping mid-pour, wearing a stunned expression. "You? Getting naked in a room with other people in it?" He chuckles. Darkly. "My, my. Please grace us with such an anomaly."

I bite down on my lip and momentarily close my eyes. If we are all half-dressed or naked tonight, I will not survive. I already want them both so badly I can hardly stand the idea that I will wake up tomorrow just as I woke up today: without knowing the experience of being with them. But short of blurting out my desires—something I'm sure the barkeep would recommend—Colden and Alexus will never know the thoughts torturing my mind.

Alexus stands and moves toward the tub, giving Colden a cocky look as he passes. "I didn't say you could watch."

There's a shift in his tone, his voice layered with something I've never heard from him. Something sensual. A little playful. It sends a chill dancing across my skin.

Colden smiles, revealing bright white teeth. "As if you could stop me."

I expect Alexus to get in the tub. I expect ten levels of awkwardness as Colden sits beside me half-naked while we listen to Alexus strip and wash behind us—misery for us both, I'm sure.

But that isn't what happens.

"Can you work your magick for me, Petra?" Alexus asks. "The water has cooled, and it's filled with Colden's grime."

Colden's smile grows wider.

"Absolutely," I answer, stuttering and fumbling about as I look for somewhere to sit my glass. My legs are shaking. It's as though I've forgotten how to function.

Colden crosses the ornate rug between us and reaches for the drink in my hand. The still-damp skin of his abdomen and blond trail of hair that disappears into his towel are right in front of my face, along with that bulge I noticed earlier.

"Flustered?" he asks with a wink, lowering his voice. "Wait until the bastard takes his shirt off."

Every inch of me feels set on fire as I stand before Colden, noticing the tension in his jaw when I meet his stare. I've experienced this moment too many times not to recognize it for what it is. He's struggling to keep from glancing down at my breasts.

I face Alexus, my nerve endings alight, my mind filling with images of the three of us naked and tangled. *Magick, Petra.* I focus on that throughout the next several minutes, trying to suffocate the other thoughts in my mind. It isn't easy to make that much water vanish and reappear, but Alexus believes in practice, that much is for certain, so he's never afraid to ask.

Soon, the copper tub is refilled. Alexus stands across from me on the other side of the vessel. Holding my gaze, he reaches over his head and tugs off his tunic.

I've seen glimpses of his scars, and the many runes carved into his skin, but he's never told me of their purpose. I know a bit about runes, though, and I'm sure these are just more signs of his secrets, signs of his past. Signs he will never discuss with me.

Beyond those marks, though, is one of the most beautiful bodies I've ever seen. Colden is regal in stature, his skin pale white, his scars petal pink. He could've been carved by the gods from stone, his face so stunning it's almost criminal. Alexus is the darkness to Colden's light. His skin is light golden brown, the deeper warmth gently fading from the kiss of last summer's sun. His powerful warrior's body is covered in mystery and thickly muscled, whereas Colden has the leaner physique of a young soldier who might also be half-god. Alexus wears the marks of battle differently than Colden. They live like brands on his skin, shadows in his eyes, and ghosts in his soul.

His hand lowers to the ties of his trousers. Nipples hardening like pebbles, I follow the movement, noticing again the trail of hair, a tempting black line drawn from his navel that vanishes into his pants—more darkness to Colden's light. I ball my fingers into fists as I glance further down where the beginnings of an erection press against his leathers. He unlaces the first tie, and as my heart pounds like a drum, I lick my lips, unsure whether to watch or turn away.

"I need you to tell us what you want, Petra," he says, as though reading my mind. "I can sense it, but I need to hear you say it. After all these many days and nights together, I can assure you that Colden and I are just as torn as you."

"It's quite evident, princess," Colden says from behind me. "But you can be honest. It's okay."

He isn't invading my space—he's an entire stride away—but I still shiver at his nearness, at being pinned between these two men. It's exactly where I want to be, and yet I'm terrified.

Still, now that my secret is no more, relief drops through me, though it quickly feels like a sinking stone. I'm glad to know they're both struggling, too, and I'm glad Alexus and Colden are intuitive enough to see my misery. But they just made it clear that it's up to me to decide where this night goes. Am I brave enough to do this? To *have* this? To walk away from it when they leave me in Reede?

"I… I don't know what I want, really," I say, my voice small. Then I shake my head, deciding to find my bravery. "That's a lie. I want to be with you. Both of you. I've wanted it for so long. Wished for it, even. I'm wishing for it now."

The room falls silent, until Colden says, "That's quite the wish."

I nod and fold my arms beneath my breasts, turning so that I can look at them both. "In my years in the Drifts and when I traveled north, I never met anyone I trusted the way I trust the two of you. I'll never have this again. I know that, and it scares me. A whole lifetime awaits me, facing people who won't see me the way that you do, not if they learn what I really am. That fear of being found out will be with me until my dying day. Until then, I know I must protect myself, and that means trusting very few people. How do you open yourself to a lover if you can't show them who you really are? If I can't show them *this?*" I motion to the markings on my face as tears prick my eyes, but I blink them away. "I also simply crave you. Both of you. I don't know how it's possible to *not* want you. I've ached so many of these nights we've shared, laid awake wishing I could feel both of you inside me, needing relief but being far too cowardly to ask for it." They both stare at me, a little shocked if I'm reading them correctly. "Don't look at me like that. You said I could be honest."

After a moment, Colden gives me a soft smile. "Always. But just so that I'm clear, you're saying that you want us both. Sexually. *At the same time.* Tonight."

My blood rushes so hard it's all I hear. "Yes. That's what I want."

Colden looks at Alexus, and I follow his gaze. The look on Alexus's face is one of indecision. I can see the conflict clearly, the war in him. A man in constant turmoil.

"Only if you're good with it," Colden says to his friend, sharing some silent conversation I'm not privy to. They often speak with their eyes alone, moving through the world like one entity at times.

"I am," Alexus finally says. "I think I need you both."

A look of surprise crosses Colden's face, but he inclines his head, again communicating an understanding with Alexus that I can't read. "Are you protected?" he asks, turning back to me.

"I am," I tell him, though only for my own comfort on this journey.

"I'm assuming that, to make such a request, you're not inexperienced," Colden adds.

"No," I reply with a smile. "I'm thirty years old, Colden."

"I know," he says, arching a brow. "But have you ever had *two* men? That's an entirely different endeavor, princess."

I can't help but notice when the front of his bath linen moves a little.

"No," I answer again. "But I trust the two of you with my body."

"That's saying a lot given what you want us to do to you tonight," Alexus says.

I shrug one shoulder. "Perhaps. But I know you won't push me further than I can handle."

Being raised in a village that didn't want me, without my parents, I came to learn a life that involved people who didn't care for me. No one was ever loving or watchful. No one ever taught me to protect myself. No one ever watched over me like the truest guardians. No one else would draw swords for me save for these two men. Draw *blood*. They truly care for me and my well-being. If I can trust anyone to gift me a night of attentive pleasure, it's them.

At the corner of my eye, Alexus pushes his trousers down his hips. This time, I watch, because it feels like an invitation. He has to all but *peel* the leather down his muscled legs, and he takes his braies with them.

All the air leaves my lungs when I glimpse his cock for the first time. He's half-hard and beautiful—*and big*. The sight makes my chest tighten, the thought of him inside me, filling me, moving in me.

I'm not the only one affected by Alexus's teasing. Colden comes to stand beside me, his bare arm brushing against my shoulder. His drink is no longer in his hand, but he looks a little drunk regardless. His eyes are glazed, as though seeing Alexus naked has mesmerized him.

"Stunning, isn't he?" he asks, and all I can do is nod.

Stunning seems like one of the only accurate descriptors for the Collector. He's enough to make a person stop breathing, to make the rest of the world stop spinning, to still a heart from beating.

All with a glance.

Alexus steps into the tub and sinks into the water. Quickly, he dips under and soaks his head before pushing back to the surface.

Wiping his face, he motions to me with come-hither fingers. "Take your gown off and get in with me."

A shiver chases down my spine. Again with the gentle commands. I am so weak to the way those words sound that I instantly slip the straps from my shoulders and shimmy out of the garment. Alexus Thibault's voice is as persuasive as any enchanter, but the way his eyes darken when he looks at my naked body is just as magickal.

Colden takes my hand, his admiring gaze skimming up and down my figure. I have a fuller shape, one that speaks of comfort and sensuality.

He just shakes his head, clearly quite happy with my curves. "You are utterly breathtaking, princess." Before he helps me into the tub, he says, "Can I kiss you first?"

I nod, and he faces me, stepping closer. Staring into my eyes, he slides his hand deep into my hair and draws me to him.

With his breath grazing my lips, my king tips my head back, and after a few agonizing moments, his cool mouth softly captures mine. His tongue slides carefully inside my mouth, as though he's making sure I'm all right with the intrusion.

But I'm so starved for him. I've dreamed of this kiss for ages. I don't have to dream anymore, though. He's here, half-naked, kissing me. So I deepen this kiss, tasting the spicy liquor on his tongue as I press my body firmly against his—my soft to his hard.

"More than a kiss," I beg him, longing for relief. "Please."

At first, all I can focus on is the torturous rub of my taut nipples against the soft, golden hair on his chest. But then his hand drifts down my back, over my ass, and he bends and grips me behind the knee. Unexpectedly, he lifts my leg, placing the arch of my foot on the edge of the tub, opening me to him.

Eyes on mine, he touches me there, dragging his fingers through the wetness gathered between my legs before slowly slipping a finger inside me. Holding on to his broad shoulders, I try to contain myself, but I can't stop the sound that leaves me. The whimper.

He kisses my throat, his tongue tracing a pattern along the sensitive skin beneath my ear. "You feel so good, princess. Is this how you've touched yourself when you've slept alone? Knowing we were just across the hall?" He pulls back and looks into my eyes again. "Oh, the things we would've done to you if we'd known you were doing this all alone, wishing it was us touching you."

He pushes my knee back a little, spreading me open further, and moves behind me. Kissing the curve of my shoulder, he slides his hand down my abdomen and returns to his ministrations, pulling me apart, exposing me. He's doing this for Alexus, giving the Collector a perfect view.

Alexus meets my stare before glancing down, that hungry look in his eyes returning. It thrills me the way these two work, the silent knowledge they share, the understanding they already seem to have of one another's needs. I long to know more, to experience more of their connection, even if just for the night.

With Alexus's eyes on me, I begin moving on Colden's hand.

"Oh, *there* she is," my king whispers against my ear as he plunges a finger inside me, then adds another. "You're going to feel so good wrapped around our cocks, aren't you, princess?"

His words are enough to make my stomach flip and my mind reel, especially knowing Alexus is absorbing every second of what Colden's doing to me.

As Colden tilts my head back and kisses me, his tongue exploring and tasting, and as I move my hips, greedily sliding along his fingers, it registers that his touch isn't warm. It's as cool as his talented mouth, the contrasting sensations between our skin sending a bolt of longing through me. Is his cock just as cool to the touch?

His movements slow. "I think I have to share. I'm sure the sorcerer wants his turn." Colden lowers my leg, keeping his arm around my waist.

Alexus's eyes have gone black as night, his features sharp. He's leaned back in the tub, the water not quite covering his abdomen. One arm rests on the vessel's edge while he strokes his cock slowly.

He lets go, and I memorize the sight of him: his full erection, every throbbing vein, and that lovely, broad head.

"He's magnificent," Colden says.

I couldn't agree more.

Again, Alexus motions for me to come to him.

"Not the... Not the bed?" I say softly, a bit curious why the bath is where things are beginning.

"The warm water will relax you," Colden says, winking again. "And Alexus will certainly get you ready. We need a little playtime to figure out how much you can handle."

Oh. *Oh my*. How much *can* I handle?

I feel eager but anxious, excited but scared. But I want this. Whatever I can have with them, *I want it*.

Colden holds my hand as I step into the tub. The vessel is large like the bed. Still, even though the tub is fairly wide, I'll have to straddle Alexus. It's the only way we can both fit.

I gasp when I settle around his hips, the hot water rising with my presence, more contrast on my skin. Alexus stares into my eyes and lifts his hips, pressing the hard ridge of his cock between my legs. The expression that masks his face happens so quickly I almost miss it, but I recognize it all the same.

Relief.

I grip the side of the tub as his eyes close and his mouth parts on a breath, the quiet rapture of a man who hasn't felt a woman in far too long. Need flickers through me, and as though he senses it, he leans forward and closes his warm mouth around my nipple, his red lips stark against my soft pink tip.

While he sucks and bites and teases one breast, he cups the other, his hand large enough to grip my entire breast. I pant as he squeezes and kneads my flesh before tweaking the tip. It sends desire straight to my core, making my clit tingle and my muscles tighten. It also makes me far too aware of the emptiness I so desperately need filled.

Suddenly, Colden is there, kneeling beside the tub. He trails a cool touch up and down my spine as Alexus worships my breasts.

I turn my head to kiss my king.

"Do you want Alexus's cock inside you, princess?" he asks against my lips, his question making me blush. "Do you want him to stretch you wide for us?"

"Yes," I moan, my voice breathy as I rock my hips against Alexus's hardness, the water lapping at my sensitive flesh only heightening my need.

"I can't blame you," he whispers with a smile in his voice, and then, "Give the woman what she's begging for, Alexus."

After sliding a wicked glance at Colden, the sorcerer grips my hips and lifts me just so, repositioning me.

Colden reaches behind me, and though I can't see what he's doing, I can feel his slightly chilled touch. He's holding Alexus's cock.

For me.

"Sit back," he says. "He's so hard and so fucking ready for you."

I can't breathe as the world narrows to the image in my mind of what Colden is doing, then to that one sensation: the wide head of Alexus's cock pushing into my entrance.

At first, he fills me slowly, inch by thick inch, but then he pauses and looks at me with a question in his eyes. "I don't want to go too fast."

"You won't," I plead, losing any control I have left. "I need you, Alexus."

Just like that, I sink onto him at the same time he thrusts in fully. We gasp at the same time as the emptiness I've wanted to be rid of for so long is annihilated. There's so much of him that I feel impaled at first, but I would gladly endure this sensation every day for the rest of my life.

Colden's gaze is like a brand, its heat focused where Alexus and I are joined as he begins pushing into me, over and over, slowly fucking me until my body shudders. I'm so close to orgasm already. So close to showing these men just how much they've affected me these last few years.

Alexus slows down even more though, a small smile tempting the corner of his mouth. "Not yet. This needs to be a night you remember with fondness. I can't have you remembering me for lasting all of a few minutes, and if you come now, I won't be able to hold out."

"I'm certain we can get another rise out of you," Colden says mischievously. "Both of you. One way or another."

Colden slips his cool fingers over the curve of my ass and further down, making me shiver. Alexus's body stiffens beneath me but quickly relaxes as Colden touches the base of Alexus's cock, stroking me in the process. It feels like he's slipped Alexus between his V'd fingers, his fingertips curling against my damp flesh with every stroke back and forth.

"So lovely," Colden says. "I'm going to lick both of you like this tonight. I'm going to put you on top of Alexus, princess, facing away from him, his cock buried deep, and I'm going to spread you wide and feast while he fucks you. Would you like that?"

Another whimper leaves me as I struggle to even nod. I've imagined many things with these two involved, but I've a feeling tonight's pleasures will still be a surprise.

"We're going to fuck you," Colden continues, swirling his fingertip around my entrance, even as Alexus pumps in and out. "Right here in this pretty little pussy. It won't hurt as much as the other way, and we haven't time to get you ready for that foray. But we can still try to give you two cocks at the same time, if you want us. It might feel a little like this."

Gods' death, he slides a finger inside me, alongside Alexus's cock.

I grip the edge of the tub so hard the copper lip bites into my palms. Alexus groans, loudly, and I'm uncertain if I can stop the orgasm that threatens, especially when Alexus slides his hand around my neck and draws me down to him as Colden fucks me—*fucks us*—with his finger.

"Would you like that?" Alexus says, making my toes curl. "Do you want us both inside you?"

My heart races and my blood pounds in my veins. "Gods, yes." The idea of them fucking each other inside me is everything.

Alexus swirls his tongue over my nipple and bites down gently, flicking at the tip. My pussy tightens in response, and my clit hardens. One wrong—or one very *right*—move, and I'm going to erupt.

Colden kisses my shoulder. "Take what you want, princess. Show us how you fuck."

I can barely stand listening to him talk that way. Either of them. It makes me feel like I could lose my grip on the entire world. It makes me feel like I'm composed of little more than a thousand unbridled desires.

The darkest kind.

Using the tub for leverage, bracing myself, I begin riding Alexus— and Colden's finger—grinding the deepest part of me against the swollen tip of Alexus's long cock.

He releases my breast with an audible pop as his fingers dig into the flesh of my hips. "Fuck, yes, just like that," he grits out. "Fuck us, Petra." He slides his hands down, gripping the underside of my ass, spreading me. Colden is still touching me. Still fucking me with his finger. He inserts another, though, working me, stretching me— *preparing* me.

I gasp and let out a small cry at the sudden, sharp sting and the feeling of fullness. It's already so much that there's no way taking more won't involve true pain. And yet the threat is enticing, the thought of two cocks pushing into me, flesh to flesh.

Again, Alexus looks me in the eyes, his face taut with lust, and I realize he likes eye contact. He likes connection. Even still, this is just sex. I can feel the barrier between us, can see the wall Colden once mentioned. It's like a shutter over Alexus's eyes. Raw sex is all he can give me and Colden—the *physical*—and I respect whatever boundaries he holds in place. If the memory of pleasure is all I can carry with me after this, then so be it. I'd rather have a memory of us like this than never having this at all.

The muscles in Alexus's jaw clench as I move on him, chasing the pleasure trapped between my legs.

"You're getting tighter," he says. "Wetter. You like what Colden and I are doing to your pussy, don't you? It's going to make you come for us, isn't it?"

Crying out, I toss my head back as my release pulses through me in hard and violent waves. Colden clamps a hand over my mouth as I come, my body clenching Alexus as I ride it out, grinding on him as though I can possibly drive him deeper.

I can't.

"Fuck him," Colden orders, kissing and licking my neck. "Fuck him for me. Fuck him so good it hurts."

I shouldn't like it, those words, but hearing them uttered at my ear as Colden holds me silent, watching me as I rock on Alexus's brutally rigid cock and Colden's fingers, makes my orgasm even more powerful. The feel of his hand. His grip on my face. Being held there, trapped between them.

I want more. *So much more.*

When the haze of passion dissipates and my orgasm finally relents, I'm left feeling drugged, my body languid. It isn't until Colden dries me off, sweeps me into his arms, and carries me to bed that I realize neither of them came.

Lying there with Colden sitting beside me, we watch Alexus dry off and walk toward us. His cock is still as raging hard as Colden's.

Colden moves to the foot of the bed and crawls up between my legs as Alexus props my head on a pillow. I shiver when Colden runs his hands up my thighs and spreads my legs, trailing chilly kisses behind his touch.

"Come on, princess. Clear your head." He drags a long lick up my inner thigh, making goosebumps rise on my legs. "That little taste of decadence in the tub was only the beginning."

That wicked mouth captures my clit in a hard suck before he plunges his tongue inside me, making me cry out again as my spine arches of its own volition. Alexus taps my lips to *shoosh* me quiet and rests one knee on the edge of the bed, angling his cock toward my mouth. A shimmering pearl of cum awaits, ready to spill from the edge of his swollen tip.

"You're going to bring all the menfolk upstairs, eager to rescue the crying maiden," he says. "I suppose I have to keep you quiet." Using his thumb, he easily pries my mouth open as Colden licks and sucks my still-tingling and sensitive flesh. I moan, helpless to the bliss flooding through me, but Alexus silences me by pushing the head of his dripping cock between my lips. *"Shhh,"* he commands, dragging his hand down his length to squeeze out another drop of cum.

Groaning, I take his tip fully into my mouth, devouring him. He groans, too, though the sound is far softer than mine, locked deep within his chest.

Gliding my tongue down his shaft, I feel that long column on his underside, as well as the veins running through all that hardness. I suck him, struggling to think around Colden's expert tongue, and now his fingers, pumping into me. I can't tell how many, but I feel stretched, like before.

He's working me again, this time running his fingers from side to side in a half circle before pushing into me deep and then repeating the motions. His touch is meant for pleasure, but also to get me dripping wet and to force my muscles to become as lax as possible. Knowing why he's doing this makes me impatient, though I know better than to rush a single part of this night.

Alexus presses his cock deeper, leaning over me, one hand gripping the headboard, the other gripping my breast. I don't know what inspires me—Colden's hand on my mouth earlier or Alexus quieting my moans moments before with his cock—but I take Alexus's massive hand and place it on my throat instead.

"Gods, Petra, yes." His fingers tighten, just a little. Just enough to make me feel that same sense of being trapped that I'd felt before, of being dominated by him and Colden. It's a desire I didn't know I possessed, a need to finally trust someone else enough to let them take control for a while.

Alexus starts to fuck my mouth then—*truly fucking me*—pinning me to the bed as he teases his cock toward the back of my throat. I can't handle all of him like this, and he knows it. I know he's holding back so that I feel thoroughly had, yet not to the point of discomfort. The muscled ridges of his abdomen are tight and flexed with his restraint.

There's a carefulness in him, too, something I can sense as he watches me, detecting what I want and need, measuring the line between too much and not enough. The only problem is that I'm beginning to feel like I will never get enough. Like there isn't anything they could do that I wouldn't like.

Suddenly, Alexus withdraws every inch from my mouth, and Colden's tongue and fingers leave my body. He sits up and then back on his heels, leaving me empty as he wipes the back of his hand across his glistening mouth. He and Alexus share a simple glance, and again, from that moment forward, their mental bond shows in the way they move, some greater awareness the rest of us don't have—not even me, a Seer.

Alexus turns, rummaging through the drawers of the bedside chest. I watch him for a moment, but any focus on what he's doing disappears as Colden crawls over me.

"Spread those lovely legs for me," he whispers. Hands braced beside my shoulders, he teases his cock at my entrance before pushing in deep, making me curse. "Oh, princess," he says on a breath, a feral look forming in his black eyes. "You are so fucking perfect. Now taste your sweet pussy while I fuck you."

I fist my hands in his damp, blond hair as he leans down for a kiss. At first, his full lips are cool and wet on mine. Gentle. But then he pushes his tongue into my mouth the way he'd pushed it inside me minutes before, and gods, I *can* taste myself. It's so arousing that I suck on his tongue the way he sucked on me, eliciting a deep groan.

There's a momentary power shift that makes my skin tingle. In those seconds, I'm in complete control of my king. I'm certain I could steer him any way I'd like.

When I release him, he gasps and kisses me deeply, hard enough that when he pulls away, my lips feel swollen.

"Do you truly want us both inside you, Petra?" he asks again, thrusting hard and deep, almost like he's trying to remind me of the punishment ahead if I agree to go through with this. "Say it. Tell me you want our cocks fucking you at the same time. Coming in you at the same time. *Say* it."

I cup his beautiful face and, through the haze of desire washing over me, I give him what he wants. "Colden Moeshka, I want you both. Everywhere. Don't make me beg."

Though another deep chuckle reverberates inside his chest, his playful look quickly morphs into a dark and sensuous expression, growing darker still the moment Alexus appears on the far side of the bed. He slides toward us and lies next to me as Colden slows his movements, leaning onto his left elbow. From this angle, he can look at Alexus and me, or he can glance down and watch his cock moving in and out of me. He takes a moment to look at all three.

I'm struggling to focus. Colden feels so damn good, but this is like an interlude, a few minutes of keeping me ready while the real show gets set to begin.

Alexus holds up a small red glass bottle with a cork and then lays it on the bed between us. "Found."

"Mmm," Colden says with a small smile. "Glorious."

I know exactly what that red bottle is. Those types of bottles live in many a bedside table here in the North, a gentle mixture of olive and primrose oils. The muscles between my legs clench, my body understanding exactly why we need it tonight.

Before I can think further about it, Alexus rises on his elbow, slips his hand across my waist, and leans down to suck my breast. I wind my fingers into his dark, wet hair, clutching him as he swirls his tongue around my nipple and draws the tip deeply into his hot mouth. Colden leans in and suckles my other breast, moving inside me in long, slow strokes.

Light and dark. Cold and heat. My king and the Collector.

Alexus looks up at me, tongue flicking my nipple.

"Gods, I wish you were doing that between my legs."

As though commanded by that one little wish, Alexus kisses a trail down my stomach and, much to mine and Colden's surprise, begins tonguing my clit, all while Colden's cock throbs inside me.

Colden sucks in a harsh gasp. An expression of shock muddled with absolute delight paints his face as he leans back on his elbow to watch his friend.

"Fuck, Alexus, are you trying to make me come quickly? Because—" he gasps again, and his hips stutter in their movement, his entire body seizing, his lean muscles going rigid. Still leaning on his left arm, he buries his other hand in Alexus's hair as his eyes close, his mouth parted.

I can still feel Alexus's tongue, but I've a sense Colden can feel it, too, and not from accidental slips.

When Colden re-opens his eyes, his gaze is transfixed between my legs, his expression filled with longing as he pulls out to the tip and goes still again, his fist tightening in Alexus's dark hair.

Alexus is doing what Colden promised he would do earlier, lavishing us both.

Colden's head drops back, his chest rising and falling hard. "Gods, have you any idea how long I've waited for this?"

Alexus lifts his head, lips glistening with a wicked little smirk, and Colden meets his eyes.

A palpable tension fills the air, the kind I've only felt a few times in their presence, when their locked gazes could electrify an entire room. It was those gazes that made me believe they were lovers, but in this moment, I realize they are something far, far more than that.

They've existed together for nearly three hundred years. They've shared everything—well, *almost* everything according to Colden. The trust they must have, the depths of loyalty and dedication and devotion—I cannot fathom. This desire I see in them is real, but it's also its own kind of love. More than romantic love. More than platonic love. And much more than sex. Their souls have been united for centuries, their very essences intertwined. They trust one another completely.

At the same time, they lean closer over me and kiss. It's as though I'm watching a private moment, reveling in the way their lovely mouths move together, a dance I can tell they know well, but perhaps one they don't perform often.

"Alexus." Colden sighs the Collector's name. "Oh, Alexus."

My king begins moving his hips again, his cock so hard inside me —so hard and stiff and swollen. I know he must be aching.

Alexus touches my clit, rubbing tight little circles as he deepens their kiss, their tongues sliding and licking, enjoying one another but also enjoying me. My taste is in their mouths, a pleasure bringing them together as one.

I touch my breasts, feeling another threatening orgasm pulsing between my legs as Colden rocks his hips and Alexus teases my clit. I can feel Colden's orgasm building, too, throbbing through his shaft to his tip. He's so, so close.

"I'm really going to come if you don't stop kissing me like this," he says against Alexus's mouth. "And I want us all to come together."

Alexus kisses him one more time, then moves to the head of the bed and props his back against the pile of pillows. He reaches for me, and I know that if I let him take me, this will all end, far too soon.

"Wait." I grip his forearm as Colden pulls out of me, once again leaving me with that empty feeling I hate. I glance at them both. "I want more of what just happened." When they hesitate, I do something ridiculous. I make a wish, then I look at Alexus, understanding that he's the one struggling to let his walls down tonight. "Please."

Alexus arches a brow at Colden, and with one flick of his finger, Colden is on him, his long, beautiful body stretched over Alexus, moving to straddle him.

Stars and moons, they're beautiful.

Alexus slides his hands up Colden's thighs, up his sides, and then he pulls him down into a bruising kiss. Heat crawls over my skin and I have to touch myself, every inch of my body aching for these two men as Colden grinds his hips, rubbing himself against Alexus. I can't see between them, but the thought makes me whimper again, my need so close that a mere image like that traveling across my mind makes me want to tease out my release right this moment.

But Alexus's hand is suddenly on my knee, and as I come back to myself, I feel their eyes on me.

"No coming," Alexus commands. "Not yet. Not until I say so. Just watch, or I'll make you wait all night for what you want."

I swallow hard, unused to this side of him—this darker side that peeks out now and again. I like it.

"Sit up," he says to Colden, and like everyone else who buckles under Alexus's voice, my king obeys.

Alexus reaches for the red glass bottle and un-pops the cork with his thumb. It's then that my attention locks on their cocks, positioned so close together.

Seeing them like this is breathtaking. Colden is more slender than Alexus, his tip a bit narrower, but he's just as long. Together, they're enormous, and yet the sight makes my mouth water and every muscle between my legs clench.

Carefully, Alexus pours a thin stream of oil on Colden's cock. I don't know what I expect, in truth, but it isn't for Alexus to set the bottle aside and begin stroking both of their cocks in his massive hand. He pumps hard, their cocks shiny and slick.

"Gods above, I cannot bear this." Colden groans and reaches for me. "Kiss me, Petra. I beg you. Or I'm going to scream so fucking loud they hear me at Winterhold."

He folds his arm around me when I move closer, but that part of me that enjoyed controlling him earlier rears her head. I glance down at their cocks, held tightly together by Alexus's fist. They're both leaking cum already, and I need to taste them.

I take their tips into my mouth, one at a time, sucking away the saltiness of their promising release.

"Fuck," Alexus says as Colden fists my hair. The tug at my roots, that gentle bite of pain, only fuels me.

Alexus continues stroking, a bit more gently, but it's as though he's feeding me, an act that ironically only makes me hungrier and hungrier.

"Stop, or I'm going to come," Colden warns, his voice breaking. "I can't—"

I pull away and kiss his mouth, but I'm fully aware of Alexus's hand moving harder. Faster. I can hear his breathing growing deeper, his quiet grunts of pleasure.

"You like his hand on you," I say to my king. "Fucking you."

"You have *no* idea," he whispers into my mouth, bucking his hips to match Alexus's tempo.

"Yes, I do," I say, torturing him. "I tasted what he does to you."

Colden only nods, as though he can't possibly form words right now.

I lean back down. This time, I only lick Alexus's cock, cleaning up a long drip on his tip. He pauses his ministrations just long enough to let me, gasping when I drag my tongue across his head. Then I'm back with Colden, his black eyes shiny, like they're coated in ice. Slowly, I push my tongue into his mouth, feeding him as he fed me, and this time, it is my king who whimpers.

He sucks my tongue, tasting the man I think a part of him has longed for all these years in some way.

"You need more of him, don't you?" I ask.

"So much more," he whispers.

"I'm not denying you," Alexus speaks up, and Colden seems to shake out of a daze. "Put your mouth on me."

Colden looks at me, eyes bright. "This is your night, yet I feel like I'm experiencing a very special fantasy birthday."

"I can join you," I say with a smile.

Together, we bow and feast on Alexus Thibault's cock. Our tongues and lips tangle as we pleasure him, taking turns sucking. When it's Colden's turn, I find I'm quite impressed by his skill. He takes Alexus to the root and groans, something that sends a jerk through Alexus's long body.

He lifts his hips, gripping Colden's hair. "I don't know what you just did but do it again."

Colden smiles around Alexus's cock, but he obeys, groaning, dragging out the sound.

"Fuck, that's it," Alexus cries, his head tipped back against the pillows. "That's all. It's time."

Colden draws back, and in one fluid and gentle movement, Alexus pulls me atop him, my back against his strong, heated chest. I realize what's happening as Colden helps position me, draping my legs over Alexus's sides, spreading me open.

"I don't think I'm going to be able to forget this night for as long as I live," Colden says, leaning down to lick me once, an oddly loving gesture. "I don't care if I live for eternity. This is going to be branded on my memory."

My heart starts hammering as Alexus bands his arm under my breasts. Colden returns to us one last time, sucking Alexus and licking me with that cool tongue that's a shock to my system, priming us, getting us wet.

He rubs Alexus's cock against me. "All you have to do is lift your hips and slide onto him, princess."

I do as I'm told, Colden keeping Alexus angled just right as I sink onto his impossibly hard length. It takes my breath, Alexus's size, giving me a moment of pause. I don't know if I can take them both or not, no matter how badly I want it.

Alexus arches his hips, pressing deep as he kisses my shoulder. "If you need us to stop, just say stop, Petra. Or squeeze my wrist." His voice is gentle, his caress up and down my arm soothing. "If anything is too much for you, that's all you have to say or do, and we'll stop."

He isn't known to be a Seer or a mind-reader, though I swear that in moments like these, I wonder if he has abilities that simply haven't manifested yet, somehow dormant.

Resting against Alexus's strong form, finding comfort in his embrace, I watch as Colden settles on his knees between us. "Alexus is going to hold both of you very still while I try to enter," he says, as though they've done this before. Surely they have? Over so many years? There had to be a woman who found her luck long before me.

Colden opens the bottle of oil—I never even saw him pick it up— and pours a little more of the lubricant on his cock, stroking himself, covering his length in a deeper sheen, one that makes his engorged flesh look that much more obscene.

The yearning inside me coils into a tight, needy ache. But the moment he grips his cock and guides himself to my body, a bolt of fear ricochets through me.

He leans down one final time and kisses me between my legs. Kisses *us.* I watch him, lost in the sight, feeling our bodies growing wetter under the warmth and attention of Colden's mouth. When he straightens, he wipes his mouth and leans forward, gaze holding mine as Alexus's arm tightens on me.

"You're sure?" he asks.

"Absolutely," I reply.

There's a sudden pressure at my entrance as he presses the head of his cock against Alexus's shaft, trying to ease his way in.

"Take a deep breath and let it out," Alexus says, and when I exhale, Colden pushes harder.

I start to cry out. Not to stop them, but from the intrusion that I so desire and simultaneously fear.

"Cover my mouth," I order Alexus.

I feel him hesitate, but he thankfully does as I ask.

"Squeeze my wrist if we need to stop," he reminds me. "I mean it."

For what feels like several minutes, I gasp and gasp, trying not to buck to get away, feeling torn in two, a hot sting in my flesh—and so much fullness. But I refuse to end this.

Alexus clings to me through it all, holding me still and muffling my cries while Colden's hands press into my thighs.

Pinned. Again. Just like I wanted.

"Fuck, so tight." Colden blinks, shaking his head as if to clear it of a daze as Alexus slides his hand from my mouth. "Talk to us, princess," my king commands. "I'm only halfway in."

Halfway? *Halfway?* I can't imagine taking all of him. And yet I can't imagine *not* doing it either.

"Just say the word." Alexus's voice is warm and soft against my ear. "Just say it and we'll stop, Petra."

I shake my head adamantly and utter a different word. "More."

Alexus presses another tender kiss to my shoulder. "So brave."

Colden runs his hands up my waist to cup my breasts. "Yes, and such a good little girl. Fucking beautiful and so damn good."

"Relax for me," Alexus says. "One more time, then we can fuck you like you want."

I try to relax, but I'm shaking. Trembling.

I wrap my hands around Alexus's wrist and hold on. "Just do it," I tell Colden. "And this is not me telling you to stop," I say to Alexus. "Just get it over with so I can have you both."

The look on Colden's face is one of respect, but also lust. Holding my gaze, he spits on my pussy, the saliva falling from his mouth in an unexpected and purposefully erotic display.

"Fuck, Colden," Alexus grits out, his cock twitching inside me, but I'm taken so off guard that I do, in fact, relax.

Then it happens. Colden pushes into me without hesitation.

A bolt of pain and that familiar hot sting returns, but my body seems to have adapted to the added girth—thanks to Colden's earlier efforts—because, though there's initial discomfort and pain, I'm not in misery like I expected. In fact, as moments slip by, the pressure of two erect cocks held captive inside me begins to feel *amazing.*

Colden smiles down at me, his eyes sparkling like they're made of stars. "Are you all right?"

I nod, and though a lone tear slips from my eye as I quiver, I manage a, "S-so good."

Alexus chuckles at my ear, then his hold on me eases. "We're going to fuck you now," he whispers, slowly beginning to move inside me. "And yes, we're going to make this feel so good for you."

Colden pours even more oil on us, then both men begin moving in a slow rhythm they don't even have to work out. They just know, reading one another intuitively.

"Do you feel what this is doing to me?" Colden asks us. "How hard I am from fucking you both at the same time? I could die come morning, and all these years of living an immortal life would be worth it, for this night alone." He sweeps a look at where his cock is rubbing Alexus's, where he's fucking us.

With every passing minute, my body eases into the invasion, the slight sting lessening more and more until pleasure completely overtakes everything else. It's as though my mind simply changes direction, sensing the utter domination and claiming of these two men as ecstasy in place of agony. I've heard that sex can blur the line of pain, but until tonight, I didn't truly understand how.

"Harder," I beg them, wishing for more.

Colden gives me a narrowed look. "Be careful, princess. If you unleash us, you might not be able to rein us back in."

"Harder," I plead again, forcing an edge of daring into my tone. "I'm not scared."

Little by little, my king and the Collector pick up their pace, pushing deeper and harder. I lie against Alexus, burying my hand in his silky hair as my body rocks atop him, my breasts moving with every thrust. I turn my head just enough to feel the roughness of his stubble on my face, the warmth of his breath.

He kisses me then. Alexus Thibault actually *kisses* me. I hadn't thought he would. From what I witnessed between him and Colden, his kisses seem like saved-up gifts he only bestows every so often. This kiss is passionate yet soft, his lips lush yet firm, his tongue curious instead of claiming, almost like he's daring to dream that I possess some greater fire I fear he won't find.

He pulls away, and after I glimpse a glimmer of disappointment, those green eyes shutter once more, locking away any window he might've temporarily opened to a deeper part of himself.

I am not the one.

I can't linger on the worry that spurns in my heart, because time blurs into nothing as the moment quickly passes and they take me. It could be seconds or minutes or hours that they fuck me, I can't discern anything except pleasure and need, my body lost to them, to their cocks, their roaming hands—warm and cool—and Alexus's kiss. I can feel their building orgasms thrumming against my walls, the rising sensation beginning to undo me, a star about to shatter.

Alexus slips his hand down my body and touches my clit as he and Colden move faster, pushing in as deeply as they can.

"Come for us, Petra," the Collector whispers against my mouth. "Come for us, and we'll follow."

His words and his touch and his kiss and the way they're thrusting into me shoves me over the edge. Alexus covers my mouth, trapping my cries before I can scream. He wraps his arm around me once again, pinning me against him as I thrash through the most intense climax of my life.

My body clenches, clutching at them over and over as tears of happiness fall from the corners of my eyes. I'm all sensation and joy and mindless bliss as I feel them coming in response, both of them pounding into me, gasping, chasing my orgasm as their swollen cocks finally spill their pleasure inside me.

I'm surrounded by muscled bodies and strong hands, curses and grunts and moans and cum, my pussy growing wetter by the second. Alexus even bites gently into my neck to silence himself through his release.

Colden doesn't seem to care who hears us. He watches, no doubt seeing their pleasure dripping from my body, uttering the word *fuck* so many times that by the time he and Alexus finally slow and then still, Alexus and I can't help but share a quiet laugh for our lover.

Still inside me, Colden lowers himself on trembling arms. We all lie there for a few minutes, embracing, unable to let go just yet.

"Are you happy?" Colden asks me. "You got your wish."

A strange feeling settles inside me and my smile falls, my happiness beginning a slow unravel. Did this happen because they wanted it? Wanted *me*? Or because I was careless with the barkeep's magick and wished it upon them?

"Hey." Alexus's voice brings me back to them. "Where'd you go?"

I shake my head, trying to force away the thoughts, trying so hard to cling to this, to Colden and Alexus.

"I think another bath is in order, princess," Colden says. "If you're up to magick."

I nod, unsure if I am just yet, though after a while, I'm soaking my sore body in a tub while Colden and Alexus bathe me with loving hands.

Soon after, Alexus carries me to the bed where Colden awaits, pulling back the covers. We lie together beneath the blankets, naked, the way I've dreamed about for so long. As Alexus curves his big body behind me, Colden nestles close in front of me, the two of them holding me and kissing me like a treasure.

Sleep calls, but before we give in, they claim me one more time, individually and without a wish. Alexus goes first, taking me gently from behind as Colden kisses me and touches me. Then it's Colden's turn. He lifts my leg over his hip and penetrates with carefulness, moaning when he feels Alexus's release inside me.

When it's over, none of us can speak, and sleep finally wins the battle. I'm the last to give in, held between two men I think I could be in love with. Two men I wish I could have like this for always.

Two men who aren't meant for me. No matter how hard I wish otherwise.

⚜

THREE DAYS LATER, HAVING LEFT THE TAVERN AND WISHES BEHIND, WE reach the icy village of Reede.

Before today, we shared one more night together in an outskirt inn, a night not created by a magickal wish. It healed a worry inside me, a fear that I'd taken something I had no right to take.

The truth is that Alexus and Colden did want me. They still do.

But the union and bond between us isn't enough. For Alexus, I'm not certain anyone will ever be enough, not until he finds the right person, a soul mate. As for Colden. I think he doesn't really know what he wants, and that he simply won't know until the answer hits him like a sledgehammer, probably unexpectedly, with someone he never would've imagined himself falling in love with.

As we ride into Reede, my glamour is up, as it will have to remain from here on. Brennan and Shannon Dulevia, the local bowyers and my contacts here, greet us, aware that the king and the Collector were set to bring a friend to Reede to set up residence. Brennan and Shannon and all else who stand nearby, wearing mounds of fur from head to foot, bow when Colden dismounts.

"Please, there's no need for that," he tells them, longing for anonymity. "We'd like to get Miss Anrova out of the cold and settled in her lodgings. It's been a long trip."

"Of course, Your Highness," Brennan says as Alexus helps me from my horse. "It's just this way."

Groomsmen take our animals, and a few younger boys, unaware that they're in the presence of a king, lug our heavy packs behind us as we walk the snow-laden road that meanders through the village. The wind is bitter, biting enough to sting the skin. I never much liked the cold, but this village is small and far enough away from Winterhold that I won't be so tempted to return.

Because I can't return. Ever.

Brennan stops at a tiny stone cottage where smoke already billows from the chimney and opens the door. We follow him inside to find a quaint, one-room home with the barest necessities: a hearth with a kettle, a bed with a few thick, woven blankets, a trunk for clothes, fur rugs spread about the floor, and a small table and single chair.

Though the cottage is warm, my stomach tightens into a cold knot. This is a home, but it isn't *my* home. My home is with Colden and Alexus, and yet the more I'm with them, the more dangerous I realize things become.

Because I would do anything for them. I would turn myself inside out for them, blacken my soul if it meant keeping them safe. As much as I love them, and I know that what I feel is love, I can't lose my goodness for them. And I would. I've felt it stirring inside me for a long time, had too many dreams of myself killing in their name.

Love, for some, can make them thrive. For me, it's a threat. No, a promise. A promise that I will turn myself into the mightiest weapon, a weapon unleashed without restraint, for the men who have captured my heart.

A very young boy—struggling with one of my packs—stares at me with wide gray eyes.

"Joran," Brennan snaps. "Stop ogling. Run along."

Joran and the other boys drop our things and leave while Brennan lights an oil lamp and turns to face us, a broad smile splitting his dark beard. "If I can get you anything, Miss Anrova, I live three cottages down. Shannon will enjoy having a new friend here."

I smile as warmly as I can. All I see in my future are lies to kind people, a life of secrecy, aloneness, and a longing that can never be filled.

Brennan leaves us, and I face Colden and Alexus. I knew this time would come, but it feels more difficult now.

They lower their hoods at the same time, their handsome faces pink from the cold.

"You don't have to do this, Petra," Alexus says. He said this to me a dozen times before we left Winterhold.

"We can get right back on our horses and go home," Colden adds.

That word again. Home. Winterhold. With them.

I strip off my gloves and bite my lip to stop the tears that have formed from falling. "I need distance from you two. The future I saw for myself was bleaker if I stayed with you than if I left. I need you to understand that. That I'm doing this for more people than myself."

War is coming. I don't know when, but I've seen it. And I've seen myself in the middle of it, ripping apart minds until their owners are nothing but thoughtless husks. I cannot be that. I cannot use Loria's blood to destroy what she made.

Colden shakes his head, still disbelieving in the war I feel the Northlands will eventually face, regardless of his treaty with the East.

"Well, there's no changing your mind then?" he asks. "Even after..."

I look at them as his voice trails, my heart breaking, and close the small distance between us. With all the love I possess for them, I press my hands to their faces.

In that instant, with our barriers finally down, images flicker through my mind. I see Alexus with a beautiful, dark-haired woman donned in warrior's armor, staring at her fierce face as though she is the universe itself. And I see Colden, clasping the face of a handsome man with hair like a raven's feathers, looking into his eyes with so much love and longing it takes my breath away.

"No," I whisper, my tears finally falling. "These last nights with you were the greatest gift. I will carry those memories with me always. But we have different paths. We must go and find them." I lower my hands and glance around the cottage. "My new path begins here."

Alexus steps close, tightens his hand at my waist, and draws me in for a kiss. He wants to want me the way I long for him to. Wants to love me enough that he would fight me before leaving me here alone. That's the kind of love he will give the dark-haired woman.

The kind that allows no divide.

When he releases me, Colden takes his place, tugging me into an embrace. "We might be weeks away, and I know you don't like to do it, but you're welcome to speak into my mind any time. If you need us, all you have to do is call to me, and I will be here."

I pull back and cup his face again, a smile managing to form on my lips. "I know," is all I say. Not *I will*, because I won't. I just can't.

They stay for a while and help unpack my belongings. Alexus inspects every part of the cottage to make certain no repairs are needed, and Colden ices over a few tiny gaps in the stones from the outside, sealing off any chance of a draft. They check the firewood and the village food stores.

Salted fish. I'm going to be eating a lot of salted fish.

That afternoon, they finally gather their horses to leave. Standing in the bitter cold, they each hold my hands and look into my eyes as the villagers watch us with curious stares. No more kisses are shared. No more pleas for me to return with them are made. Alexus simply brushes his thumb across my cheek, his eyes glassy, and Colden squeezes my hand.

"You have a piece of my heart, princess," he says. "Always."

"And you, mine, my king."

Sadness fills his eyes, enough that he rips his teary gaze away and mounts his horse. Alexus nods at me one last time and swings up onto his animal.

The pain that lances my heart as I watch them ride across the white plains and vanish is the most brutal wound Loria's gift has ever brought upon me. Because if I'd just been born a normal girl, I could've been with them the way I desire, blissfully ignorant of futures I have the power to change.

In my cottage, I sit by the fire for a long time, absorbing the silence that will become my closest confidant. Alone, I stare out the single, small window, crying with an aching heart as I watch the falling night descend.

There truly is no darkness so great as a night sky over the Iceland Plains midwinter. Except the darkness I foresaw in my heart. The darkness that made me choose this life over one at Winterhold.

I can only pray to the Ancient Ones I made the right decision.

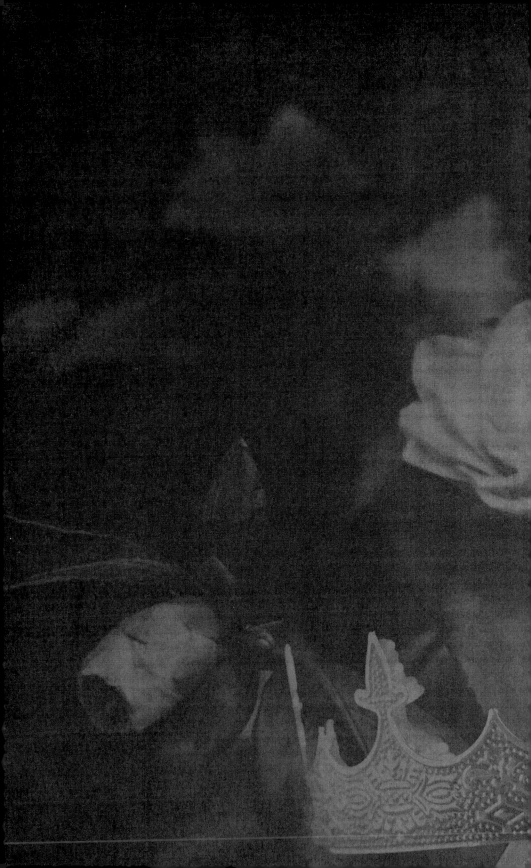

PARAMOUR

Colden & Nephele's First Time

❧

Three Years After Nephele's Collection

NEPHELE

"P leeeeease? You're making me beg for something I shouldn't have to beg for."

Colden glances up from his book. He's lying in bed, already undressed, and tucked under the covers for the evening, as though it isn't barely after dark on my favorite night of the year here at Winterhold: the Midsummer Festival.

He drags his hand from beneath the covers and arches a brow, skimming his dark gaze over my red gown. His attention lingers for the briefest moment on the small swell of my breasts peeking from the scooped neckline before quickly slipping back to my face.

"I'm sure you'll catch the eye of some lucky lad tonight, especially wearing *that*. You don't need me tagging along, spoiling your chances."

As if I'm looking for a lover tonight. I can't say I'd be against it, but no one in the village has captivated me enough that I would willingly let them take what I have to give. Except for the king lying before me, and he isn't the slightest bit interested.

I sit next to him on the edge of his bed and examine the book clasped in his hands. There's no title on the worn, red cover. "What is that?"

He snaps the book shut and smirks. "A dirty book. That I rather enjoy reading from time to time." He taps the tip of my nose. "But not when pestering little girls are in the room."

I return his raised brow and push my chest out a little. "I'm far from a little girl. Or have you failed to notice?"

"Apparently so. Perhaps because I'm approximately twelve—or is it thirteen?—times your age. Math never was my strong suit. You may be twenty and five and feeling older and wiser, but you're still a youngling to me."

"As is everyone else in the world!" I throw up my hands. "That's not the point right now. The point is that I have no one else to go with me, Colden, and you're the king, for gods' sakes. Everyone would love to see you."

He groans and drops his head against the mounded pillows behind him. "If you had any notion how many of these parties I've attended. Can you not take Alexus?"

When he looks at me again, I make the most awful face. "Alexus is not fun at parties, and you know it. He sits with his beer in the shadows and broods. *Broodingly*. You *know* he won't dance with me either."

Colden laughs. "He can dance. Slowly. He just won't."

"Yes, well, I'm not looking for anything slow tonight. I need…" I take a deep breath and blow it out. "Fun."

"That new bowyer from the plains seems to fancy you. He keeps coming around. Perhaps you should go find him."

"Joran Dulevia? No, thank you. He's handsome and all, but the ladies say he's a horrible prick. Besides, I don't want to go with him. I want to go with *you*."

I take his hand between mine. Sometimes it strikes me that in three short years, this deadly hand I loathed when I first came here is now the hand that I constantly find myself reaching for, sure and comforting.

Again, I say *please,* but this time I draw his hand to my chest.

A sigh of relent leaves him as he tosses his dirty book aside and stares into my eyes in that easy way of his. He shakes his head. "Gods-damnit, you hold far too much power over me, Nephele Bloodgood."

I squeal and bounce on the edge of his bed before hurrying to his oversized wardrobe where I swing open the carved doors. "I'll find you something lovely to wear. Silver, maybe? Purple? No. *Blue.*" I reach for a blue satin dress jacket and black pants I'm not sure I've ever seen him wear. "Blue is definitely your color."

"Whatever you think. So long as I'm more comfortable than I am pretty."

When I look over my shoulder to say something snarky, he's standing from the bed, his back to me—*completely naked.*

I can't look away.

He's beautiful, of course. I've thought that since I first met him. I've seen him shirtless a time or two in training, which was breathtak-ing. But *this...* The long, lean muscles stretching down his tapered back. The tight curve of his perfect ass. The soft, golden hair on his long, muscular thighs. He seems more powerful like this than any other way I've ever seen him, even sweaty and half-naked, with a glint of mischief in his eyes on the training field, bearing dual swords.

It's... overwhelming. Enough that not only does my pulse pound but my mouth waters, too.

Colden opens a drawer beside his bed and slips his book inside. I gulp when the way he's angled affords a glimpse of even more of him, certainly more than I've seen before tonight. It's a side view, but I think... I think he's half-hard.

Something clicks in my brain. He was in bed and undressed when I came into his room unannounced. Reading a dirty book. With one hand beneath the covers.

I interrupted him.

"It's not polite to stare."

His voice rattles me out of my daze. Startled, I blink up to meet his eyes, my face burning. "I... I wasn't—"

"Yes, you were." A sly grin curves his lips as he grabs a shirt from another drawer and holds it over his private parts before strolling toward me. He stops only inches away, and suddenly there's simply too much of him in this room. He takes the suit from my grip. "I'll get dressed and meet you in the south garden in half an hour?"

I clear my throat, paint on a fake smile, and pray my face looks a little less than utterly mortified. "That sounds perfect."

The moment I skirt around him, I groan inwardly and roll my eyes at myself. Who stares at the king's cock? Me, apparently.

"Oh, Nephele."

With my hand on the doorknob to his room, I turn back. "Yes?"

He's already slipped into his trousers, though they remain unlaced, hanging low and loose on his hips. The blond trail of hair from his navel to his... pretty bits... draws my attention, but I force my stare to remain on his face.

"I lied earlier," he confesses. "I haven't failed to notice anything when it comes to you."

My heart trips over itself, and my blush grows even hotter as I smile, this time genuinely.

"I'm glad," I tell him.

Then I slip out into the hall.

⚜

I CANNOT STOP LAUGHING.

By the time Colden and I make it to the top of the stairs leading to his chambers, I have to pause to catch my breath.

I grip my side, tears in my eyes, my cheeks aching. "Gods' death. It hurts."

Colden slings his jacket over his bare shoulder and wipes at his eyes. He's still laughing, too, even as he leans against the balustrade, his muscled torso shadowed by the dim light. His tunic was discarded and left behind at the festival, with good reason.

"Payback is going to be brutal," he warns. "Alexus Thibault will undoubtedly make us pay for that."

"His *face* when you rubbed your nipples. He was half-livid and half-horrified."

"You'd think he's never had a lap dance before, and I know better, believe me. I was there."

"Just never one from you!" I try to walk down the hall, but I can't see because my eyes are squeezed tight from laughing so hard. I bump into the wall next to Colden's door, and then he's there, too, pressing his hand above me, his face flush with humor, his black eyes bright in the candlelight illuminating the darkened corridor.

"*Shhh.*" He presses his finger to my lips, making me shiver when he pulls away. "Someone might be sleeping."

Though I doubt that's the case since most everyone is still at the festival, I take a deep breath, press my lips together, and try to calm myself.

As our hysterics quiet and our breathing returns to semi-normal, I become aware of Colden's nakedness again, his crushing nearness, the delicious scent of him, wild winter laced with summer's musk and blackberry wine. I suppose, in the end, that's what's to blame for what I do next—*the wine*. Because I did have a few glasses at the festival, making me a little more relaxed than usual, a little braver. Certainly bolder.

I arch off the wall. Just enough that Colden's knee slips between my legs.

His smile falls into a more serious mask, his gaze locked with mine as he tilts his head. "Careful, love. That's a dangerous look you've got in your eyes."

His voice always sounds rich and wonderful, but tonight, it's dark and smooth, sex on velvet.

Taking a chance, I press my hands to his bare chest, feeling, for the first time, the curve of muscle there, the smooth, cool-to-the-touch skin, despite the summer night we just abandoned. He doesn't stop me.

Daring to take even more liberty in the moment, I slip my hands up to his shoulders and thread my fingers into his blond hair. "Dangerous, how?"

He leans closer, licks his pretty lips, and presses his knee against me, making me gasp. "Oh, I think you know."

I don't give myself a second of deliberation to do anything in that moment except kiss him.

He flinches when my lips collide with his. Shocked, I'm sure. But then his mouth begins working in tandem with mine, our lips and tongues learning a new dance that sets my blood on fire. It doesn't matter that we're in a hallway with more bedchambers nearby, including Alexus's. Nothing matters in those minutes, save for the need to get closer to one another, a need to feel skin on skin.

I rub against his leg, the sweet friction causing a deep ache to stir and build. In response, Colden runs his hands up my arms and over my shoulders, drags them across my breasts and up to my throat, and cups my face.

He pulls back from our kiss, leaving me breathless all over again. "Birthbane?"

"Yes. Always."

"Me, too." He runs his thumb over the shape of my lips. "Tell me what you want from me tonight, Nephele. Tell me, and I'll do my best to give it to you."

"Isn't it obvious?" I ask with a small smile, stroking myself once against his strong thigh. "I've never truly been with a man. I want my first time to be you."

Colden shakes his head as if to clear it. He then drops his knee and looks at me as though I've sprouted a horn from my chin. "What did you just say?"

Voices echo from the stairs. Colden snaps his head that way, then looks back at me, a decision hovering between us. Quickly, he opens the door to his room, takes me by the arm, and drags me inside.

I press my back against the door while he tosses his jacket on a nearby chair and stares at me with wide eyes, hands resting on his narrow hips. "You're a *virgin*, Nephele? I already felt like I was committing some horrible wrong by desiring you. This makes matters *so* much worse."

I frown, remembering what he said earlier tonight about our ages. "First of all, you've slept with other people, Colden. Did their age matter? Why am I any different? And secondly, I *know* I mentioned that I have never *been* with a man. It was this past winter, in fact. We were in the library. You were telling me that I should give Lorance the groomsman a chance."

He screws his face into a scowl. "The difference is that *none* of those other people have been you. A Witch Walker under my care. And… I don't recall any talk about you being a virgin."

"I told you that I had never lain with a man, and my first wasn't going to be Lorance who perpetually smells like horse!"

A blank look takes over as I watch his mind working, trying to remember. "I suppose what I heard was *I've never been with a grooms-man.* Not *I've never been with a man.* You're twenty and five and fucking beautiful as the day is long. How, in Loria's name, has no man wooed you to bed by now?"

My brows dart up. "I never said that none had wooed me to bed. I said I've never truly been with a man, and I want the first to be you."

He looks utterly perplexed by this. "But…*why?*"

"Again. How is this not obvious? You're…" I gesture at him, standing there like a half-naked god. "You!" "I take a deep breath and sigh. "And I don't know what I'm doing in the least when it comes to sex. But I know that if my first time is with you, you'll make certain it's a night I will never forget, unlike anyone else in this village."

He drops his head, rubs the bridge of his nose, and mutters something mostly unintelligible. Something like… *Oh gods, this again.*

When he looks up, his mouth curves down at one side, and one sharp eyebrow raises. "Playing to my ego, I see."

I shrug, pinching my fingertips together. "Perhaps a bit. Is it working?"

"Of course not." He narrows a look on me. "All right, maybe a little."

After too many moments of awkward silence, he reaches out and takes my hand. "Come here."

I let him guide me to a chair by the fireless hearth where he sits and tugs me into his lap, which is absolutely all right with me.

"Listen. I am beyond honored that you would want me to be your first *real* experience," he says, sounding so polite. "But perhaps you need someone with a bit more—" he glances around the room as though lost and looking for an exit "—*stability.*"

"Oh, yes. Because Winterhold is ripe with unattached, stable men. It's practically overflowing with them." I lightly smack at his chest. "Like who? Trei the greasy bookmaker? Sam the butcher, with blood under his fingernails? Varin, the bladesmith's apprentice? He pets his sword and his cock more than he would ever pet me, and that's the opposite of what I need."

Colden laughs. It's a quiet laugh, but a laugh, nonetheless.

I push a lock of hair behind his ear and gentle my voice. "I told you. I need a man who will make my first time memorable. Who will be patient and teach me and pleasure me and prevent it from being something I will forever regret."

He takes his hand from the arm of the chair and places it on my hip. "You assume I'm a grand lover, then."

"I know you are. Word spreads. From people of all stripes. And I know *you.* I know I won't be fucked and forgotten. I know that it will matter that it's good for me and that I'm happy afterward."

"But why tonight?" he asks. "Why have you said nothing before now?"

I shrug. "I don't know. I've thought about it before, far too many times. But in all honesty, tonight is the first time I felt like you really saw me. Saw me and wanted me. I felt it, and so I kissed you and hoped you didn't scold me and send me to my room like the little girl I am not."

He touches my face, trailing his fingertip along my jaw. "I just need you to understand that *this*... This is..."

"Not love," I say.

He slips his hand into my hair, his long fingers curling around my neck. "No, I do love you, Nephele. You have become a best friend over these last three years. A confidant, like no other. I trust you as well, and that is rare for me. Yes, I've had my affairs, but other than Alexus, there's been one other person before you in the last *century* who I trusted as much." A shadow passes over his face. "But beyond casual intimacy, fun sex, and friendship, I am not capable of giving you what you deserve. I haven't been capable of that in a very long time."

"And what *do* I deserve? A husband? Ten children running about? A cottage to care for and fields to harvest? What if I don't need or want any of that? What if all I need is someone to be a comforting set of arms when I'm sad? Someone to listen when I need to talk? Someone to laugh with, and someone to take me when I need to be taken? A settled, domestic life is good for many, Colden, but I don't know if my mother raised me to be one of those women. But what's more... *I'm lonely.*" I rub my fingertips over his brow. "Like you. I search for any joy I can find, even in a drunken festival. I want to *feel* something deeper, to be wild with bliss, to share what I've only ever given myself with another. And I want that person to be you."

He looks sad. Not the reaction I meant to provoke.

"You know I want you," he says. "I don't know how anyone could be in your presence for long and *not* want you. But I need to know that I won't hurt you. I would never forgive myself."

"I'm not fragile. And I know what I have with you. Your friendship is precious to me. I'm aware that your heart isn't part of the deal. Mine isn't either if I'm honest. But you do make me happy, in our own special way. And if I must get naked in front of a man and bare my all, I fear I can only do it in front of you."

He smiles. "That comfortable?"

I nod. "That comfortable."

He frowns again. "Have you ever seen a man fully naked?"

I roll my eyes at him. "Yes. Of course."

His shoulders scrunch up. "I didn't know. I'm confused by this entire situation."

I can't help but giggle. "Then ask what you need to know."

He lets out a huff of a breath. "Have you ever even touched a cock?"

"Yes." I smile and waggle my brows. "A handful of times."

"Oh, you're clever. I see what you did there." He winks. "Tell me what it was like. What did you actually *do?*"

He says those words as if he isn't sure I know what I did at all.

"Well, the first was awful. I was a young girl, maybe fourteen. I touched him and ran away, horrified. The second and third... I was still a girl, but a bit older. One was in the dark behind a barn, so you have me there. I don't really know what happened. I touched him, he grunted, and then we got scared and ran. The other, well, my mother caught us behind a tree just as he was about to gasp for glory, and that was that. He never looked at me again. The fourth, however, was when I was twenty. We were watching the stars and one thing led to another. He liked my breasts and touched me through my pants. I stroked him until he spilled in my hand. I rather enjoyed that one."

Colden blinks at me, most likely at my forthrightness, biting into his lower lip. "And the fifth? *Was* there a fifth?"

My cheeks heat as I summon honesty. "Yes. It was Varin. Two summers ago. He brought Alexus a new sword. I saw him and we chatted, and he came to my room. Talking led to drinking which led to kissing that led to touching, and touching led to more kissing on my part. Just not with his lips. I let him finish, but not in my mouth."

"Where, then?" he asks, his voice a bit huskier than before and thoroughly interested.

I drag my fingertips down my chest, touching the line of cleavage between my breasts. "Here."

Colden arches a brow and takes a deep inhale, the hand at my hip tightening. "And did he bring you the same pleasure you brought him?"

I shake my head. "It was as though he didn't know how. He touched me, inside and out, but in all the wrong places and all the wrong ways. I grew tired and wasn't going to instruct him, for gods' sakes. He was a grown man."

Colden laughs a little at that. "But you have also pleasured yourself, yes? You said before…"

"Oh, yes. Of course, I have."

I swear the midnight in his eyes darkens at the thought.

"And did you make yourself…"

"Come?" I whisper close to his lips, leaning into him as my heart starts beating harder. "Many times."

A low groan leaves him. "Godsdamnit, Nephele. You are far better at this than you believe."

I tighten my hand in his hair. "Reward me, then," I whisper. "Show me what you do to good girls."

He grips my chin and looks into my eyes. "I do vile things," he says. "You might not be quite ready for all that yet."

"I'm ready for more than you know." My blood hums and I raise a taunting brow. "Defile me, my king."

Eyes sharp, he reaches for the laces tying my bodice and unthreads them, one by one. When the pressure releases, I remove my stays, and Colden helps me pull my dress and smock down around my waist.

"Come here, you vixen." He draws me close and kisses me, his lips cool and wonderful, his tongue gently exploring, tracing and tasting every curve and line. It's simultaneously the most arousing and most tender kiss I've ever experienced.

I'm already swooning and breathless when he pulls away and cups my breast, studying me and touching me like something he's never before seen. Then his mouth is on me, sucking, biting, and licking my rosy tip in a rhythm I swear tugs on some invisible string that leads straight to the bud between my legs.

As though he's fully aware what sensation he's inspiring, he slips his hand beneath my skirt. I drop my head back as he caresses me through my undergarments, teasing and tugging, rubbing and flick-ing. It's torture, that thin layer of fabric keeping him from me.

I lift my head, watching with eager wonder as he swirls his tongue around my nipple. "Colden."

"Mmm?" He drags his teeth over the tip, making me whimper with want.

"I desperately need you to touch me."

"I *am* touching you," he says with a wicked grin. "Quite scandalously."

"You know what I mean."

"I do. And I can tell." His strokes between my legs grow rougher. "Your sweet little cunny is soaked for me."

My core clenches, and I tighten my thighs around his hand, gasping from the shock of pleasure that bolts through my clit.

His hand stills. "What's wrong?"

"Nothing," I reply on a rushed breath. "It's just… No one has ever spoken to me like that before."

He arches his brow. "Oh my. That one little word made you bear down? Then you're in for quite the fun tonight."

He withdraws his hand from my skirts and stands, sweeping me up with him. He carries me next to his bed, where he sets me on my feet. Unexpectedly, he pulls up a chair and sits down.

"Finish taking your clothes off for me," he says. "Slowly."

Oddly, I find it ridiculously erotic being told what to do. Obedience and submissiveness are not parts of my nature, and yet I have no resistance to Colden Moeshka. He could demand anything, and I believe I would do it.

I reach for the sash at my back, untie it, and begin peeling off my skirts and other layers. It takes the time it takes, which is, I realize, part of the pleasure, so I draw it out with certain movements. Curving my spine. Running my hands over my breasts, my hips. Colden watches every second, stroking the erection hidden in his black trousers, though I can see the firm outline, the way his hand slides up and down that impressive length.

When I go to remove my lace undergarments, Colden says, "Turn around when you take those off."

My face heats. I'm slender and strong, but I carry weight in my backside, an asset that has spurned many lingering looks, crude comments, and sneaking slaps over the years. For the first time, though, I actually *hope* it spurns all those things.

I turn and decide to make a grand show of it. Slowly, I slip the lace over my curves, dragging them down my legs, and kick them away when they reach my feet.

Colden's hands are on me in a heartbeat, skimming up my thighs. "This ass does wicked things to me."

He cups my bottom and squeezes, making me blush and throb all at the same time. The cool press of his lush lips kissing my lower back makes my nipples harden.

Tenderly, he trails his mouth down my curves and gently bites my ass, slipping his fingers between my legs, stroking my ache. "I want you to show me how you touch yourself," he says. "Exactly. So I know what you like."

In truth, though I feel so at ease with Colden, this gives me a moment of pause. It seems so salacious, and yet something about the indecency of it all gives me a thrill, a sense of power I haven't experienced before.

I crawl onto the bed, providing a view that makes Colden groan deep in his chest. Gods. I'm naked and exposed before the Frost King's hungry eyes, longing for him, my body pleading for his touch. After a lifetime of imagining anything other than this when it came to him, the last few years—and tonight especially—feel like a strange dream.

I sit facing him and spread my legs for my king anyway. He shakes his head as if in awe. "Fucking devils, Nephele."

"Now it's your turn," I tell him, loving how enthralled he seems.

He unlaces his trousers, taking his time as I tease him, touching only my thighs and the small tuft of hair at my apex. When he finally frees his cock, I swallow hard, desiring it instantly.

Need coils tight in my core as I begin working my body, rubbing my fingertip in quick circles over my clit.

"I usually have my crystal," I admit.

All of us women in the castle, and many others, purchase rose quartz crystals from a lady who lives near the Mondulak Range. She journeys here once a year with her smooth-as-glass stones, honed into pleasurable shapes and sizes.

Colden rubs his thumb over his tip. "Mmm. I would love to watch you fuck yourself that way. Do you ever ride it?"

I dip my fingers into myself and begin shifting my hips, fucking my own hand, feeling suddenly empty and needing relief. "Yes," I breathe. "Often."

With that, Colden stands and strips off his pants. It's as though the knowledge that I've certainly fucked—just not a *man*—alleviates any fear he might've had about being my first.

A moan leaves my lips as he kneels on the bed. "Thank the gods."

He chuckles. "I'm still not done."

Eyes locked with mine, he lifts my hand and sucks my fingers into his mouth, cleaning both that were inside me just moments ago. Another *zing* bolts straight to my clit, my blood burning. He looks starved, like my taste is the sweetest nectar.

When he finally lets go, he leans down and kisses me. I tangle my hands in his hair, suck on his tongue, and arch my hips.

"Please," I whimper. "I need you inside me, Colden."

"Mmm. *What* do you need inside you?"

He lowers himself, resting some of his weight on me, and I finally feel him, so hard, nestled right between my legs.

I know what he wants to hear. I just don't expect saying it to make me mindless.

"I want your cock," I answer, writhing, trying to reach what he's keeping at bay. "I want it so much."

He shifts to the left, leaning on his elbow, and trails his other hand down my body, pushing my knee up. After opening me to his eyes once again, he flicks his fingers over my clit and then pushes one inside me.

I gasp at the feel. He has such lovely, strong hands. The hands of a lover and a fighter. I clench around him as he strokes me, making me breathless.

Colden leans down to my ear. "One finger. One truth. I'm going to come inside you tonight. Right here, in this pretty little cunny."

I make a small mewling sound, a weak whimper that doesn't feel like me at all. Yet I can't do anything else.

Colden pushes a second finger in and begins a steady thrusting, in and out, curling his fingers at just the right spot to make me quiver. No instruction necessary with this man.

"Two fingers, two truths," he says. "The first one… When I'm done coming inside you, even after you've already orgasmed until you can't think straight, I'm going to fuck you again. In some incredibly obscene manner."

"Promise?" I move against him, sliding up and down his fingers, matching his tempo, wishing he would just touch my clit. That's all it would take for me to shatter.

"I swear," he answers.

"What's… the second… truth?" I manage to say.

He nips my ear with his teeth. "You still have a crystal?"

I bite my lip, my skin growing hotter and hotter against Colden's cool body. "Yes. In my room."

I feel him smile against my neck before he looks down at me. "Wonderful. Because one day, when you're ready, I'm going to watch you ride it, then I'm going to kneel behind you, and I'm going to fuck you in that stunning, tight little ass while your pink crystal is buried in your cunny. Would you like that?"

Gods above and below.

"Yes," I groan. *"Yes, yes, yes."*

He brushes his thumb firmly back and forth over my clit, my flesh all but preening for his attention. At the contact, I instantly orgasm, arching off the bed, tilting my head into the pillow, screaming out as he flicks his thumb faster and leans in, swallowing my cries with his mouth.

I grip his wrist, sure that this pleasure pulsating through me will end any moment, but it doesn't. It's brutal and unrelenting under Colden's expert caress, an ongoing destruction that I want to happen over and over and over again.

Eventually, his thumb slows, and the quaking and quivering inside me ease. When I float back down from the high of his touch, I'm panting as though I've been fighting for my life.

"I'm..." I scrub my hand through my hair, searching for words that won't seem to find me.

"Delicious," Colden finishes for me, licking his fingers again. "Beautiful. And so fucking tempting." He kisses a chilly trail up my throat, making my nipples peak so hard they hurt. "I think this might've been a very wise arrangement."

I angle my hips toward his, desperately needing him buried inside me. "Please, Colden. Stop making me beg. I've been begging all night."

A small laugh trips off his lips. "Patience, love. Lingering makes it all the better. The torture is half the fun." He kisses me again. His mouth moves languidly, as if we have all the time in the world. I suppose to an immortal man, we do. "I would very much like to put my tongue inside you. Do you want that?"

"Gods, yes." I don't mean to reply so quickly or with such fervor, but he meets my eyes and smiles when I do.

"Eager little thing, aren't you? If you want something, all you must do is say it."

I have said it, I think to myself. But I decide against complaining when he sucks my nipple into his mouth, his talented tongue teasing me.

"I like to hear you say filthy things just as much as you like to hear me," he adds.

He kisses his way down my body, making my pulse quicken. I rise on my elbows. I'm not sure if there's etiquette to this, but I want to see him if I can.

Colden looks up at me. "You like to watch?"

"I'm… I'm not sure. I think maybe I do."

His smile grows, and he kisses the inside of my thigh. "I think maybe you do, too."

Gently, he tugs my hips forward, tilting my pelvis upward, angling me better. We lock gazes for a long moment, then he lowers his head and drags his tongue up my center like he's licking melting cream from a cold treat, pausing at my clit. The groan that leaves him as he slides his tongue back and forth over that bud of pleasure makes my body tighten in response, the sound and feel of his needy moans so erotic. So hungry.

He licks lower and pushes his long tongue inside me, fucking me in a way that is better than I ever imagined, and with far more skill than I might've ever hoped for.

I've never felt like this. Never felt so entranced as I am by watching Colden feast on me like I'm the last meal he will ever know.

I thread my fingers into his hair and clutch his head, pressing him closer. It bends my mind that I'm already so close to release again, that I can't control anything about my body as I grind shamelessly against his mouth, loving the way it feels to have his face between my legs, the sense of dominance it gives me.

"Don't stop," I plead, but the moment I say those words, he looks up and lifts his head, his red lips glistening in the candlelight.

"I want to make sure I get to feel you come on my cock. We must be a little sparing with the orgasms until I know how many times I can set you off in a night."

That sends a thrill up my spine. I'm both excited and a little scared to think about what that might be like, learning how much my body can take when it comes to Colden Moeshka.

I drag him back up to me and manage to flip him to his back.

"My, my, I like it when you're rough." He grins, big, as do I, just before I kiss him, sucking my own pleasure from his lips.

This kiss is just as feverish as when he was between my legs, but everything seems to shift when I finally slip my hand down and close my fingers around his cock.

"Fuck," he groans, clasping my face. "I didn't realize how badly I needed you until tonight. How much I've ached for this."

With that confession, I stroke him, hoping that I'm pleasuring him. I'm assured when he curses again and closes his eyes, biting down on his plump bottom lip.

I glance down. Varin is a lovely man, physically, but Colden is an entirely different creation. He has a pretty cock, plush and pink, the skin unbearably soft, covering inches and inches of rigid delight.

I find that I rather love it. That thick vein running up the underside of his shaft. The swollen head that looks somewhat aggressive. The impossibly stiff nature of it, the way it curves so slightly you could almost miss it, how it looks a tad bit threatening. Something in me comes alive at the sight, wanting to be fucked with that cock until I forget my name.

As I stroke him, a pearl of cum slips to the slit of his head. It's shocking how that one little drop of pearly white liquid can make my mouth water again, and even more bizarre, compels me to slip down between his legs and take him into my mouth.

"Oh, fuck, Nephele." He, too, rises on his elbow to watch, pushing my hair back for a better view.

I can't say that I know what I'm doing, but instinct takes over quickly, as does the deep hunger I feel for this man and his body. I take him as far into my throat as I can, then I pull back out and stroke him, swirling my tongue around his engorged tip.

"Fuck, that feels wonderful," he whispers, watching closely, his voice suddenly ragged as I flick my tongue over his firm head. tasting the salty proof of his desire.

"I want you to come in my mouth," I tell him, sucking the tip.

I've heard tales. Some women love it. Others do not. I wasn't sure about myself, especially after feeling the need to pull away when I was with Varin. But Colden? I want it. I *crave* it.

"Believe me." He traces his thumb over my lips as I suck and lick him. "I would love nothing more than to fuck that pretty mouth until cum spills down your chin. And I will. In time. But tonight…" He curls his finger at me. "Come here, little vixen."

Obediently, I crawl up his body, straddling him.

"Is this what you want our first time to be like?" he asks with a smile. "You get to choose."

I think about it. I'm sure there are many ways to have sex. I know of some, of course, and I want to try them all. Eventually. But tonight? Tonight I need release, and I know exactly how to chase it down when I'm riding my crystal. I have a feeling that riding Colden will make my orgasm even easier to claim.

"I *do* want it like this," I tell him, leaning down, pressing my naked body against his. "I need you deep."

He slides his hands down my back and over my ass. "Put me inside you, then. Fuck me the way you wish."

I reach between us and find that angling our bodies is far easier than I imagined. In seconds, I'm sinking onto him, the throbbing head of his cock opening me.

We both sigh at the joining. I rise on my hands and arch my back, rolling my hips, taking him inside of me inch by delicious inch. He teases my nipples with his tongue as I work around his hardness.

"Look at you taking all that cock," he says against my skin. "Stretching that sweet little hole so I can fuck you so very hard."

I quiver down to my toes. "I'm going to need you to talk to me like that every day."

He laughs. "Like at breakfast? You want me to lean over and whisper filthy things in your ear? How I'd like to spread you across the table and tongue fuck you? Stick my cock inside you and fuck you in front of everyone?"

I take the last inch of him, filled to the brim, and I swear, I cannot think of anything else than the image he just placed in my mind, seeing him pinning me to the table, his beautiful cock thrusting in and out of me while everyone watches with lust in their eyes.

"What are you doing to me?" I whisper, my voice rough and trembling with need. "I feel ravenous."

"Good." He pushes his hands into my hair and kisses me. "Because I'm not going to stop until you're thoroughly satisfied, which means we could be at this for a while." He thrusts his hips, making me cry out. "I have no complaints," he adds.

Again, he slides his hands down my body and grips my ass. I'm unprepared for the onslaught he delivers, the way he begins with a shallower assault that steadily deepens and quickens, each resulting thrust reaching the deepest part of me, a part I've never reached. It comes alive when the gentle curve of Colden's cock strokes it.

He sucks my nipples, too, and dips a fingertip into the wetness we share before dragging that same finger up and over the hidden part of me that no one—not even me—has ever entered.

He pauses for a moment, rubbing the slickness onto me, and then pushes in. "Just a little," he says. "Just to give you a taste. I couldn't resist. Your ass is a temptation all its own, Nephele."

I gasp for breath, my pussy clenching his cock, stimulated by an intrusion that doesn't even involve those parts of our anatomy. There's no pain, much to my surprise, but there *is* torture. Because I'm already coming undone, becoming malleable and compliant under his talented care as he fucks me in two different ways, teasing with his finger and thrusting his cock in the most sensual rhythm.

"I think you like it," he says. "I think you like your king fingering your tight little ass while he fucks that perfect pink hole, making you his plaything."

I shake my head, feeling half-wild, feral. "I love it. I'm yours, Colden. Make me your whore."

Colden looks into my eyes, and though I see a glint of deepest lust shining there, he says, "Never a whore. But you can be my paramour if it suits you. The secret can make it feel all the more exciting. Especially when I bend you over and fuck you spontaneously in the middle of the day, when anyone could walk in and see how thoroughly I've corrupted my favorite witch. Would you like that,

Nephele? My cock in your cunny and my thumb hooked in your ass while you come all over me in the library? I would make you lick me clean."

A sound leaves me that I don't recognize, a guttural moan saturated with unquenchable longing. In response, Colden sucks my nipples again, flicking his tongue and biting harder this time, until my clit stiffens and throbs, pleading for the violent release I know lies ahead. It's as if my body and mind are pleasure troves and Colden Moeshka knows exactly how to explore every nook and cranny.

"I'm going to come." The words rush out of me, and for a moment, I wish I could suck them back in. I fear he'll stop, and my orgasm is *right there.* I can feel it teetering, just waiting to obliterate me.

"Mmm, fuck me, then. Punish your cunny on my cock for waiting this long to tell me that you've desired me. Then I'll punish it some more."

The next few minutes feel like an out-of-body experience. I do fuck him, so hard, rocking and grinding on his dick until pleasure rips me apart.

I gasp around the sensation, my entire body seizing from the intensity. This orgasm is cataclysmic, more than anything I've ever been capable of giving myself. It's as though nothing else exists but us, like I can pinpoint the height of every known desire to this brutal, pulsing pleasure, like the universe's heart is pounding between my legs.

When it ends, I can barely hold myself up. I can feel Colden smiling, feel his hands soothing me, hear him praising me—*good fucking girl, my sweet little vixen, my precious little witch.*

I'm so lost in bliss that it takes a second to connect what he's doing when he gently turns me onto the bed, on my stomach.

"I just need a few more minutes," he says, hovering over me, rubbing his cock between my legs. He leans down and kisses my ear. "Can you take it?"

I feel like I've been turned inside out, my muscles lax, but I push myself up to my knees, dragging a pillow under my breasts so I can keep my upper body on the bed. "Always."

Colden follows and rubs his hands over my hips. "Fuck, Nephele. Your ass is going to consume my dreams, I swear it."

I gasp as he gently hooks his thumb inside me, just the tip, his fingers splayed across my lower back. Then he pushes all that cock inside me, dragging it out to the tip before slamming back in.

I grip the covers in my fists. He's so impossibly hard. I feel every inch of it like this, every thrust forcing my mind to memorize the length, the girth, how long it takes for his head to slide over that sweet spot inside me. His thrusts turn to pounding, his balls slapping against my clit, awakening new need in me all over again.

Suddenly, Colden wraps his free hand in my long hair and uses it to tug me up from the bed, angling my head back, trapping me in his hold. I rest my weight on my hands and let him have me.

"Touch yourself," he orders, pushing his thumb in a little deeper. "Let's see if you can come one more time for your king."

Gods' death. I wouldn't have thought it possible, but as I touch myself while he rides me hard, pleasure builds. I feel it building in him, too, swelling inside his cock, making every thrust tickle me from the inside out.

His tempo increases until he's slamming into me so hard and fast the heavy bed knocks against the wall, over and over. I can do no more than utter unintelligible sounds as my body spasms and clenches, squeezing him through an orgasm, wrenching his own release from his body.

"Fuck yes, Nephele," he cries out as he pumps into me. "Fuck, you're making me come so hard, love. Gods. Fuck, fuck, *fuck*."

I can feel the warmth of his spill, the way I grow wetter between my legs, slick on my inner thighs. I writhe and whimper in his hold, tears breaching the corners of my eyes as everything slows and his hold on me gradually relents.

Afterward, Colden cleans us both in lavender water from the wash basin, then tucks me into his comfortable bed, lying behind me, holding me in his arms.

"Are you all right?" he asks.

I smile, though if he could see my face, I'm sure he would see the disbelief there. "I'm blissed out of my mind. So yes, I'm *all right*. Are you?"

He laughs against my ear, that same quiet chuckle from deep in his chest that I'm beginning to familiarize with his intimacy. "Of course, I am. My body wasn't the one being defiled. Though you are always welcome to try, if you'd like. I'm a good sport. I take as good as I give. Always up for the task of pleasure."

"Why is that?" I inquire, suddenly curious about this man that I know but feel like I'm only truly beginning to understand. "I mean, outside of the obvious."

I feel him shrug. "Three centuries of living can get... boring. Time becomes trivial. You begin to feel a great distance from your fellow man. And the normalcies of life that can feel new and comforting to most people simply lose their novelty. A sunrise is nice, but when you've watched thousands, it just isn't the same. You are always looking for something special on the horizon."

"But sex?" I ask. "Why doesn't it lose its novelty?"

"Because an orgasm is an orgasm. It transports me to a place that nothing in this world can touch. For those far too brief yet somehow eternal minutes, my mind carries me to a paradise where euphoria reigns. I think of nothing else but that—*euphoria*. Immortality is even momentarily forgotten, chased away by a rapture so true it's as though I've entered another realm."

Damn. I understand that now. I felt it tonight. Truly.

"So it feels like an escape," I reply.

"Most of the time. It allows me to forget, for a short while, my circumstances. It's a balm to a never-ending life. So yes. I reach for it often." He kisses my neck sweetly. "But tonight didn't feel so much like an escape as it did an arrival. Like I've found a safe place that makes me feel things I've forgotten how to feel. It's been decades since a kiss made me imagine a different life. But tonight, your kiss did that."

I perk up at that and turn over to face him. "Whose kiss did that to you?"

He lifts a brow, and one side of his mouth quirks up. "I'll never tell. Just someone I shared a long night with many years ago in a faraway land. His smile made my stomach twist with far too many feelings. And his laugh… it hummed in my bones. He felt like home, which was strange, because I hardly knew him. And when we parted, I felt nostalgic for a thing I never even had. I think because I allowed myself to dream of what it would be like to take him and run away from everything. But it wasn't meant to be."

I can hear the sadness in his voice, and it breaks my heart. "I'm so sorry you lost him."

Colden pushes a lock of hair off my forehead. "It's all right. I've survived this long."

"I want to ease that pain for you. I can be your home if you'll let me."

He smiles softly. "I'd like that very much. But I want you to under-stand something."

I run my hand over his shoulder. "I already know, and I feel the same way. This isn't romantic love. This is friends with very nice benefits."

He chuckles. "Yes, as I said, it's a wonderful arrangement. But that's not what I meant."

I frown. "Go on, then."

He grazes the backs of his fingers across my cheekbone. "One day, you'll meet someone who turns your world upside down. He's going to walk into the room and alter everything about your world with his mere presence. You might want to hate him, but his smile will eventu-ally thaw your icy heart. And you might want to kill him, but his kiss will set you on fire in a way that leaves you ready to burn down anyone who threatens him. He will change you, and you will fall in love with him. And when that happens, I don't want you to fear anything when it comes to me." He takes my chin in his hand. "Don't ever give up on someone you feel that kind of spark with because of me."

"That's how the man you spoke about made you feel?"

"Yes." Sorrow fills his dark eyes. "Much as I wish otherwise, no one has ever felt like him."

I say nothing more. Colden said many years had passed. His love could be gone now, taken by time that is a cruel dictator over Colden's existence.

I reach for him and pull him toward me. He puts up no fight, even smiling as he slides atop me, resting on his forearms.

"My paramour." He kisses the tip of my nose. "Thank you for this. For tonight. And any other night you choose to give me."

I slip my hands up and tangle them in his hair. "Many. I choose to give you *many*."

He arches a brow. "Until you meet *The One*. When he arrives, you'll walk away from me with no guilt and live a happy life. Swear it."

I don't know love like that. The closest I've ever been to it was seeing the relationship between my parents. It feels like a far-way thing for me. An impossibility. But I give Colden what he needs anyway.

"I swear, my king. But for now, you'll swear to defile me often and vigorously, in the most daring of places."

A delighted grin spreads across his handsome face. "I swear it."

He presses his erection between my legs and winks, then he rips the covers off us and grabs me, whisking me across the room, carrying me like a child, my legs wrapped around his waist, my arms around his neck. When he opens the door to the balcony that overlooks the south garden, where people still mill about, and beyond to the dwindling festivities, a swift, cold breeze rushes past, blowing out the lanterns hanging on either side of the door, casting us in shadow.

I let out an uncontainable squeal at his magick, and his choice for our first lewd act.

Colden laughs but covers my mouth. "I can't fuck you in the wide open if you howl like a wolf, woman," he whispers. "Tame yourself. We're going for clandestine sexual acts in the vicinity of the public, not everyone thinking I'm murdering you."

I giggle against his hand, and he uncovers my mouth before setting me down on my feet. Gripping my waist, he spins me toward the balcony wall and the gardens.

My eyes bulge. "Like *this?* Here?"

"Oh yes." He lifts a hand and caresses my nipples, while the other grabs a handful of my hair. "Lean forward, hands on the wall. Hold on as best you can. You'd better be quiet, too, or I'll have to spank you."

The next thing I know, he's rubbing the tip of his cock up and down my slit. I gasp when he enters me in one brutal thrust.

Colden lowers his fingers to my clit as he begins fucking me in the balcony shadows, all while villagers and servants linger two stories below.

"Let's give the night our first show, Miss Bloodgood," he whispers against the back of my neck.

I smile and spread my legs wider for him.

And we do.

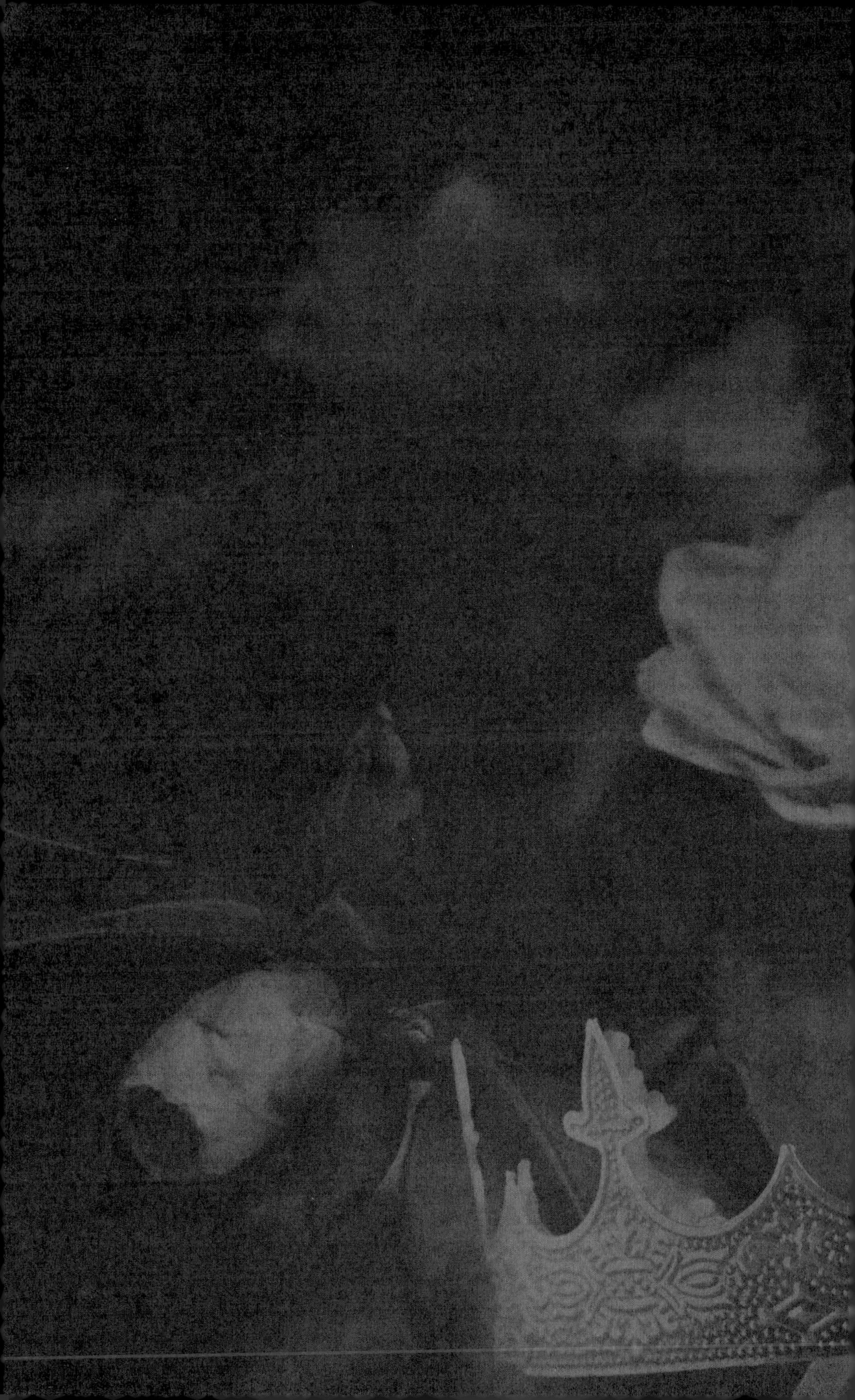

RATTLE THE CITY

From City of Ruin

❧

A Continuation of the Final Love Scene Between Raina and Alexus

ALEXUS

I t's early evening when we meet at the main courtyard for dinner with Fia.

We've scrubbed all proof of our journey away and have been groomed by the palace's maidservants until we look like we haven't been through any difficulty at all these last days.

The outside table—decorated with colorful glass lanterns and tall vases of red flowers—is set for eleven, with Fia residing at the head. She's dressed in black tonight, regal and lovely.

On the side of the courtyard sit musicians with stringed instruments including a harp, each one playing their part in a quiet song. Raina sits beside me, smelling like a rose and dressed in red again, her neckline plunging to her bellybutton.

I lean over to whisper in her ear. "That dress might be the death of me. Who needs food? All I want is to take you back to our room and make love to you for the rest of the night."

A soft blush touches her cheeks, something that might always make me swoon.

"We are guests," she signs, keeping her gestures small and between us. *"And so present we must be."*

And yet, she drags her hand beneath the table, from the top of my thigh to my knee and back up a little past halfway, sliding inward, teasing just the tip of my cock.

"Evil woman," I whisper, and she just smiles.

I'm so glad to see that smile. These are not the easiest of times, and when she checked the waters earlier today, Vexx had arrived in the East, and she still couldn't see Finn. Worry is eating at her, but I'm hoping that tonight provides a little distraction.

"A toast," Fia says, standing at the head of the table with her glass raised in the air. "To the future," she says. "May we be the shining lights who change the days to come."

We clink our glasses of sparkling wine, and the dinner attendants begin passing platters of food around.

"Where's Joran?" I ask Nephele who sits across from me. I point to the only empty place setting, the one beside her. Everyone else is here.

At my question, she chugs her wine.

"No idea, really. Maybe he wasn't hungry." She fidgets with the ruffle running down the front of her jade green dress, then her hand moves to a small ruby pendant hanging from her neck that I've never seen.

I sense a lie. I know her. Perhaps they had an argument.

"Well, I'm famished," Rhonin says, plucking two bread rolls as the basket passes. Helena smiles, sitting close beside him.

"With all that moaning coming from your room earlier today," Keth says, voice low so that Fia doesn't hear, "I can imagine why."

Zahira smacks at Keth's hand, though she wears a smile, and Rhonin turns so many shades of red that I'm certain one of them matches Raina's dress. Everyone seems happy, save for Nephele who looks nervous and on edge. I'm certain it has something to do with Joran.

After dinner, Raina and I walk the terraced courtyards, still sipping wine, before we head back to our room. Standing at the vanity table, I slip off my shoes and strip off my tunic and iron key, neatly laying everything aside. There's already a low fire burning in the hearth to ward off the desert chill, and the candles around the room have been lit.

When I turn around, I don't expect to see Raina standing a few feet away, already naked, holding a small golden jar and wearing a rather erotic smile and a display of bright witch's marks. But that's what I find, and I couldn't be more pleased.

I shake my head in admiration of her lovely body and move toward her, returning her smile. Standing close, I tap the top of the jar. "What's this?"

She unstops the cork, carefully, and hands me the jar. I should've remembered. Fia is a woman of tradition.

"Fever Lilac dust." I hold the jar to my nose to smell that cloying scent, laced with hints of rose and vanilla.

"*A gift,*" she signs. "*From Fia.*"

"Do you remember my story about this?"

She arches a brow. "*What do you think?*"

I wrap my arm around her waist and draw her against me. "We can't use too much. That's the only rule."

Though I'm glad her mind is on us, and that she feels like using it at all.

She makes a face, questioning me, asking why.

"Because, if I paint you in this like the couple from the wedding will do tomorrow night, we won't leave this room for a month. We still have a king and a world to save."

She pinches her finger and thumb together, squinting one eye.

I can't help but laugh. "Gods, you are so adorable. Yes. We can still try a little."

It is exceptionally difficult to keep myself from covering her in golden dust from head to foot. Trying to think with reason, I lead Raina to the bed and lay her down. Crawling over her, still wearing my black trousers from dinner, I sprinkle a tiny amount of dust between her breasts, right over her heart, where two simple flourishes curve over the swell of her breasts.

The dust spreads quickly, glittering her skin with a soft,

golden sheen. Using a small taste of my magick, I draw my hands over her breasts, her shoulders, down her arms, feeling her skin pebble beneath my palms. Then I move lower, straddling her ankles as I rub more dust over the curves of her legs and hips.

It's such a sensual experience, touching her this way, taking my time to feel her curves, to memorize every little dip and valley on her body. Before I left them behind, I sketched images of her in my journals from memory. But I think I would like to draw her like this, posed for me so that I might be forced to notice everything. Every scar. Every freckle. Every witch's mark. The sleek line of her spine. The dimples at her lower back.

Already, she's breathing heavy, massaging her breasts, tweaking her nipples. The sight makes my blood rush and my cock hard as steel.

I move between her legs and use my knees to knock hers wider. She opens for me without any resistance, revealing that slick, pink center I'll never get enough of.

Carefully, I sprinkle a little more dust, right over her pussy. I rub her gently at first, working the dust into her flesh, watching her writhe as she grows wetter and wetter for me. I can feel the dust working on me too. A heady arousal that feels like we're in another world, just the two of us.

Kneeling there, I thrust my fingers inside her, fluttering them with a tickle of my power, and she arches off the bed. Her lips part on the sweetest gasp. After long moments, her eyes meet mine, hazed with desire as I work her deep before finding that magickal little place inside that sends her reeling.

"Do you like it when I fuck you like this?"

She nods, a silent whimper visible on her face. It makes me smile as I bend down and drag my tongue up the length of her slit.

"And you like it when I lick your pussy?"

She shoves her fingers into her hair, nodding again, working against my hand.

"Do you like it when I talk to you like this?"

Another nod, and this time, her hands move into *my* hair.

I lean back down and devour her, fucking her all the while with my fingers, sucking and nibbling her perfect little clit until she's grinding against my mouth, seeking the magick on my tongue.

When I pull back to look at her, to see that golden skin shimmering in the firelight, her eyes are all but on fire. She shoves up and pushes at me, grabbing the jar I sat aside. I obey and crawl off the bed.

My feet no sooner hit the floor than her hand is on my chest, and she's driving me backward until I'm pressed against the wall.

I smile, and she holds my gaze while unlacing my pants. Quickly, they drop to my ankles, and I kick them aside. Raina pours just enough Fever Lilac dust in her hand, then she sprinkles the gold powder over my chest. Using both hands, she spreads it over my shoulders and arms, down my torso, and then she's on her knees— where I think she wanted to be in the first place—gripping my cock with both hands, staring up at me as she twists her wrists, working me in a way that makes me yearn to be inside her.

She strokes me, and the moment she puts her mouth on me, I feel my control slipping. I slide my hands into her hair, ready to fuck her lovely mouth down to her throat. But I pause.

With a tender touch, I brush my thumb over the curve of her bottom lip as she stares up at me with those hungry, dark blue eyes. The sight of her on her knees before me, naked and ravenous and golden, spurns my deepest desire.

But there's something else about seeing her like this. Something that makes my blood heat in a different way.

Anger, the fire of a thousand suns, an emotion that shouldn't be anywhere near this moment. But it is, and I need it gone.

Before she can protest, I reach down, sweep her up in my arms, and carry her to bed where I lie beside her and draw her to me.

"This is better," I tell her.

She pushes up on her elbow, dark hair framing her beautiful face, confusion writing itself into the lines between her brows. *"Did I do something wrong?"* she signs, a glint of hurt in her eyes.

"Gods, no." I sit up against the pillows and clasp her face. "Raina, there is nothing I want more than your mouth on my body." I lean in and kiss her. "I have ached to take you that way more times than you can count since that night at Starworth Tor. It's just that..." I swallow the tightness in my throat as I search for words, a reason why I stopped her that doesn't sound like madness. And the answer hits me. "You bow to no one," I tell her, my voice graver than it has any right to be tonight. "Do you hear me? Not ever. Especially not to me."

She crawls up my body and straddles my hips. Not another word is said as she takes me inside her, then leans down, one arm around my neck as she moves slowly, taking her time, taking me deep.

I was too eager moments before, so I haven't yet asked, but I think tonight we both might need tenderness. I can feel it in the way she kisses me, as though that simple connection is enough for her to enter my soul, to memorize who I am, who I've become under her care.

I don't hide anything. I have no fear anymore. Any darkness, she has destroyed with her light. Every shadowy, gloomy place inside me feels remade because of her. I feel healed.

She tightens her fingers in my hair and presses her lips to my throat, tasting the skin over my pulse as her other hand traces my rune. I fold my arms around her and hold her tight, moving with her, and a different kind of instinct takes over, something so intimate that we begin to move in a beautiful rhythm, like when we were in the pool at Starworth Tor. Every movement is fluid, every thrust met with slick grace, our hands and mouths finding that sensual rhythm. It's a dance, one our bodies have learned these last weeks, but tonight it's perfected.

Raina kisses me, her mouth brushing mine, the soft drag of her bottom lip enough to give way to sweet pleasure.

I plunge my hands into her hair to the wrists and inhale her. This kiss is so much more than just a kiss. It's a promise. An oath. I already know that before she presses one word to the skin over my heart.

"Mine."

"Yes," I whisper. "Always. El om ze pera. Lohanran tu gra."

She pulls back, and I see the question in her eyes, the recollection.

"I was supposed to tell you what that means when we were in Malgros."

She nods, eager for me to continue. "It means, *there is no other*. You are my only temple. I love you, Raina." I've said those words before, when things were different, but tonight, I can see that she hears me. That my words are etching themselves across her heart. "I meant it," I tell her. "I swear I have loved you all my life. And when we are gone from this world, I will love you still."

"I love you the same," she signs, and I cannot stop the smile that breaks across my face. My heart feels discovered. Like a lost thing finally found by the one meant to hold it.

Tears fill her eyes, and when they fall, I kiss them away. Again, we begin our dance, making love as though we might never have the chance again, lost in a euphoria that makes it feel as though we're floating among the stars.

Suddenly, a strange feeling comes over me. I grip her hip.

I can feel her.

I can feel her through the bond.

Clasping her face, I stare into her eyes. Now, when I look for her in my mind, she's there. As though she never left.

The threads of our magick begin weaving together, a tight braid chasing along the bond.

I shake my head, confused.

"I healed the bond," she signs, laughing and weeping. *"I did not know if I could."*

It is impossible to express the joy I feel. I'm not certain even Raina would understand it. But this—being with her—feels like my fate has finally arrived. The overwhelming relief of this night is incalculable, because the thing most precious to me in this world is with me, in my arms, and she's mine.

Hungered like never before, I turn her over, pressing a kiss to the smooth skin beneath her delicate collarbone that used to bear her rune. That still does, I suppose. Inside.

"I hope you aren't sleepy," I tell her as she completes the tangling of our magick.

She smiles and shakes her head, and I bury myself inside her "Because tonight," I whisper, "we're going to rattle this city."

RAINA

Time blurs thanks to the haze of Fever Lilac passion.

Alexus makes love to me, slowly torturing with his body and his magick. Worshiping.

His temple. His *only* temple.

I believe those words.

Our bodies move in perfect time, every kiss and touch marked by its own intimate desperation. The need we share is so intense that tears of relief spill from my eyes with each orgasm that crashes through us.

It happens three brutal times—once with Alexus on top of me, another with him lying behind me, and a final event with me astride him, so lost to sensation and connection that time seems to stop when we finally climax.

After that third collision, we come down from the high of bliss for momentary rest. That's all it is, though. A few short minutes of reprieve.

"I need water before I wither." Alexus leans over me, that dark, enchanting face so entrancing. "You?"

I shake my head, fist my hand in his hair, and drag his mouth back to mine. He tastes like sex and the vanilla of the Fever Lilac flower carrying us through this perfect night. I can't get enough.

But he pulls away. "Water," he says with a smile in his voice. "Then more sex."

A pout twists my face as I trail my fingertips down his muscled chest, his abdomen, and into that silky trail of glittering dark hair below his navel. I don't want water. I want *one* thing, and he's about to take it away from me.

A sexy smirk curls the edge of his mouth. "You naughty temptress. That dust is having its way with you, isn't it?" When I graze my fingertips along the length of his cock, that smirk unfurls. "Give me two minutes."

Reluctantly, I let go of him. He rolls off the bed and struts across the room to the ewer and basin, then pours a glass of water and tilts it to his lips.

I lie atop the sheets, head propped on a stack of pillows, watching him. He's so tall, so naked, so glistening with sweat and gold dust. His hair is loose and tousled, hanging in waves just above his broad shoulders. That wide, scarred back—marked with a wheel of runes—tapers to a narrow waist and the tautest, roundest ass I have ever been so blessed to see.

Drunk off him as I am, I still register the coolness of sweat on my skin, the heat of the fire crackling in the hearth, and the carnal glint in Alexus's eyes as he turns around and pins me with that emerald stare.

He sits back on the massive wooden writing desk and unfolds his long body like an invitation, feet shoulder-width apart. His cock is half-hard, his balls hanging heavy between his legs. He's lovelier and more enthralling than any man has a right to be.

A thought flashes through my mind as I study him. I'm not against being taken across a desk. In fact, I imagine it, being ridden hard, and it only makes the hunger and ache inside me worse. My body responds, tightening, wanting something to clench. Wanting *him.*

I bite down on my lip, trying to stave off my desire, but it's no use.

The Fever Lilac has me locked in this sex-addled state, and even if it didn't, I'm too addicted to Alexus Thibault to let this moment pass.

With one brow cocked mischievously, he lifts the glass in my direction. "Want some?"

The innuendo in his sultry voice is clear, and suddenly, I'm parched.

In answer, I crawl off the bed. For those first few steps, the muscles in my legs tremor, and I worry they might not hold me long enough to carry me across the room.

But Alexus's cock twitches against his inner thigh, and his gaze flares at the sight of me, and before I know it, I'm standing between his knees, taking long swigs from the glass as he rests his hands on my hips, kisses my shoulder, and waits with the calm patience only a three-hundred-year-old man can possess.

When I finish, I set the glass on the basin table and thread my fingers into his hair. We share a lingering look, one that speaks a thousand words without any utterance. *I love you*, it says. *I need you. Take me. Break me. Mold me. Fuck me.*

I kiss him, relishing the taste of his sweet mouth, sliding my tongue over lush lips, slick and cool from the fresh water. Greedy, I reach down and stroke him, deepening our kiss as he draws me ever closer, those strong hands holding my waist.

How I love the feel of him. That smooth sheath covering all that rigid delight. That firm head, and the tiny pearl of longing that always greets me. It takes mere seconds before he's hard as the stone beneath our feet.

If I had any modesty before, any propriety, it's now gone, because I can't stop imagining him standing behind me, pushing into me until I can't think around the pleasure.

And so I break our kiss, and in brazen fashion, step to his left, where the top of the desk is clear, and drape myself across it. I spread my legs wide enough to give him quite the view and all the access he needs.

I turn my head to look at him, my fevered cheek pressed against the cool wood. His eyes are bright with love and lust in the firelight.

Turning toward me, he runs a rough hand along the curve of my back and down my ass, cupping my bottom. "This is a braver move than you realize. Have you any notion what it does to me to see you like this?"

I rise on my elbows and shake my head. *"Show me,"* I sign.

As though that command is all that's needed to spur him into action, he stands. I expect him to nestle himself between my legs and begin, but that isn't what happens.

He lifts my right leg, placing my knee on the desk, opening me more fully. Then he kneels, sliding one hand over my hip and down my thigh while the other rests atop my raised leg, gently holding it in place.

"Fucking perfect," I feel him murmur, his breath warm against my skin. "Arch your back for me. Let me see all of you."

The second I obey, a low growl rumbles from his chest.

He tongues my clit and sucks it into his mouth, alternating between that and biting my lips, devouring me from behind, much the way he did our first night at Winterhold. I'd been taken so off guard that night, having the Witch Collector feasting on me in such an erotic manner, to have my body open and vulnerable when it had never been so boldly explored before. It scared me that I loved it as much as I did, and that I wanted so much more from him.

When pleasure crested and I'd tried to crawl away, Alexus had dragged me back to his mouth and continued his assault, ultimately knowing that my true desire didn't match my physical reaction. I'd needed relief and wasn't sure how to endure the journey to get it, other than to escape it all together.

But I didn't fight him. It was *that* act, the act of yielding all to a man I trusted with my very life, that heightened each moment forward. The feeling of relinquishing control to someone who could show me what bliss truly is. I almost came from that alone. From that tiny bit of domination.

Tonight is no less consuming or startling. He's been inside me. Released inside me.

And he doesn't care.

I am the only thing he needs. The only thing that will satiate this blinding hunger. There are no boundaries tonight because the Fever Lilac has obliterated them all. Pleasure is everything, and the love and trust between us is overwhelming. There isn't a part of me that isn't his, no part of me that doesn't want to please him.

I grip the edge of the desk and move along his tongue as he feasts and groans into my damp flesh.

But things begin to change. *Alexus* begins to change. I feel it in the way his tongue grows more demanding, his mouth more eager, more starved. It's in the way his hands move, fingers no longer caressing but digging into my thighs.

"Fuck yes, Raina." He plunges his tongue inside me, then drags it up the length of my center, that slow, smooth scrape almost too much to endure. "This is mine," he proclaims. "My clit. My pussy. My ass. All of it. *Mine.* Do you understand?"

Emphatically, I nod, barely able to summon a coherent thought. If I know anything, however, it's that I am indeed his. There isn't a single cell in my body that doesn't know this as truth.

And he is mine. I've felt that way for a long time now, though tonight I feel it on a different level. I'm still just as protective as I'd been that night at the thermal pools, probably more so. But now there's a special unity between us, something even more possessive and all-encompassing.

He has my heart. My body. My soul. My trust. My love. My devotion. My entire being.

And I have his.

Finally, he takes one last taste and stands. With his hands gripping my ass, he spreads me open and rubs his thumb over the most intimate part of me. I gasp at the contact, waiting and wanting as he teases my slit with the head of his cock, rubbing it around my entrance.

"My little honey hole," he says in that deep voice, and I swear to the gods I melt across the desk.

Alexus tugs me back into form, and in one swift and punishing move, he impales me, rooting his stiff cock deep inside me. Reflexively, I grip the desk's rounded edge and try to breathe.

Hard and fast or deep and slow. He hadn't asked me that question tonight. I usually answer *both,* and I suppose our lovemaking is a blend between the two options. But tonight, everything before this moment has been Alexus Thibault's brand of tender. His brand of gentle. It was wonderful and passionate, and my heart feels so full from the connection we share.

But this shift in the air…

This shift in him…

I don't know what to expect. I've glimpsed his more animalistic side in moments of anger, and to a degree when we've been intimate. But I want more than a glimpse. I want him to stop tempering his lust, to unleash that part of his nature on me. To use me. To plunder my body. To fuck me into a state of utter oblivion. I can always feel him holding back, as though I'm breakable.

Slowly, he wraps my hair around his hand and tugs me up, pressing his other hand atop the desk as he leans over me. Gods, he fills me so completely, his cock stretching me.

"I feel what you want along the bond." My face heats as he trails kisses down my neck before returning to my ear. "Have you done it before? It's not so simple as what you envision."

I shake my head because it's the honest answer. Nephele has, with Colden, and she swears it's bliss. But as for me, I've explored my own body, a little, but Finn and I never ventured into that territory save for touching and teasing. It seemed too much. I didn't want to let Finn Owyn have *all* of me. In truth, I held back so much from him.

And yet the idea of Alexus taking me that way? It seems right, and tonight, I hunger for it. If anyone will ever know me that intimately, it will be him and him alone.

No sooner does that thought strike me, another hits. He knows what I desire isn't simple because he's done it before. Of course, he has. After three-hundred years, it would be impossible that he hasn't.

I shouldn't be jealous of the woman from his past who was lucky enough to experience Alexi of Ghent giving himself over to such passion and power, the woman—or women—he claimed in the manner I long to experience.

And yet I envy them. Was it Fleurie? *I can't think about that.* Can't let my mind go there. It's probably wrong of me, but I want to be the sole person to have ever been pleasured by him this way. I want something of him that has never belonged to another. Only to me.

"Remember that the yearning you're feeling tonight is even more powerful under the haze of the Fever Lilac," he informs me. "So be careful what you wish for, because I fear I might not have enough restraint to do anything but grant your every desire."

And I don't have the control to do anything but beg that he do just that.

Images rush through my mind and along the bond. Images that have tortured me for weeks, in waking and in dreaming. I try to be reasonable. Wise. Careful in what I show him.

Just like our first time, nervousness and anticipation swell within me, but I trust this man so wholly. He *will* give me what I want, and he will make it divine.

A harsh breath leaves him as he utters my name, that husky voice raw and rough. "Are you certain?"

He presses his cock into my core, and I nod against his grip.

He kisses my neck again, dragging his teeth over my fluttering pulse, licking the sensitive place just beneath my ear. "I'm going to fuck you here then. There's something about having you spread across this desk I can't resist. I need to come in you like this." He brushes his mouth along my cheek. "I'll give it to you so good, Raina. I'll give you all you can possibly take."

Tears of overwhelming pleasure well in my eyes as I angle my face to kiss him, panting into his mouth. I grip my breast and tweak my nipple as he begins moving inside me. The building desire is already that intense, enough that I need all the sensation I can get.

His hold on my hair relaxes, allowing me to brace myself on the desk again. But that's the only reprieve he offers.

Alexus begins his torture anew, pumping into me, sinking deeper with every thrust, even as his magick begins crawling over me.

Through me.

It's a cruel form of pleasure. With each punishing thrust of his rigid cock, Alexus's power teases my body. It feels so real. Like a hungry tongue working my clit and laving my breasts, guiding me to the brink of orgasm but refusing to let me plummet over the edge.

And yet I love every moment of his sweet torment.

More, more, more, I think along the bond.

Harder, harder, harder.

Deeper, deeper, deeper.

He splays his warm hand across the small of my back, and I feel something liquid dripping onto me. When I look over my shoulder, I catch a glimpse of Alexus spitting, just enough to wet me. I don't know what to think of myself, because that sight makes me tighten around his cock in a crushing grip.

He brushes his thumb over me again, wetting me where no one else has ever touched, rubbing small circles. "This is what you want, isn't it?"

I nod and push back against his touch, trying to claim what I need, but I'm too tense.

As though sensing the issue, Alexus says, "Fever Lilac eases discomfort. Important for many wedding nights. Relax. Breathe. I've got you."

My body responds with trust, tight muscles loosening and uncoiling as I take deep, calming breaths.

"There you go," he says, gently easing the tip of his long thumb into my ass.

Though there's a small bite of pain in the beginning, it dissipates quickly. He slips deeper, and the sensation that follows is mind-altering. To be so filled, so claimed, so penetrated—by the man I love—is everything.

"Someday soon, I'll give you more," he says. "Do you want that? To feel my cock here?"

"Yes," I manage to sign, needing him to know just how badly I want to experience that feeling.

Pinned beneath his grip, his thumb buried deep, Alexus begins moving again. His thrusts become longer, dragging his thick cock out to that broad tip before sinking back into me so hard each impact inches the heavy wooden desk across the floor, scraping at the stone tiles.

Gods, it hurts. The good kind of hurt. The kind only he has ever given me. I'll feel him tomorrow, and the next day, too, and perhaps the day after that. A constant ache between my legs that will remind me of every second of this night.

"Hold on," he commands, and I grip the desk as though my life depends on it.

He uses his right hand to pin my knee to the desk as his left hand presses on my lower back, that thumb working me as he slams his cock into me over and over, giving in to the carnal need singing in the bond between us.

This time, when my orgasm threatens, his magick doesn't relent. It pulses through my clit, a brutal vibration that sends me crawling again, doing my damnedest to flee such unfathomable pleasure.

And again, Alexus prevents my escape.

"If you try to run," he growls, his right hand clasping the back of my neck as he lifts his knee to the desk behind me, trapping me with his weight, "I'll only chase you. And I'll catch you, my love. And fuck you even harder. You can make damn sure of that."

These words. His voice. There's a change I can't register. Un Drallag, perhaps? That is the darker side of him after all, the side he so desperately wants to forget and bury. A side that feels like temptation to me. It sends a rogue chill coursing over my skin.

To push him to the edge, I try to move away again, using my grip on the desk to propel myself forward. He jerks me back and *tsks.*

"You like this, don't you? The chase. Being at my mercy." He leans down and drags his teeth across my shoulder. "I like it, too. Too gods-damn much. But you don't get to pull away from me without punishment."

He straightens, and his hand comes down on my ass, harder than ever before, sending zings of ruthless sensation shuddering through me.

I come instantly. Brutally. Erupting under the touch of this magnificent man and the waves of power pouring off him, power tangled with my own magick, humming in my veins.

As Alexus's orgasm builds, throbbing inside me, my body squeezes him in spasms, coaxing him to the brink. I close my eyes, still reeling, and move along his shaft. Harder and faster.

The sound that tears from his body when he comes brands itself into my memory. It's a sound torn between agony and sweet relief, a roar that brings with it a stunning surge of magick.

Wind rips through the room as his thrusts turn wild, sending sheets of parchment fluttering and the drapes whipping. Even the paintings hanging around the room clatter on their hooks, and the writing implements and ink pots, nestled in a wooden tray atop the desk, tumble to the floor.

The walls tremble, Fia's palace rattling under the power of Un Drallag's release.

It lasts longer than what should be humanly possible, so long I can hardly take it. With deep groans and grunts, he spills into me over and over, until his pleasure runs down my thigh, and he withdraws his thumb from my body.

But just when I think it's over, he wipes his release up my cleft, and suddenly there's pressure where his thumb had been.

"Just a taste of what you're asking for," he says, spitting on us again before pushing the head of his cock into my ass with a rugged groan of ecstasy that drives me wild.

He slips in easier than I imagined, and I gasp hard at the feeling, that same initial bite of pain followed by intense fullness. Thanks to his earlier ministrations, I feel more than ready, though. For this few inches, at least.

And so I move against him, needing more, and slide my hand between my legs, teasing my clit. We work together like that, gently pushing the limits, his cock still impossibly hard and thick.

As our rhythm intensifies, his grip on my waist grows firmer as he pants behind me like a man ready to explode. He begins thrusting shallowly, carefully moving a little deeper. I'm still only taking less than half of him, though it feels like so much more.

I don't expect our orgasms to arise so quickly, but Alexus begins moving faster, and they roll in like a tide, each wave promising to eventually destroy us.

When my pleasure crashes, I pound my fist on the desk, gasping, uncertain if I can bear this, just as Alexus says, "Fuck Raina, I'm coming again."

Magick roars through the room and pounds through me, and together, we are annihilated by sensation as the world stops for us once more.

In those long moments, tears spill down my face, because I feel Alexus so thoroughly in the bond, our magick so entwined. I feel his unyielding love for me, his deep appreciation for my trust, the overwhelming pride that I am his, and the comfort that I don't fear any part of him. He treasures me. Treasures *us*.

After several moments, he lowers his leg and gently eases mine off the desk. My entire body is shaking. I can't think clearly, but I know I can't stand on my own. If not for the desk and the hold Alexus still has on me, I would collapse.

Tenderly, he withdraws from my body and lifts me into his arms, carrying me to bed. I feel him cleaning me, smell a hint of lavender, sense the cool touch of a damp cloth on my face, my neck, my breasts, my stomach, and finally soothing between my legs. I register little else until he crawls in bed beside me and draws me to him.

All I know is that I gave Alexus everything tonight, and I would do it a thousand times over.

"We rattled the city," I sign against his chest, smelling the lavender on him as well. The Fever Lilac dust is gone, save for a few specs glimmering on his abdomen.

He tugs the cover over us and smiles against my hair just before kissing my forehead. "That we did, my love."

There are no more words after that. No worries or fears or concerns about tomorrow. No thoughts of gods or wars or death or destruction.

We curl around one another, our magick still tangled, the shimmering threads glowing brightly as the lighthouse beacon in my mind's eye.

And we sleep.

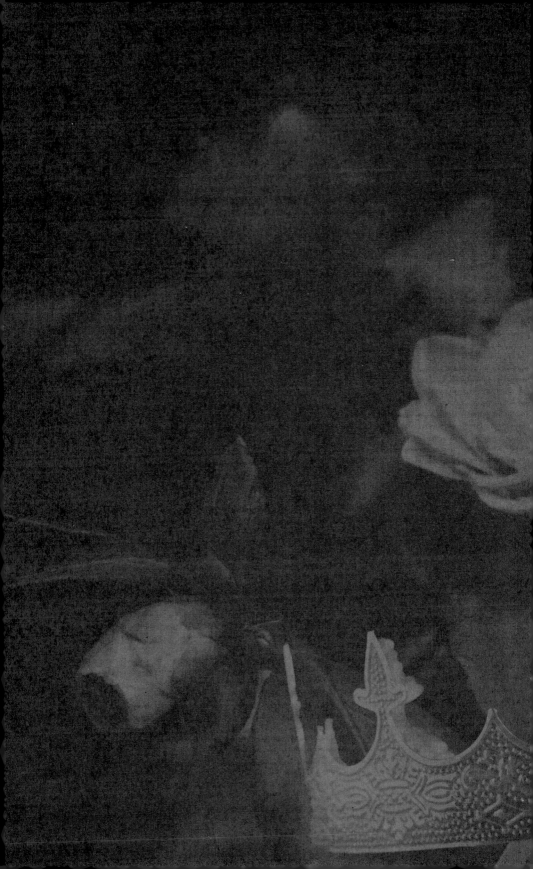

ALEXUS'S DREAM

From The Witch Collector

❦

A Glimpse into Alexus's Memories
Alexus & Raina

ALEXUS

I have known cold.

Years and years of long and unkind winters in the North, but I'm not certain I've ever known cold like this.

Lamp in hand, I bring Mannus to a halt and dismount, my booted feet crushing through a snow drift that reaches above my ankles. Surrounded by an orb of faint light from my lantern, I gather the heavy blanket around my shoulders and trudge against the wind and falling snow toward the women.

I still don't know how to feel about the blacksmith's daughter. Something is wrong. Something I've yet to place. She carries a stench my mind remembers from many years past, an odor that sparks a warning in my mind, but it's an impossible thought. *Impossible.*

"You have fire magick, yes?" I say to the girl.

She bristles, as though the sound of my voice offends her. "I'm not good at fire magick."

Her tone is harsh and bitter. Rude and quick.

"You don't *have* to be good." I grit the words through cold teeth. "I just need you to help me get a fire going." I glance at Raina, shivering beneath my cloak against Helena's back, and jerk my chin toward

Mannus. "There's a rocky overhang over there. I'm hoping this is Nephele's doing."

I have to believe it is. Even if I don't feel her here, I have to believe she will somehow protect us from freezing to death out here.

As I stalk back toward my horse, the blacksmith's daughter scoffs and speaks two words she isn't wise enough to keep quiet. "Foolish man."

Perhaps I'm only tired, or perhaps I'm irritable from the blistering cold. Whatever the culprit for my easily roused temper, I halt and turn around, lifting my lamp so I can see Helena better in the darkness.

She knows nothing about me save for that I am the Witch Collector, a title I've never wanted. But in moments like these, the legend surrounding me often dampens the bravery of those who consider speaking so unguardedly as Helena. I suppose I've become used to such deference, because her blatant disrespect pisses me right the fuck off.

"I'm wiser than you think, girl. You would do well to remember that."

Clenching my teeth, I bury my irritation and find shelter for the horses beneath the tallest part of the stone overhang. It's the shape of a crescent moon, perfect for shielding much of the wind.

After the animals are settled, I gather any dry wood and brush I can find, which proves to be a task though not impossible. When all is said and done, I've collected a hefty armful of under-limbs from a dying tree, broken branches shielded by needly boughs from the weather. Some are damp but will hopefully light.

Back at our makeshift camp, I dump the kindling on the ground where Raina has cleared the ground. She sits an arm's length away, huddled beneath my cloak. I can feel her watching my every move as I shield the oil lamp and begin the work of taking flame from the wick using the wool from the tinder box. When a rough wind sucks away my flame, I try again, but the wind blows the tiny fire to nothing.

"Gods' death." I snap the glass door on the lamp closed. "I can't risk losing the only light we have." I take a seat beside Raina, sensing her attention moving toward her friend who sits across from us, oddly silent. There's an easy way and a hard way to survive the cold tonight. The easy way lies with her, yet she makes no effort to help. *"Fulmanesh,"* I say to the girl, trying to prime her into action. It seems unlikely, but perhaps she's still in shock. "That's the word for summoning fire," I remind her. *"Iyuma* if it needs urging."

"I told you, Witch Collector," she all but hisses. "I'm no good at fire." She gets up and, without another word, heads to the far corner of the overhang. Wrapped in the gambeson, she turns her back to us amid the shadows, as though she's going to sleep.

Raina scrubs her hands over her knees, then starts to push off the ground to join her friend. I can sense her concern, but I sense something else in the air, too. Something that screams at my instinct.

I reach out and capture Raina's dainty wrist in my grip, halting her from leaving my side. But the moment she turns those dark blue eyes on me, I let go. Not because I see anger there, but because something dead inside me flares to life when I touch her, let alone when I look into her eyes at the same time. It's too much connection, a dangerous combination that might make me want to do something I have no business doing when it comes to her.

I'd give just about anything to understand what I'm feeling for her, but there's no explaining it. No reason for it. It's ridiculous and overwhelming. I tell myself she's only awakening an old part of me, the man who could become a master player at seduction when seized by the sultry gaze of a beautiful woman. But I am no longer that man.

"Let her rest," I sign, a little too uneasy about her friend to insist she help us. *"Perhaps she needs to sleep it off."*

"We need fire," Raina replies, her hands and fingers moving stiffly.

"We'll *get* fire. Even if we have to conjure it ourselves."

I tug the blanket tighter over my shoulders and attempt to build a fire with the contents of the tinder box again, but unfortunately, it's no use. My hands are so cold they're shaking, and the wind that slips under the overhang makes the effort impossible.

To save what light we have, I close up the lamp and shove the tinder box aside, burrowing beneath the blanket as an idea strikes me. "I can show you how to summon fire," I offer. "You might not like it, but I can show you. One time, that's all it takes. After that, with some practice, you should be able to seek out fire threads for yourself."

In the pale light, I swear her cheeks grow pink with warmth. *"I know what must be done to see them,"* she signs.

I can't help but lift my brows at that. "Yet you don't know how to summon fire? Who taught you how to see the threads but didn't take the time to help you master them? Or is this another skill I had no idea you possess?"

I glance at Helena, buried under the gambeson, sleeping as though we aren't in the middle of a frozen nightmare. She must've taught Raina a few things when it comes to fire magick. Or maybe it was someone else. The lover she lost to the fire. It doesn't matter. I feel a strange dislike at the thought of anyone but me teaching her anything.

"Not a skill, and I cannot see them," Raina clarifies. *"I only know what is necessary to do so."*

"Or you think you do. I fear you might've had an inadequate experience." The moment those words leave my mouth, an image of her staring up at me, face soft and lips pillowy, hungered eyes reflecting golden candlelight, flashes through my mind. It's so fast—there and gone. Not a memory, but perhaps a longing.

It's the last thing I should do considering the struggle I feel when it comes to her, but I open my arms anyway, holding the blanket out, and spread my legs. "Come here. Let me show you."

Her reservation is obvious, a war in her wide eyes and turmoil on her face. But after several moments of indecision, she moves toward me regardless. It seems I'm not the only one doing things I shouldn't be doing.

To make the position more comfortable, I scoot until my back is against the stone behind me, and Raina carefully fits herself between my legs. It's unnerving how much I want to draw her to me, to feel every curve of her body against mine. But the blanket and closeness will provide much needed warmth for us both. At least that's what I tell myself as I fold my arms around her.

"You can relax," I say near her ear, smothering a small smile. I know she loathes being so close to me, but I sense her thawing when it comes to the idea, so I can't resist poking fun. "This is far easier if you're not stiff as a tree. As long as you don't try stabbing me like you did that scarecrow."

She cuts a murderous look in my direction. *"I am frozen."*

"Frozen or not," I say after a laugh, "we need heat or fire if I'm to help you harvest the strands. So you might as well get comfortable. Body heat it is."

She glances at the lamp and widens her eyes. Even without words, I know what she's communicating.

"No lamp," I reply, wishing I was still capable of providing light so we didn't have to depend on that singe flame flickering in the lantern. "If it blows out, we'll be in total darkness, and believe me, collecting fire threads from body heat isn't something you want to do in the dark if you're worried about touching me. Now sit back and cooperate. The faster we gather the threads, the faster you can warm yourself by a fire and not against me." I lower my voice. "Since I'm clearly so horrible to be near. Your friend is a wretch and smells like an unemptied chamber pot, and you chose to ride with her anyway. I'm not sure how to feel about that."

She glares at me even harder, but I just smile.

"Come on. Stifle your pride. It's bitter out here." When she still hesitates, I say, "Am I truly so awful that you would rather die than be near me?"

She rolls those lovely eyes and finally relents, leaning back against me. We're both shivering, but soon enough, the shaking eases, and I'm left completely unraveled from this simple moment of closeness with Raina Bloodgood.

To soothe her *and* my nerves, I rub my hand from her wrist to her shoulder to create more heat. She feels so small beneath my touch, yet so very familiar. So very right.

I try to ignore the way my heart skips a beat when she turns in my arms, facing me, and begins doing the same to me. Her touch isn't quite as reverent or admiring as mine, but the feel of her hands on my body…

A small wind rushes over us, chasing away the thought, and I curve around her like a shield to block it out. Once it passes, I pull back, placing a few inches between us. Unexpectedly, she relaxes against me again, quickly erasing any distance.

"Close your eyes and keep them closed," I tell her, trying to focus enough to continue the lesson I'm supposed to be giving. "Then touch my chest. Right over my heart."

She lifts her hand and pauses for a moment before finally resting her palm exactly as I instructed.

Gods, she *must* feel my heart racing.

"Imagine strings," I say, hoping to distract both of us from her obvious effect on me. "That if you move your fingers delicately, like playing the harp, you can lure those strings right through my skin and into your grasp. You can do this with flames, too. Some witches, mages, and sorcerers can even harness fire threads from storms. There's much power in the air during a storm. Heat and light. Fire threads can even be gathered using glass and sunlight. You just have to focus and summon them. They will come."

She flutters her slender fingers against my chest, and as the connection between us forms, growing warmer and warmer, she looks up at me with surprise.

"Close your eyes, you little rebel." A smile tempts the corner of my mouth, and a grin tugs at her lips as she obeys. "Now, *fulmanesh*," I whisper. *"Fulmanesh, iyuma tu lima, opressa volz nomio, retam tu shahl.* Think of my heartbeat. The force of life within me. Reach for the deepest part of me. Keep strumming, just like you are now. Then close your eyes and repeat those words in your mind. *Fulmanesh, iyuma tu lima, opressa volz nomio, retam tu shahl."*

Instead of repeating the words in her mind, she signs them against my chest, repeating them over and over. *"Fulmanesh, iyuma tu lima, opressa volz nomio, retam tu shahl."* Fire of my heart, come that I may see you, warm my weary bones, be my place of rest.

Again, something inside me—something so dormant it's as old as the god that hides within me—sparks to life. These words... They meant something to me at one time, something I just can't remember. But I try. As she repeats them, signing them against my heart, gods do I try. But I don't know what I'm looking for, and even if I did, it would still be shrouded in the shadows of centuries long past and mostly forgotten.

A broken breath shudders out of me, my hand resting on Raina's wrist. "Do you see the threads yet?"

I need her to see them. I need her to stop tapping those words into my soul.

Thankfully, she nods.

"Good. Now give me your hand." When I pull her fingers from my chest, I *feel* the threads leaving me, tugging at my core. The sensation sends a shiver over my skin, like she's tethering me to her, even though I know that isn't what's happening. Another broken breath escapes me, and I cup her hand in mine, palm up, blessedly stilling her fingers. "Very good. Again. In your mind only. *Fulmanesh.* Think it."

Her face falls into a mask of concentration, and in seconds, a small flame bursts to life above our hands. Clearly sensing it, she opens her eyes and jerks upright, that bright stare landing on me.

I jump up, dropping the blanket in the process, and take the tinder from the tin. Squatting, I stuff the wool between two pieces of wood. "Now. This is the hard part," I tell her. "Just send the fire over here."

She gapes at me as though I've gone mad.

I stalk across the small space between us and settle behind her on my knees, cupping her hand and aiming it toward the pile of twigs. "It's mental. You *will* the fire where you want it to go. Like most any magick, it will do what you want once you've harnessed it. Think of the thing you want most in this world," I say against her ear. "This can strengthen your magick. It's where true power comes from. We often hold the most will for our strongest desires."

The wind blows stronger, and a blast of snow whips through her hair, making her tremble in my arms. Suddenly, the flame flickers out.

Raina opens her eyes and turns a look over her shoulder, panic clear on her face. *"I can try again,"* she signs.

I can't help but frown, but not out of disappointment. Out of confusion. "What happened? You were doing so well."

She shakes her head and turns away from me, drawing her knees to her chest like a child.

The need to soothe her again is strong enough that I run my hand over the curve of her back. "It's all right. I imagine we'll have plenty of cold to practice in these next few nights."

I go back to the kindling and tinder box, my hands shaking harder now. It takes at least a dozen tries or more, but the flint finally strikes and a tiny flame catches the wool and holds. That's only half the job, though. I keep working, building the flames higher, until a true blaze warms and lights our shelter.

Relieved that we most likely won't die tonight, I blow out the lamplight to save the oil, toss the blanket over my shoulders, and sit close to the fire. Raina nods at me in thanks, her own relief visible in the softening lines of her face, before getting up to check on her friend. When she returns, she sits beside me, sinking into my cloak and holding her hands near the heat.

"Sorry," she signs after a while. *"I tried."*

I nudge her with my shoulder, proud of her regardless. "I told you. It's all right. We're going to live. Besides, you came so close. It isn't easy, fire magick. You made it look that way, though."

"Until I lost it."

I shrug. "Again, at least we'll live to try another day."

After a time, she says, *"Fire magick would have been useful in the vale. All those winters."*

"I'm sure. But magick like that has a tendency to spread, taught from parent to child, friend to friend, mentor to student." I pause, unsure about my next words, but it's a lesson I feel needs reiterated. "Fire in a village can be dangerous."

I don't mean to bring up terrible memories, but our paths will part after this, and I've just begun the teaching of fire magick. She has to understand how dangerous that sort of power can be, even when it feels like it's no more than a party trick to light a bonfire. It can have devastating consequences. Moreover, the conjuring of a flame is only the beginning of fire magick's potential.

When sadness flashes across her face, I change the subject, hoping my point has been made well enough. "Your ability. You're a Seer, a Healer, *and* a Resurrectionist? What is that like?"

"Seer, yes," she signs. *"Healer, yes. But Resurrectionist? No. Is there such a thing?"*

I can't help but laugh at the face she makes, but any humor dies fairly quickly. Surely I wasn't mistaken when I saw her chanting her mother back to life. "But on the green, I saw you..."

"I heal," she says. *"But I have never brought anything or anyone back from the dead. I have saved animals from dying, and you, but that is the extent. I am not very skilled. I thought my magick was secret. I taught myself."*

"You've done well to make it this far with such complex abilities without a teacher," I say, wondering why her mother did what she did. "And yes, being a Resurrectionist is a thing. It's usually a darker type of magick and a form of necromancy. I wasn't sure about you. The line between healing and resurrecting is often thin. It seemed that was what you were doing—or trying to do—with your mother."

There's a certain pain in her eyes, the same pain I saw when we stopped in the wood to camp that first night. I mentally scold myself for not being more careful with my words, constantly reminding her of her mother. Sometimes, grief feels strange for me, even grief in others. It's like an old friend to me. Something I don't fear but accept. I've lived with grief for so long, grief for a life I can't even remember anymore.

Before I can ease the discussion in a different direction yet again, she does it for me. *"What happened to your magick?"* she signs. *"Why can you no longer use it?"*

Ah. The question I dread most. Time for this conversation to end. "It died. A long time ago."

"When you were a child?" she presses.

The wolf inside me laughs, his spirit roiling under my skin, all that godly darkness mocking me. From the way Raina looks at me, I fear she can see him in my eyes. It wouldn't be the first time someone noticed his presence.

"Something like that," is the only answer I offer before I lean back and lay flat on the cold ground, staring at the stone ledge above. "Enough questions for tonight. You must be tired. Get some rest while you can."

Thankfully, she doesn't push for more information as I close my eyes and pray for sleep. I know she's curious about me, and she has every right to be. And gods, a part of me believes I could talk to her all night if we were in any other situation. But there are some things I just cannot share, and those seem to be the things she's most curious about. I am not a puzzle to be figured out. More a tomb to be left undisturbed.

I have a feeling, however, that Raina Bloodgood isn't the kind of woman to leave well enough alone.

ALEXUS

I lean against the doorframe of her room, watching quietly as she stands before her floor-length mirror, dragging a bristled brush through her long, dark locks. I've missed her more than I ever imagined I could miss someone, and now she's here, within reach, dressed in nothing but a white silken gown, stark against her suntanned skin.

"Beautiful as ever," I finally say, announcing my presence.

The stunned and elated expression on her face when she spins around is everything I'd hoped for, proving these last months have not been a dream. That smile reminds me of the moment I saw the sun break through the clouds after twenty days of rain at sea, the moment I knew I was close to home.

After a toss of her brush onto her dressing table, Raina launches across the room. I smile and pick her up as she crashes into me, throwing her arms around my neck and squeezing tight.

"You act like you missed me."

She draws back to look me in the eyes as I carry her into the room and kick the door shut. We're the only ones in the library at this late hour, but I want privacy just in case someone decides to pay a visit downstairs.

With her hands in my hair, Raina crushes her mouth against mine, and *any worries that have haunted me prior to this moment fade. I move us toward the bed, ready to lay her down and ravish her the way I've imagined.*

But then we're suddenly back in front of the mirror.

The moment has altered, a shift in time and emotion, from happy and hopeful to uncertain and filled with unanswered longing. I'm dressed differently, as is she.

I stand behind her in a fine, black suit, staring at her in the mirror. The only sound in the room is our breathing and the crackle of the fire in the hearth. She's wearing nothing but her cotton dress slip, her crimson satin gown discarded and crumpled nearby on the floor. She's breathing so hard, her blue eyes locked with mine as I trace my finger over the curve of her shoulder and under the strap of her garment.

"Do you want me to finish undressing you?"

Long moments of hesitation pass, but Raina never looks away from me, not even when she finally nods her head in answer.

I lean in and drag my teeth over her earlobe as I slowly lower the strap from her shoulder. Her nipples are already peaked beneath the thin gown, making me ache to see them, to taste them.

Beneath my fingertips, chills chase across her skin. A sigh leaves her as I drag my tongue up the side of her throat and carefully lower the other strap.

Her slip doesn't fall, the stretch of her full breasts keeping it from dropping to the floor. Her body is all dangerous curves now, muscular from training yet softer in places from Cook's meals. I want to kiss every inch, learn her body the way I might memorize a map.

Hooking my thumbs in the fabric, I pull the slip down over her breasts, achingly slow, watching in the mirror as her naked torso is finally revealed. The candlelight and firelight illuminate her like a piece of treasured artwork highlighted beneath a chandelier. She gasps when I take her breasts in my hands, her attention focused as I grip and knead. The sight is erotic, and I can tell that she likes watching, yet this is only the beginning.

"Do you know how long I've wanted to see you?" I ask. "Touch you?"

She shakes her head and stretches her arm up, curling it around my neck, drawing my mouth down to the sweeping line between her ear and shoulder.

Show me. *That's what she's saying to me.* Show me.

I kiss her there, making no effort to be gentle. I suck and bite and lick as I tease her nipples hard between my fingers, hyperaware of the way she moves against me with every new assault. My cock hardens, wanting release, but I remind myself that I've waited for this for months. Much as I want to give in, right now I crave the agony of blinding desire more than relief.

I press my erection against her, a promise of what awaits. Raina shifts her ass against me, rubbing, and boldly drags my hand down her abdomen and between her legs. Even through the linen I can feel her heat, how wet she already is for me.

"I've imagined this," I confess. "There aren't many things I haven't imagined when it comes to you. Making you come where I can watch every moment has been a recurring dream, though."

She meets my stare in the mirror. For a moment, a question lives there, but then she blinks it away and slides her hand atop mine. Again, I can read her face so plainly, even without a single word signed.

Show. Me.

"Are you sure?" I ask. "Because what I want to do to you would be vile to many."

She faces me. "You have no idea the things I would let you do to me," *she signs.*

Just like that, we become all hands and lips and teeth, kissing with open-mouthed sighs as we strip away my jacket, vest, and tunic, my trousers and braies, followed by the remains of her slip. I lower my head to her breasts, suckling one at a time, my balls growing heavier and heavier by the second. She clutches my hair, letting me have my way, until she can no longer endure.

She tugs me up and kisses me, trailing her fingertips down my torso. She's all but panting when she pulls away, admiring the hills and valleys of my body, muscle formed from too many years of training. I flinch when she twirls her fingertips in the hair below my navel, and then moves to boldly grip my cock in her hot little hand.

She strokes me with gentle pressure, the look on her face one of happiness and perhaps a bit of disbelief, as though she can't believe she's finally touching me. I understand. After so long, I feel the same way.

On an exhaled breath, I press my forehead to hers as she continues, gliding her hand from root to tip, over and over, her thumb catching every drop of cum that pearls at the head. I could lose myself so quickly, only to rise and do it again—inside her, on her, in her mouth. I want her in every way.

But first...

I tip her face up and look into her eyes, expecting a reflection of unease. I'm a lot of man to handle, yet there's not even a sparkle of worry in her gaze. Then I realize...

"Do you still have the crystal I gave you?"

She arches a single brow and lets go of me.

Ah. Now I see a glimmer in her stare.

"Did you think I would not use it?" she signs and returns to her stroking.

The thought of her doing such a thing in this room, right above me, makes the desire inside me turn molten.

"I hoped you might," I whisper, thinking of all the nights I lay wondering if she was indeed relieving herself with a crystal carved and polished to match the size and shape of my cock. I wanted it to be true. Wanted her to be taking me in some way. But I still doubted she even kept it. "Where is it?" I ask, my cock twitching in her hand.

Reluctantly, she lets go of me once more and turns toward her dressing table. I'm enchanted as she walks the short distance—by the way her ass sways, the sweet cleft between her legs, the way her long legs stride so elegantly. I study her curves, the way her waist dips, the lines of muscle in her back.

She opens the top drawer and retrieves the wooden case I gifted her months ago. When she lifts the lid, the pale pink quartz nestled in its bed of red velvet, is revealed. Raina drifts her fingertips across the crystal and looks up at me with a gleam of curiosity in her gaze.

I grab the cushioned bench at the foot of her bed and move it so that the end faces the mirror. I know exactly what I want. I just hope she wants it too.

Straddling the bench, I sit and pat the empty space in front of me. "Come here. Bring the crystal."

Her eyes widen for a moment, but after the realization of what I'm about to do sinks in, she obeys.

Without further reservation, she positions herself between my legs, the crystal clenched in her hand. I move her hair aside and kiss her shoulder, running my hands along her thighs, feeling goosebumps rise in my wake.

"Are you nervous?" She shakes her head adamantly as I cup her breasts, which makes me smile. "Excited?" I whisper, teasing her nipples, and she nods.

Gently, I cup the back of her knee and lift one leg at a time, placing each one atop mine, exposing her fully to us both in the mirror. Her chest rises and falls fast as I slip my hand between her legs again, though this time there is no barrier, nothing to stop me from feeling her. From seeing her.

"I'm going to make you feel so good," I whisper as I slide my fingers between her lips, opening her, spreading her wide, relishing the feel of her slick, hot flesh. "Look at you." I flick my fingertip back and forth over her clit, making her flinch as she arches against me and curls her arm around my neck again. "So fucking perfect. I knew you would be."

I have to touch her. After all this time, I have to be inside her, in any way I can.

Her eyes flutter closed as I circle her entrance, then I push a finger inside all that damp, tight heat. I stroke her first, feeling every ridge, learning her before I begin pumping in and out slowly.

"Open your eyes," I demand. When she does, her gaze is already hazed and heady. "I want you to watch what I do to you."

Again, so obediently, her attention lowers to where I'm touching her. It doesn't take long until we fall into a rhythm—the punishing glide and curl of my finger, the hungry rocking of her hips. With every thrust, I can feel her need rising higher, sense her pleasure building, a flood threatening, just within my reach. But I'm not ready to give her that sweet relief. Not yet.

Withdrawing, I reach for the crystal. Raina takes a deep breath and hands it over, looking a little shaken, either from the sudden absence in her core or because she anticipates what comes next.

Or both.

I'm pleased to find the stone cock is already warm with magick. Perhaps my little trick at Wendolyn's shop worked after all. I have to know.

"Does it vibrate?" I inquire. "When you command it?"

"Gods, yes," she signs, and I smile.

"Well, that's my magick, and tonight, I command it, all right? No vibrating until I say so."

She nods submissively. It makes me desperate to pleasure her.

The rush of want that courses through me the moment I run the head of the crystal between Raina's glistening lips is inexplicable. Her arm falls, and she grips my thighs, bracing herself.

"Relax, love. I'll be gentle."

And I am. I take my time teasing her, sliding the wide tip up and down, getting it wet, circling it around her clit, edging her toward bliss but guiding her back down before we get too close. When it's time, I want her wild with passion and need, thrashing with an orgasm the likes of which she has never imagined. I want to watch as she shatters into oblivion, a memory I know I will never lose.

Carefully, I slide the crystal inside her. Just the head at first. I think to be easy, but she begins rocking again, greedily taking the cock into her body broad inch by broad inch, fucking it, showing me just how comfortable she's become with this version of me.

"That's a good girl. Fuck that lovely pussy."

I don't expect her to buck harder and faster, but she does, as though my words drive her.

I pump the crystal deeper and nip at her ear, teasing her nipple with my other hand as she rides. But it isn't long before I can watch no longer. When I pull the crystal free from her body, I'm met with an almost scathing glare. I smile and lift her knees off mine before standing, only to move before her spread legs and kneel like a sinner at a god's altar, ready to bow and worship.

Raina grips the bench behind her with one hand and runs the fingers of the other through my hair, studying my face with a rumpled brow. I see her silent question, and it reminds me how much I love that I've learned her so well.

"I'm beginning to understand who deserves my bent knee and who does

not," I explain. "But even if you were to cast me away, I would still want this."

She opens her legs a little wider, curves her hips upward, her dainty feet on tiptoe. It's an encouraging invitation seeing her spread for me like this, one I would never deny. I kiss a hot trail up one leg, taking in the floral scent on her skin, the chills left behind by my stubble, until I reach that divine, pink slit, soaked and beckoning. She smells so good, a sweet musk, and she's positioned perfectly for fucking or devouring. My mind can't determine which my body needs most.

As much as I want my throbbing cock buried inside her, I draw out the agony a little further, pushing the crystal root-deep inside her instead. Raina gasps, her fingers tightening in my hair, just against my scalp.

Our gazes meet—her eyes are glazed with lust—and as though linked by some invisible mental connection, she tugs my head down, urging me to taste her, even as I'm already lowering my mouth to her core.

At the first touch of my tongue to her flesh, we're both lost. If I could taste only one thing ever again, it would be her. I want to drown in her, to fall in and never come out.

I give in to the natural dance, the assault and retreat of the cock in my hand matched by the flicking of my tongue against her clit. I fasten my mouth on her, working that little bud, deciding that perhaps we will both come more than once tonight. We have to. Because I must taste her. Must lap up every drop of her pleasure.

Raina falls back to her elbows, panting. She's so beautiful, even outside of this moment. Even when she's working in the library in her tunic and breeches, her hair pulled back in that severe bun. But here? Now? Naked and in the throes of passion?

She's utterly resplendent.

With my mouth still latched to her clit, I give her a wink and send a command to the magick cast within the crystal, all while sending a trickle of my power through my tongue. Raina's hand darts out and grips my shoulder.

That's the only warning before she comes. It's instantaneous, as though all I'll ever need to do if I want her like this is lick her with a little magick.

Feeling like I might come myself, I watch as she writhes, her head thrown *back, her hips rolling her pussy over and over the crystal as my mouth plays. But soon, she comes down off the high of orgasm, both our movements slowing, until I remove the crystal, suck her release off the tip, and cast it aside.*

Her eyes darken as I gently draw patterns on her wet lips with my tongue, tasting her, dipping inside for a feast. I look up, over the softness of her belly to the mounds of her breasts, her skin illuminated by golden candlelight.

I focus on her face, all that dark hair cascading to the floor. I'm ready to carry her to bed, to sink deep into her warmth and fuck all night, to whisper all the things I've wanted to say for so long.

I care for you. I want to love you. Teach me how.

But the image morphs. The golden light drenching the room blurs to a dark, white world.

And I wake up.

❧

I BLINK THROUGH THE HAZE OF A DREAM.

I don't remember much, only that the woman now lying in my arms, folded inside my cloak and blanket, was there as well.

But she was very naked. Much unlike our current situation.

Raina's head is nestled firmly against my chest, her arms tight around my waist. I don't recall when we met in our sleep, when she crawled into my reach, nor when our legs found their way to one another, tangling like the limbs of lovers. But I don't mind waking like this, with her next to me. I do, however, mind that my cock is stiff as a marble hilt.

I lie still and will away my erection, but with every minuscule shift of her body against mine, it becomes a pointless fight. I can feel her heat where my thigh lies cradled between her legs, and her breasts are pressed firm to my ribs, our heartbeats so close.

The need to piss strikes, though, and my erection finally begins to soften, but not before I sense Raina waking. She goes rigid in my arms, only pressing closer to the very thing I was trying to hide.

"Good morning," I say awkwardly, and she tenses harder, if that's even possible. I can't help but laugh under my breath that we're in this predicament in the first place, and that neither of us knows how to get out of it. But I try. "Breathe, Raina. It's all right. The world isn't going to crumble because you touched me. A lot, I might add, but still." I lower my head to her ear, unable to resist the urge to tease. "Also, you're very warm, and I rather enjoyed your company if that's not obvious, but now that you're awake, could you please disentangle your legs from mine? If I don't piss, we're both going to be in trouble."

She quickly jerks away and sits up, as if my skin is scalding. I know she's embarrassed, but there's little to be done for it now.

Before I head toward the wood, I fold my side of the blanket over her shoulder to save some of our heat. Again, an image strikes me, a remnant from the dream, of lowering the strap of her dressing slip over her bare shoulder.

It wasn't real, I tell myself as I walk away from her, much as a part of me wishes it were. It was only a dream. Nothing else. In the oblivion of rest, my tired mind was granted a haven, and Raina stayed warm enough to sleep.

That's all that matters.

But as I stare over the dark, white world beyond our camp, I'm reminded of words spoken to me many moons ago by an old friend: *The universe conspires. If someone is meant to be in your life, Fate will find a way to place them there, as well as in your dreams, that you might recognize their essence when your paths finally cross. That you might understand something greater than you is saying, "Look. Listen. Pay attention. Here is your past. Your present. Your future."*

As I head back toward camp, I try to do all those things. To believe that Raina Bloodgood's presence—even beyond the fact that she's already saved my life—holds an even higher purpose for me.

There's only one way to find out, and that's to keep moving, with her at my side.

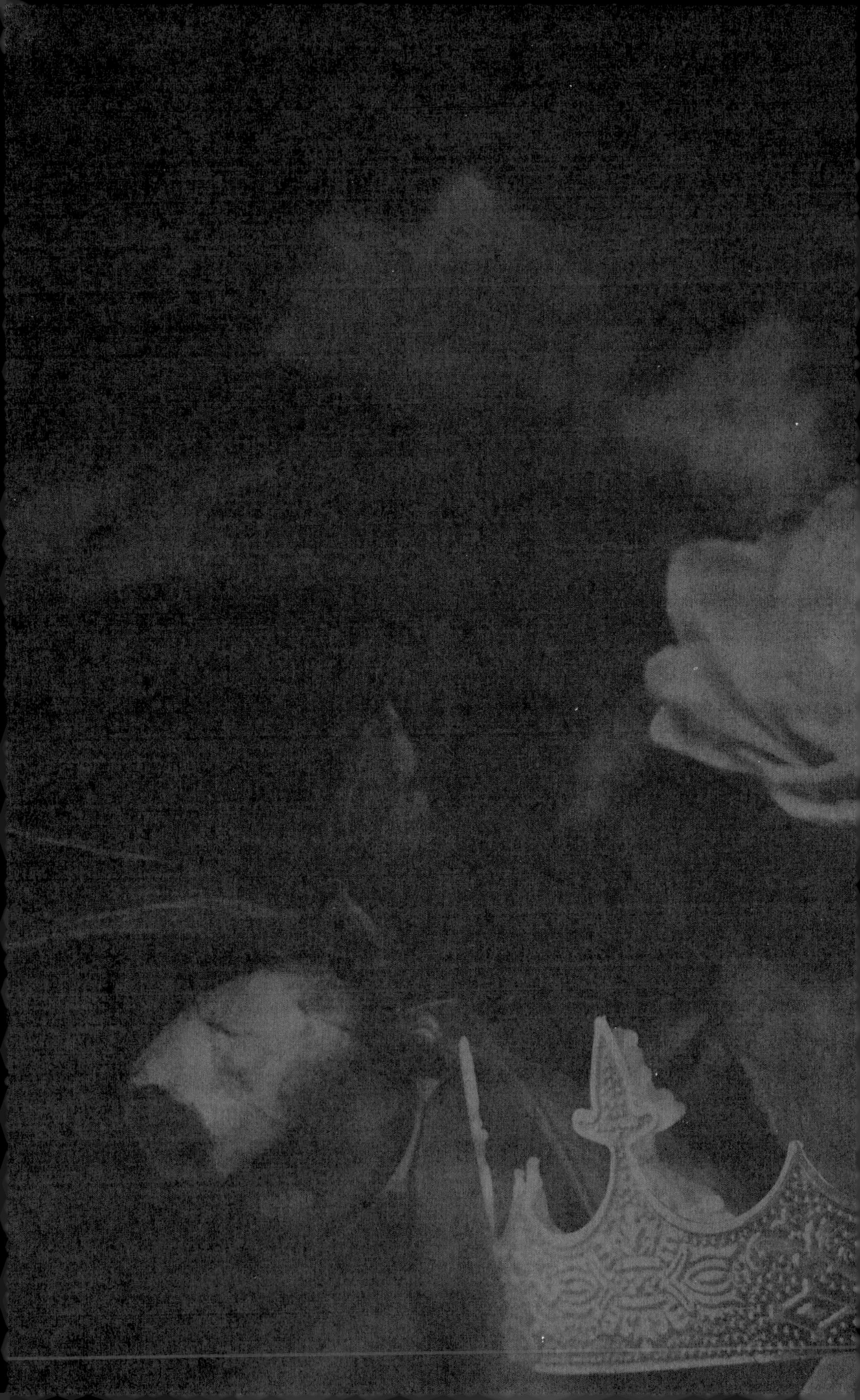

TO KISS A PRINCE

Thirty years before the East's attack on the Northland Valley, an immortal king met a newly crowned prince.

It did not end well.

Or did it?

COLDEN

The Eastland Territories are much like I expected, thanks to Alexus's first-hand knowledge and detailed descriptions.

The Mishan port is as intimidating as he claimed, what with its near-constant shadows, spitting rain, and black, jagged mountains being the welcoming site. The people working the docks are watchful when we arrive. Curious and cautious, yet kind and accommodating. As we travel deeper into the kingdom, I find that same curiosity and hospitality with every stop, exceeding anything I could've imagined, even once we reach Quezira.

Our driver delivers us to an inn along the edge of the lower quarters, one whose owners have already prepared for our stay. People loiter nearby, as though waiting for a spectacle, but seeing us must be enough, because once we're spotted, they scatter. It seems the whole of the territories knew we were coming.

After we're settled, I head out into the rainy night and roam the cobbled streets and taverns for a few hours while Alexus burrows alone in his room with his books and journals. He insisted on accompanying me for this trip, but it's clear that being on Eastland soil again, even after so many years, is difficult for him. He once had a life here, an existence he only partially remembers, though it seems he recalls enough to make this visit quite painful. Sadness and loss have etched their way into his expressions, ever since we spotted the East-land shore from our ship.

Quezira at night teems with more people than any city in the North. I drink too much and flirt too much, but I end up chatting with a barkeep about the rainy and humid weather in Quezira and her favorite summer and autumn festivals before heading back to the inn.

The next morning, we leave just after dawn, much to my pounding head's displeasure, careful to bypass Min-Thuret, a temple Alexus won't even acknowledge with a glance, much like the rest of this city. Per my request—for my friend's sake—we're to meet the newly crowned Prince of the East at his home in Vale instead, a town further inland, and a place Alexus *did* visit as a child and later as a young adult, but one that holds no bad memories.

That he recalls, anyway.

We've already been on the road for eight days, and our driver says it will take another week to reach Shara Palace from Quezira. It's a journey that leads us across rugged yet beautiful landscapes of forests and rolling green valleys, the land verdant and lush. Though our driver is determined to outride the clouds, we stop and rest a few times at various villages, each one just as prepared for us as the people of Quezira had been.

"I truly imagined they'd all want me dead," I say as we begin the last stretch to Vale on a blessedly sunny summer morning.

Chin resting on his loosened fist, Alexus sits across from me, staring at his former homeland through the window of our fine carriage, a vehicle sent to the Mishan harbor by the prince himself.

The memories in Alexus's eyes shine bright as we pass a few wary villagers shepherding sheep, watching our conveyance rumble along the road. "You're a legend to them." *Like he used to be.* "A mythical being mentioned only in their fireside stories about the Land Wars. Now they're seeing you in the flesh, a man who bested King Gherahn's forces. A man blessed by the gods." He glances my way, his rugged face softening. "They're fascinated, my friend. Not murderous."

By his letters, their new prince seems fascinated too. No more fascinated than I am when it comes to him, however. This unknown prince who swayed an entire kingdom to seat him as ruler.

Not a king. A *prince*.

It's strange, to say the least. Strange enough that I felt the need to leave Winterhold and investigate in order to ensure King Regner's former treaty with the North would remain intact after his death. That's the greatest security I have for my people outside of our meager defenses. We simply don't have the masses to build an army that could endure war with the East. We have magick. Veils. Shields. And the Northland Watch along the coast. But I don't trust that any of it is enough.

I'm asleep when we actually cross into Vale's borders that afternoon. Alexus wakes me with a few nudges of his boot against mine.

"Damn," he mutters as he stares out the window. "She's just as I remember."

I scrub my eyes and study the lay of the land. The landscape is flat, the city sprawling around what must be Shara Palace, a massive white stone structure perched regally on the only hill for what must be miles. At each corner of the edifice stands a round bastion tower, replete with tall cupolas crowned in shimmering gold. Multiple chimneys protrude from the central rooftop, and rectangular and arched windows delineate the six floors of this monstrous residence that has been passed down to Thamaos's kings and queens for centuries.

We cross through the gatehouse and over the moat, until soon, our carriage approaches the graveled courtyard. As we circle toward the entrance, I spot an entourage spilling from the main doors.

Alexus points toward the palace. "That must be him."

My gaze snags on a young man stepping from the palace into the sunlight, straightening his fine, green jacket as he runs his fingers through short hair that's as thick and dark as the night itself.

"My, my. I certainly hope so." When the carriage turns and the man vanishes from view, I look over to find Alexus watching me with narrowed eyes and a smirk. "What?" I shrug. "I didn't picture such a dashing fellow, that's all. It's nothing."

He cocks a brow and folds his thick arms across his chest. "Are you *really* trying to lie to me right now?"

I begin fretting with my hair and inspecting my rumpled attire, wishing I'd made more effort this morning. "I'm not lying. I expected…" I check my breath and slip on my discarded blue jacket. "Fine, I don't *know* what I expected. But it wasn't—"

The carriage comes to a halt, and there, just steps from my window, stands the most handsome creature I've ever laid my eyes upon. Hands behind his back, he eyes our conveyance, a warm and welcoming smile resting on a set of full, red lips.

He's tall. Not quite as tall as me, but I can't beat him by much. His frame is lean, though his shoulders are broad, his stance relaxed and his feet shoulder-width apart. His sun-warmed skin has a subtle olive tone that creates the most alluring shadows along his sharp cheekbones. And that dark hair? In the afternoon's rosy sunlight, I can make out strands of deep bronze and copper, not to mention a pair of darkly lashed hazel eyes with bright flecks of green.

"Fuck me," I mutter, and Alexus groans.

"I really hope he doesn't," he says. "But knowing you, he'll be swooning before dinner. I give it three days before you've completely disarmed the poor man."

I smile and slap a firm hand on his shoulder. "Now *that's* the spirit! Who says wars can't be won and rulers swayed with a little good-hearted flirtation? My gods. Where has *this* Alexus been all my life?"

He rolls his eyes and checks his clothing—his long sleeves and high collar—making sure every marking on his body is well covered. "Let's just get this over with. I'm already missing Winterhold."

With that, a footman approaches and opens the carriage door. Alexus steps out first, nods once, and bows to the prince. He then extends a hand toward me.

"My liege," he announces.

The moment I exit the carriage and unfold to my full height, my eyes lock with those of the prince. An expression of utmost surprise crosses his face, and his warm, genuine smile spreads wider. I feel like an idiot, because I grin, too, and begin moving toward him with such ease one would think I've known him forever.

He moves toward me as well, like there's a magnetic force between us, drawing us together. We stop once our boots are a short step apart, our gazes still fixed, our smiles still wide.

"The mighty King of the North." He extends his hand in greeting, his voice a lovely sound to my ears. "It's so good to finally meet you, Your Highness."

I tear my eyes from his and stare at his perfectly manicured hand. He's brave. Trusting. Everyone knows I'm the Frost King. They might not know all the details surrounding my immortality, and they may know nothing of mine and Fia's curse, but they know I hold the power to harm with what they believe is a god-blessed gift.

A *Neri*-blessed gift.

As I take the prince's hand in mine, he doesn't so much as flinch at the cool touch of my skin. Instead, he looks me over, quickly though appreciatively. I know that look. He likes what he sees and wonders if there's even more than meets the eye. If we were alone, I would assure him there is.

When his stare meets mine again, his fingers tighten gently around my palm. I can't help but think how much I like the feel of his strong grip, so much power hidden beneath such soft skin.

His hazel eyes glitter in the sunlight, his stare expectant, and I'm snapped out of my thoughts. *Say something, you imbecile. Speak!*

Unfortunately, though I'm fairly certain I'm already smitten enough to tumble this man until neither of us can walk or think, I find myself at an unusual loss for words.

"Call me Colden," I finally say. "I'm no one's *Highness*."

"No one's?" he asks with a curious tilt of his head.

I smile. Am I sensing innuendo? I certainly hope so.

"No one's."

I think to ask his name, what I might call him, but I bite my tongue. Rumor holds that he has no name, not one he shares, anyway, and no royal lineage. It's a way of placing himself on neutral ground with the common people of this land, which is admirable, I suppose. A tactic I've never seen and one that clearly worked. Though as with all else surrounding his reign, something about it stings odd.

Alexus nudges me and clears his throat. I suddenly realize that we're being watched by the palace staff and my closest friend, all witnessing me and the prince ogling one another like two pubescent boys.

Fine. It's me. *I'm* the pubescent boy.

Reluctantly, I slide my hand from the prince's grasp and look to my right where a hard, wide glare awaits me. "Pardon my rudeness, this happy gentleman is Alexus Thibault, an old friend and advisor. Don't let that brooding scowl fool you," I say drily. "He's a ball of fun."

Alexus indeed scowls at me as the prince turns and extends his hand, his hazel gaze changing from one of sparkling admiration to one of narrowed thought. "Alexus Thibault." His dark brows crumple. "Have we met?"

Alexus's face is a mask of calm, a facade of deception that hopefully no one but me can see. He accepts the prince's hand, though he pulls away quickly. "We have not, Your Majesty. Much to my loss, I'm certain."

The prince lingers a look on Alexus, as though he's still trying to place him. At least I hope that's what's happening, because I'm not sure the direction this meeting will take if he delves into Alexus being the Witch Collector, a fact I'm sure isn't news, but a connection his mind needs to make. I really don't want to discuss the protections and fortifications we have in place.

After long moments, the prince turns back to me. "This is my staff," he says, much to my relief, gesturing to the people half-encircling us. "They've been instructed to make certain your stay here is nothing short of splendid. I hope we can show you both not only the beauty of the Eastland Territories but the uniqueness of its people as well."

Not a single face around us looks unhappy. In fact, everyone wears a smile, clearly glad to be part of the prince's new rule. I want to tell him that I'm fully aware of the East's unique qualities and even some of the magnificent people it has birthed, especially the one standing at my side, brooding personality and all.

But I am also aware of its darkness. The hold Thamaos has forever had upon this land. It's hard for me to believe their path will change with one simple appointment of a prince. That's why I'm here, though. To seek answers.

"We look forward to our stay," I reply, lifting my eyes to the palace. "Shara is quite a lovely estate."

"I'd love to give you a tour," he says, and with the simplest gesture, his staff begins filing back into the palace. "But first, let's get you both settled in your rooms. I'm sure you're exhausted from your journey." He motions again, and two footmen begin gathering our things from the carriage. Alexus, being the guarded man he is, grabs one of our bags as well—the one hiding his precious weapons and journals—and falls in step so easily with the attendants, following them inside.

Left alone, save for two armed sentries at attention near the doors, I expect the prince to guide me into his residence. Instead, we stand there, still trapped in this magnetic sphere that won't seem to let us move away from one another. To make matters worse, a warm breeze washes over us, ruffling his hair and drenching me in his scent. Gods, he smells like the outdoors—all pine and moss and clear streams. Musk and sandalwood and... *man*.

"You're much younger than I ever imagined," he says innocently.

"As are you." I lift my chin a little. "But looks can be deceiving, can't they? And haven't you heard all the tales about me? I'm over three hundred years old. *You* are the youngster in this dynamic, my friend."

He laughs. "I suppose I am. I just meant... Well, I didn't expect you to be *so...*"

"Handsome?" I eventually supply when he doesn't seem to know what word to use. "Beautiful? I'm rather used to this conundrum when I first meet people. I receive both compliments, too, and I appreciate either one. So don't feel uneasy."

"Beautiful. Shockingly *beautiful*." His cheeks turn a soft shade of red and his eyes go wide, as though realizing what he just said. He takes a deep breath and exhales, scrubbing a hand down his face. "Gods above, forgive me. I can't believe I spoke that aloud. That was improper and *much* too forward."

I shrug it off, flattered and encouraged. "It wasn't improper. Very little will *ever* be improper with me. And, I rather like forward. The more forward the better, actually."

He crosses his arms and leans in, clearly embarrassed, yet trying to recover. "Is that so?"

I match his stance, hearing the provocative tease in his tone. "Absolutely," I reply, more than willing to play this game. "It makes things *much* easier."

"*Things*, you say?" He arches a brow, a sexy smirk at play on those kissable lips.

"Yes," I say with a smile. "*Things.*"

There's no hesitation in his next words, words that fall from his lips low and smooth. Words that only fuel the spark already ignited within me as his eyes flick up and hold mine.

"I'll have to remember that."

My attention falls to where his tongue darts out to wet his lips, a pretty slip of pink, and my blood heats, my cock twitching in my trousers. I've been with my fair share of people and felt the tug of lust and attraction many times, though rarely so instantaneously as this. Fia is the only person I recall ever mesmerizing me so completely from the first glance. I was a young soldier with a desert princess gazing into my eyes. Anyone would've been utterly enchanted.

This is different. For one, I may appear as such, but I am no longer a twenty-year-old man learning his way around the world. There's a pulse between me and the prince, a recognition I don't understand, our bodies inordinately aware of one another.

Oh, the things I could do to this man—the things I *want* to do to this man—and we've only just met.

"Might I show you to your chambers now, Colden?" he asks, and I try to decide if he's being bold or hospitable.

Only one way to find out.

I gesture toward the main doors and paint on my most wicked grin. "Why, I thought you'd never ask."

2

COLDEN

When the prince and I arrive at the top of the stairs on the third floor where the guest rooms are located, Alexus is waiting outside what is apparently my door. His massive frame is leaned back against the ornate moulding, arms folded over his chest, his booted feet crossed at the ankles. My dark knight. My guardian in black.

My cock-block extraordinaire.

The prince and I pause at the end of the hall and glance at one another, our previous chat now thoroughly ended. He'd been pointing out certain aspects of the grand residence of Shara, to which I offered sincere admiration and interest, especially when he said, *"I hope you like your chambers. The bedding is new and exceptionally comfortable."*

So much for asking if he'd like to help break in the mattress.

Alexus straightens as we approach. "I don't know if you saw anyone downstairs, but I was told dinner will be served within the hour." He reaches over and opens the door. "I put your things on your bed, and the staff has provided a wash basin. I thought we might need to clean up before dining."

All of which translates to: *Get rid of him so we can talk. Also, I made sure your room is safe.*

The prince presses his hands together. "Ah, yes. The staff has been working all day preparing quite the feast for your arrival. Shall I help you settle in, Colden?"

The moment draws out as I consider my answer, the air between the three of us awkward and tense. By the way he's clenching his jaw, Alexus looks like he could bite a steel blade in two. His disapproval for my attraction to the prince is blatantly obvious.

It isn't jealousy. I used to wish for that, that he would see me in a different light than just an immortal friend. And though we've explored certain temptations over the years, his heart is sealed away, something I accepted long ago.

To him, this visit with the prince is strictly *business*. Nothing more. The boundaries surrounding such things are clear and firm, one of those being: *No more fraternizing with gods, goddesses, godlings, kings, queens, princes, or princesses, Colden. It can only lead to trouble, so keep your dick in your pants.*

I'm sure he's right, and that I should absolutely keep my dick in my pants when it comes to the prince. But this life would feel even longer than it already does if I tamed *every* desire.

I'd settle for a kiss. One taste of the prince's tempting lips. I might not even like it. I might feel nothing. Not a single spark. But I'm not against trying.

Alexus stares at me, and I can see the answer he wants me to provide to the prince's question. It's written all over his annoyed face.

"I'm sure I'll be fine on my own," I reply with a slight bow of my head. "But thank you."

I swear I catch a hint of disappointment in the prince's expression, though he smiles, runs a hand down the golden buttons of his brocade vest, and draws his shoulders back. "Wonderful. Then I'll leave you to it." We exchange nods, and the prince turns to go, though he stops and turns back. This time, however, his eyes don't fall on me.

He focuses solely on Alexus. "Mister Thibault, you're certain we've never met?"

Alexus doesn't move, but I see his brain working in those next few moments, and I recognize the suspicion in his eyes. "Not to my knowledge, Your Majesty. Pardon my boldness, but I know so little about you. I'm not sure where our paths could've possibly crossed unless you've visited the North."

The prince's face changes, a sudden mask altering his openness, shutting it away. "No. I've never set foot on the Northland Break. You just seem so familiar, that's all."

I lean into the door frame, resting my forearm across the moulding above Alexus's head. He cuts a look at me. "It's the black hair and green eyes," I say, gesturing to the prince. "When I first saw you, I thought to myself, *This handsome fellow could be Alexus's kin.* Quite similar features."

"I'm sure that's all it is," the prince says with another smile, though this one doesn't reach his eyes, and he doesn't sound entirely convinced. "I'll see you both in the dining hall shortly, then?"

We nod, and once the prince disappears into the stairwell, I level a look on my friend and lower my voice to a whisper. "I don't need a babysitter."

He arches a brow, matching my tone. "I think otherwise."

"Nothing would've happened save for a little innocent teasing. We just met, for gods' sakes."

"And yet I can already see the way you look at one another. You two would've never made it to dinner if the gazes you shared were any indication."

"And that's a problem *because?*"

He glares at me. "Do I really need to answer that?"

With a roll of my eyes, I push through the door to my room. Alexus follows, closing it behind him. My pack is on the bed, just as he said.

Alexus stalks to the window and peers over the vast countryside.

"There's something off about him. I can't figure out what it is, but it's there."

I jerk the luggage close and unlace the straps. "I detect nothing but a nice, young fellow who happens to be the new prince of your former homeland."

He huffs. "Nice? That's not what I call any of this. He could be trying to seduce you for political reasons. Did you ever think of that?"

"Of course, I did!" I shed my jacket and dig for my royal blue tunic and gray trousers. "I was rather hoping he'd seduce me right out of my clothes and into this—" I pause and look up, taking in the gargantuan four-post bed that could have been more fun than this conversation. "My gods. You certainly know how to ruin a good time. Remind me to never bring you along on trips like this ever again."

As I rip off my shirt and head to the wash basin, Alexus moves to the bed, stretching out and propping his feet up, hands behind his head. "If I weren't here, there's no telling what disaster you'd end up in. There are at least a few members of the Brotherhood in this palace somewhere. I'd bet the rest of my days on it. If I'm right, and I'm sure I am, they're watching every move we make. Even if you can't see them, I promise you they're around."

"And what am I to do about that?" I run my fingertips through the still-warm water. "We've discussed this. It's best to come across as no threat. You're the one acting like a godsdamn bodyguard."

"Which is my job. They don't know me, though, and I doubt they can sense my power with it bound up for Neri. You, however, are a different story. They'll be even more suspicious now that you and the prince have clearly formed a liking for one another. All I can advise at this point is to go about the business we agreed to discuss. Make certain he plans to honor Regner's treaty. Then, get any info you can on the prince himself and his plans for the Territories. Will he continue in the way of the Eastern kings with the Land Wars? Or is he truly planning to set this break on a different path than it's ever traveled before? Do all that first, and then fuck him if you must. But his attraction to you and yours to him shouldn't interfere with what we came here to do."

I splash water on my face and grab a small lump of soap in the shape of a raven. It smells like lavender and vanilla.

I scrub it between my hands until a lather forms and smear it over my cheeks. "Fine. I'll get the treaty issue sorted tonight. Then tomorrow, I'll get even more information out of our host." Another splash or two and I reach for a linen, drying myself before I face Alexus. "But remember. Seduction is *my* game. If we want answers, I might as well use the prince's interest in me to our advantage. If he's as curious as I think he is, he'll take care of the Brotherhood. It's a game I can't lose."

"So long as you don't forget that it's just that," he replies. "A game. It's temporary, Colden. It's nothing real."

Again, I know he's right, but that doesn't mean I have to like it. Nothing is *ever* real. Ever *mine.* Nothing is *everlasting* when you're immortal, save for this difficult existence.

Alexus leaves to tend to his own appearance while I finish washing and dressing. Wearing the royal blue tunic, replete with silver stitching, I stare into the gilded mirror above the vanity table and comb my hair, smoothing the soft waves.

Perhaps I'm doomed to spend eternity as someone who only ever enjoys the exhilaration and romantic notions surrounding love rather than true love itself. Perhaps I'm simply incapable of devotion like that. Flirting and teasing and the excitement of a new partner and good sex might be all I'm destined to know, and maybe I understand that deep down, which is why I've learned to enjoy all of these things to the maximum effect. I've learned to find happiness where I can. To chase it. And today, happiness lies with the Prince of the East.

Temporarily. Just like Alexus said.

Dinner is much like I imagined, save for a few things.

One, Alexus was right. There are three men dining with us that weren't present when we arrived, and though they're not donned in official garb, the look on my friend's face tells me all I need to know.

They're members of the Brotherhood.

Second, there's no talk of the treaty, and no time to slip in the mention. The Brotherhood controls the conversation with the most mundane discussions, much to my annoyance. Alexus and I share several glances, all of which say: *Tonight is not the night.*

And third, the prince seems to have lost all appetite. He picks at his food like a child ordered to be polite, a child who would rather do anything other than eat the meal before him. It makes me wary to eat it myself, but the other men don't hold back on serving heaps of meat and roasted vegetables onto their plates. We also pour our wine from the same flagons, so poisoning doesn't seem to be a fear I should worry about.

When dinner ends, Alexus bravely occupies the members of the Brotherhood, pretending to be fascinated by their ages-long sect. If anyone understands all there is to know about them, it's him.

Wine glasses in hand, they exit the dining hall and head for the smoking parlor, while the prince and I stand awkwardly in the main hall.

"Might I interest you in a stroll through the gardens?" he says. "The night is lovely."

I raise my wine glass. "Sounds perfect."

Alight with lanterns, the gardens are immense, a vast stretch of gravel pathways, fountains, statues, trees, and flowering shrubs. Together, we walk leisurely through the balmy night, under the stars.

The prince slips his hands into his trouser pockets. "These gardens were designed by Queen Iberta, some six hundred years ago. She named the palace after her only daughter."

"Fascinating. Queen Iberta was King Theron's only heir, yes?"

He turns a sparkling look at me, a small, surprised smile. "You know Eastland history?"

I shrug, feigning innocence, though I see a way into a conversation we need to have. "I know a little. The whole royalty bit has always interested me. You see, I might carry the title, but I'm no king. It certainly isn't in my bloodline. My parents were poor sailors who lived in the Western Drifts. Also, Winterhold is a lovely place, but it can't rival this."

"It isn't the blood in your veins or the luxury around you that makes one a leader, though," he replies. "Guiding a kingdom is a duty, one I think you're honoring quite well."

We stop near a massive fountain, and I meet his eyes. "What makes you say that?"

"You've led the North for nearly three hundred years and protected your people. Not to mention you're here, aren't you? To see to it they remain protected?" He rakes his hand through his hair. "Listen, I'm aware we need to discuss the treaty King Regner held with you, and I plan to sign my name to it tomorrow. I won't do anything but uphold his wishes, so you needn't worry. The North hasn't been part of the Land Wars in quite some time. There's no reason that should change now."

Hearing those words brings relief, sort of, but…

"Does that mean the Land Wars will continue?" I ask. "Or is the East finally finished with Thamaos's ridiculous plot to claim the Summerlands? He's been dead for as long as I've ruled the North. Perhaps you're the man who will end the madness that has forever infested his kings and queens?"

His eyes soften, those dark brows turning up in the middle. "Forgive me, but I cannot speak of my kingdom's political endeavors with you, Colden. I've been a prince for all of six months. I'm still learning so much, but one thing I know for certain is that I cannot share privileged information with the King of the Northland Break, treaty or no treaty. Please understand."

"Fair enough." I wave it off, pretending to be more uninterested than I really am, and sip my wine, glancing back at the palace. "You know, you and I have a lot in common, I think."

"How so?" He motions for us to continue our walk, and we head toward the rose garden, our boots crunching against gravel.

"Well, as I said before, I have no royal lineage, no blood right to lead the North. And you have no royal lineage either, correct?"

He offers a sidelong glance and a smirk that says he knows I'm fishing for information. "None."

"So see? I have a feeling we're the kind of men who simply do what must be done, which is why I'm hoping you'll change the Eastern Territories for the better." I pause and add, "From what part of the territories do you descend?"

He stares ahead into the night, a dark lock of hair falling over his forehead. "Everywhere, really." He goes quiet then, as though debating whether or not to continue giving me such personal information, though he does. "Would you believe me if I told you I was a vagabond before this?"

"Not in the fucking least."

He laughs. "Why not?"

"Because! Look at you. My gods, you're too damned handsome and charming to be a vagrant, roaming around and *unattached*."

He smiles again, softer this time, and his eyes glitter as we pass a lantern, the look on his face one of remembrance. "I was a man of the land for many years. Very much alone. One with nature and my prayers. They were eventually heard, I suppose, because I simply wanted to *matter* in this life. To *do* something or *be* someone who would leave a lasting impact. Being here—being the Prince of the East —it feels like a calling. What I was born for."

My eyebrows dart up at that. "So noble. I could probably learn a lesson or two on accepting duty with such grace." A moment passes. "How old *are* you?" I inquire. "You said you were a *man of the land* for many years. You don't look like you've had many years to begin with."

A sudden discomfort comes over him, a noticeable tension in his tightening spine. "I've had more than you'd think. Wasn't it you who said looks can be deceiving?"

I study him, feeling like I should be seeing more than I am right now.

"I'm...twenty-six," he goes on.

"Forgive me," I say, pausing and waiting for him to face me. When he does, I continue. "I didn't mean to make light of your years alone because of your youth. Your story just fascinates me. A young man—a vagabond, no less—becoming the prince of a powerful kingdom. It's the perfect beggar to riches tale, though I imagine it must be surreal to be where you are now."

He nods. "Most days, I wake up and can hardly believe this new and amazing life is really mine. Though I can't imagine it's any more surreal than being immortal. You seem to live a rather...*exciting* life."

I give a small laugh at that. "It probably does seem that way. Then again, what's the point in living forever if you're boring?" My quip doesn't receive the smile or laugh I was hoping for, so I take one more sip of my wine. Liquid courage. "Tell me, does the perfect prince have a perfect princess to share this new and amazing life with?"

Now he tames a threatening smirk, keeping his sparkling eyes on mine. "No, he doesn't."

"Perhaps a prince of his own, then?"

The corner of his mouth lifts in a dashing, crooked half-smile that makes my heart skip a beat.

"No," he answers. "Not yet, anyway."

I wink. "Just checking."

With that revelation hanging between us, we keep walking. The prince shows me through the fragrant rose garden, insisting I smell several blooms, and takes me to see his favorite statue, one of two men facing one another, their foreheads touching, their hands entwined.

"Why this one?" I ask as we stare up at the sculpture, its white stone illuminated under the moonlight. We'd passed another statue of two men in the throes of passion. I rather liked that one.

"They seem so close," he answers. "The connection between them is captured so well." He steps forward and points to their hands. "Look at their fingers, the way they seem to be caressing and holding to one another at the same time." He then points toward their heads.

"And if you look closely, you can see they're staring at each other's mouths. There's such longing on their faces. Such tense need."

I swallow hard, seeing what he means. The physicality is there, but when I look closer, *deeper*, it's impossible not to feel their yearning, their sweet sorrow, their...*love*.

"I should head back," I say, my words tumbling forth without any warning from my godsdamn brain. "I'm suddenly quite tired. Perhaps these last several weeks of travel are finally wearing on me."

Once again, disappointment crosses his face, and I'm stunned by how much it bothers me.

"But of course," he replies. "If you can find your way back, I might stay out here for a while. I often miss the outdoors, and rain season will arrive soon enough."

"Certainly." I fidget with my wine glass. "I'll see you tomorrow, then?"

"Absolutely. I have plans for us."

"Splendid! Can't wait!" Without asking him to elaborate, I turn to leave. But then...

"Colden?"

I stop and, after a deep breath, turn around, my heart beating wildly. How I want him to ask me to stay, though a part of me desperately needs to go.

"I'm really glad you're here," is all he says.

꽃 3 꽃

COLDEN

The next morning, the complicated feelings I endured the
night before have thankfully disappeared. I'm quite good at
burying notions that require introspection. My most
complex thought as I dress for the day is how I'm going to stop my
stomach from grumbling.

To solve that dilemma, Alexus and I stroll downstairs, following
the aroma of a hearty breakfast. The prince is in a meeting, or so
we're told, while we're encouraged to dine to our hearts' content.

It's shocking that, in a residence of this size, so few people are
actually here. The staff, yes. But outside of them, there are those three
members of the Brotherhood we met last night and the prince—and
Alexus and I, of course. But that's all I've seen.

"In the past," Alexus says quietly when I inquire about this oddity,
"kings and queens used Shara as a summer home. Lots of hunting and
time outdoors, trips to Orr Valley, and baby making, but little else.
The rest of the year was typically spent at Min-Thuret."

"Is it weird?" I ask, prowling around the walls he keeps so well
erected. "Being here again?"

He shovels a bite of eggs into his mouth. "Weird enough. It mostly seems like I've never walked these halls. It's been so long, and so much has changed."

I know how he feels. Time has a way of eating memory. What I recall of the Western Drifts from three centuries ago seems like a vague and distant dream. Nothing about that time feels concrete anymore. Any familiarity is thanks to my recent visits to the archipelagos, as though my early years spent there never happened.

It isn't long before we're gathered from the dining hall by one of the staff and led to a grand office on the second floor. It's just me and Alexus, for now.

Curiosity seizes me instantly once our guide is gone, so I stroll by the massive desk positioned in front of a floor-to-ceiling arched window and consider digging around in its drawers. I know I should probably behave, lest I get caught, but the temptation is so strong. There's so much I want to know about the prince. Surely he hasn't hidden the truth about who he is from *everyone.*

While I'm weighing my chances and discreetly shuffling papers for a better view at their text, Alexus drifts around the outer walls where several framed portraits hang side by side.

"Who is he?" I ask when I notice him pause, shove his fists into his pockets, and stare at one portrait in particular. The man in the painting looks strong, proud, and stern. Broad shouldered and barrel chested. He's older, with short, graying hair, and by his attire, it appears he's royalty. They all are.

"This would be the infamous King Gherahn," Alexus says.

I stop my rifling, sensing the weight of the moment, and walk over to stand at his side. With a spiteful eye, I study the man who probably hated Colden Moeshka the Soldier as much as Neri did.

"So *this* is the bastard who made your life miserable and who probably wished me dead more than a few times," I say.

"The one and only."

Alexus's expression is hard, his gaze distant, lost in an attempt at recollection, as it has often been since we arrived on the Eastland shores.

I open my mouth, to say what, I'm not sure. What is there to say to someone who's staring into the eyes of a villain from their past? A villain who ripped them from their family and changed the course of their entire life, memorialized in portrait, like a regal, just leader?

Before I can think of any words to utter to my friend, the prince enters the room, followed by his three *advisors*. Dressed in riding gear and another fine, green jacket, he looks a little tense, his hand wrapped tightly around a scroll sheathed in a bronze casement.

He pauses and inclines his head in our direction, glancing quickly at Gherahn's painting. "Good morning, Colden. Alexus. I hope you both rested well." He holds up the casement. "I have King Regner's original treaty. As I told Colden last night, I'll sign the agreement just like my predecessor. I simply wanted the pair of you to witness the occasion."

Alexus and I share a glance. This is what we crossed the Malorian Sea for, the assurance that this treaty, which has protected our land for so long, will remain.

It's over and done within minutes, much to my satisfaction. It is indeed the same document I signed so many years ago. I do, however, find it interesting and more than usual that the prince's signature, though written with the most elegant penmanship, reads: *The Prince of the East.*

The prince re-rolls the parchment and slips it back inside the casement before handing it over to one of the men from the Brotherhood. Then, his attention falls solely on me.

I think back to when I exited the carriage and realize this is something about him I think I love. The way he can make me feel like the only other person in existence.

No one ever looks at me that way.

"I thought you might enjoy a ride through the countryside," he says, his face bright, any previous tension having vanished. "I've already had the groomsmen prepare the horses, if so."

Alexus rests his meaty arm across my shoulders and displays a rare grin. "We'd love that, actually. We'll change into our riding boots."

Disappointment freezes the prince's smile. I feel it, too, having thought for a brief moment that we might have more time alone, excited at the prospect, though also a bit uneasy after all those *feelings* last night.

"I still don't trust him," Alexus says as we walk down the corridor toward our rooms. "There's just something about him. He's almost *too* good. *Too* innocent. To be an Eastland ruler, that is."

"And you don't think I can take care of myself? I doubt those Brotherhood bastards will ride with us, so if the prince tried anything at all, I could turn him into an icicle in a matter of seconds. You and your brawn and dagger aren't needed, my friend."

He doesn't listen, though. Together, with the prince, we head down to the stables, and together, with the prince, we head out across the open landscape on horseback. It's a beautiful day, and a beautiful ride, filled with exploration and a few stops, including lunch on a blanket by a stream that could've been much more enjoyable had Alexus stayed at the palace.

The next few days are much like this one. We wake, eat, and then the prince takes us both on excursions into various parts of Vale. We go for a day-long hunt in a nearby forest and visit the village and its many fine shops. We even ride over to a nearby settlement where the blacksmith and tanner are said to be the best in the land. The prince gifts each of us with daggers made to our specifications and fur-lined leather coats to take home for the coming winter. The people are friendly and steeped in Eastland traditions.

Our evenings are spent dining on the best food and wine I've ever tasted, including meat from our hunt—though the prince still hardly eats—followed by drinks in the parlor. Alexus relaxes enough to tell a few of our more interesting tales, keeping the prince thoroughly enthralled and entertained.

With each hour I spend in the prince's presence, I care less and less that I know so little about his past or that he has no name, at least one he doesn't want to share. I *like* him. His demeanor. His voice. His smile. His laugh. The way he walks. The way his hands look when fisting his horse's reins. The way his strong back flares when he pulls a bow. The way he interacts with his people. There isn't anything thus far that I *haven't* liked, and I don't know how to feel about that.

Typically, when I have stirrings for another person—*physical* stirrings—it's short-lived. Something always ends up irritating me, whether it be neediness, or true insight to their character, or a clinging personality. It varies. But no one is perfect. No one ever even feels like they *might* be perfect. Not even close.

Until now.

The most imperfect thing about the prince is that he rules the Eastland Territories.

On our fifth and last night at Shara Palace, I stop Alexus before we go down for dinner.

"I'd like some time alone with the prince tonight if you could so kindly make your exit at an opportune time."

He crosses his arms over his chest and stares at me with that smirk of his. "I knew this was coming."

"You did not."

"I did. You can't help yourself."

"I want a kiss, that's all. Nothing more. I'll be satisfied with just that."

He cocks a brow. "We leave first thing tomorrow morning. What good will come of a kiss now? Temporary, remember?"

I throw up my hands. "How can I possibly forget when you keep reminding me? I'm fully aware nothing can come of this, Alexus, but it doesn't *have* to. For some of us, something is better than nothing. To feel some spark of closeness and attraction and desire. You manage to shut that out, but I can't. I have become the man I am because of the connections I can still forge with other people. I *love* sex. And I *love* kissing. And flirting. And teasing. And all manner of things you never do. It makes me feel alive and more human than the undying *thing* I am." I grab his black lapels, and after a few moments of deep breathing, I smooth them and lower my voice. "Please, just make yourself scarce tonight so I can have this one small memory to carry home."

He reaches up to hold my wrists. "I don't want to see you get hurt, Colden. That's all. The physical things you just mentioned are understandable and normal. But I haven't seen you look at anyone the way you look at the prince. It worries me that you're going to leave here a torn man with a torn heart."

I scoff and lower my hands. "Never. My heart is not involved, you should know that by now." I wink. "But other body parts are completely in play."

He huffs a small laugh. "You're impossible."

"I very much am. I'm also persistent." I bat my lashes at him. "Will you please leave me alone with my prince tonight?"

He shakes his head. "As bad of an idea as I think it is, yes. I will vanish at just the right time."

I smile, glad that I'm finally getting a chance to do what I wanted from the first moment I saw the prince: steal a kiss.

4

COLDEN

Alexus doesn't let me down.

We share an early dinner with the prince and his council in order to allow more time to rest for our coming travels. Afterward, the prince offers a last, short stroll of the gardens, inviting *both* Alexus and I, as he's become accustomed to my friend tagging along.

Thankfully, just as we step onto the veranda that spans the length of the palace, Alexus asks to be excused for the night, stretching the fakest yawn I have ever seen. The prince, of course, dismisses him, wishing him a good night.

Finally, we're alone.

"I'd love to show you the rooftop if you're willing," the prince says. "We've been blessed with such perfect weather during your stay. It would be a shame to not show you the sunset from the top of Shara."

"I am *more* than willing," I reply with a quirk of my lips. "Lead the way, Your Majesty."

By the time we reach the rooftop, the sun is already halfway set, warming the sky in shades of deep orange, pink, purple, and red. The prince strolls to the balustrade and stares out over the land.

"Beautiful, isn't it?"

"Stunning."

My eyes should be glued to the mesmerizing scene, but I can't help glancing around. The roof is covered with stone pots and trellises overflowing with fragrant roses and lit with ornate metal and glass lanterns. But the most interesting part of the decor is the double loungers lined up side by side. Four, in fact. Covered in soft cushions. For sunset viewing parties, I suppose.

I head to the nearest one, wine glass in hand, and take a seat, propping my feet up, crossing them at the ankles.

The prince turns around, an instant smile lighting his face as I sip my wine. "Can I join you?"

Mmm. His voice. It falls a shade deeper when we're alone. Smoother. Like honeyed whisky.

I pat the cushion beside me. "I would be quite sad if you didn't."

A bolt of excitement races up my spine when he takes his seat next to me, his body mere inches from mine. I can feel his heat, smell the lavender and vanilla on his skin and in his hair.

We stare at the sun-painted sky in silence for a while, and I make myself focus and soak in the warmth. I will ache for this sort of heat soon. I ache for it often, though more so when winter comes.

As the colors fade from the horizon and the sky grows dim, the prince suddenly says, "Does the perfect king have a perfect queen?"

It's such an unexpected question that I blink over at him, sure I heard him wrong. "Pardon?"

He laughs. "Does the perfect *king* have a perfect *queen*? Or *king*? I'm only inquiring, like you did."

"No," I answer, probably far too quickly. "No queen. No king, either. No one."

He bobs his head, as though deep in thought. "Interesting. I found myself wondering. About you and Alexus, mainly."

"Oh, gods, no. We're *very* close." I pause, trying to figure out how to describe what we share. I settle on, "As close as two friends can possibly be. But we're just that. Friends."

"Truly? He's awfully protective of you to only be a friend."

I shrug. "He sees it as his duty to protect his king." *And to make sure I live so he lives as well.* "He drives me mad sometimes, though his heart is in the right place. But again, no. We aren't lovers if that's what you're asking."

Not really. Another topic that's far too complex to truly explain.

With darkness falling around us, I meet his glittering eyes. "I was hoping that would be your answer," he says. His face suddenly morphs, a bit more serious. "I've worried about it all week. From the moment I first saw you step out of the carriage."

My brows rise of their own volition. "Is that so? And here I thought you hardly noticed me, all while I was ogling your ass from every angle."

He laughs, but then he meets my eyes, and everything about his expression sets my blood on fire. "Oh, I noticed you. Surely you could tell. I've hardly looked away from you this entire week." His gaze travels over me, intimate as a touch. "You're quite possibly the most beautiful man I've ever seen. I'd be lying if I said I didn't want to see more."

I swallow hard, my pulse beginning to pound. "Careful, now, Your Majesty. I wouldn't advise flirting with me, unless you like kissing boys, because I've struggled all week as well, and I'm about two seconds away from—"

Before I can register what's happening, the prince leans forward and crushes his mouth to mine. Blindsided, it takes several moments to make my brain work, for my head to tilt the right way, my lips to soften and part for his eager tongue. But then it's over, those first awkward seconds of learning the tempo and shape of our kiss.

And it is divine.

The prince's hand slips into my hair, gripping the roots, and I cup his face, my wine glass forgotten. This kiss is a heady thing, more than I imagined it would be, everything about his mouth tempting me.

We kiss like two starved animals, sucking and biting and licking. I could stay right here, just like this, for eternity. The feel of his plump lips held between mine is that delicious. That perfect.

The wildness between us changes, though. The desperate hunger eases, just enough that our kiss turns softer. Deeper. Slower. An exploration. A tasting. I am utterly lost to it, this divine kiss, a kiss that feels like all that beautiful light earlier, bright and shining and warm, cascading through every part of me.

I turn my body toward his for more contact, and suddenly he presses closer. His hands are everywhere, sliding under my tunic to caress my naked skin, brushing across my nipple, then dragging down, down, down, trailing the length of my thigh before cupping the curve of my ass.

Unable to stop myself, I grip his waist and tug him toward me, gasping into his mouth when I feel the ridge of his thick cock against my hip. It's bold, but I grab his hand and press his palm to my own erection, needing him to feel how much I want this. How much I want *him*.

He traces the outline of my cock, from my throbbing head to my tightening balls, squeezing me through my trousers until I exhale a sob of pleasure. With our mouths still connected, I flip him over, using the weight of my body to press him into the cushions. He spreads his legs to welcome me and whimpers when I rub my cock against his. I swear to the gods, that whimper is the sweetest sound I've ever heard.

I grip his hands and drag them over his head, deepening our kiss. When I pull back a little, he catches my mouth with his, keeping me from getting too far.

"Colden," he whispers, arching his hips toward mine, pressing his hardness against me once again. "Please," he says, grinding. "I'm begging you."

Please. Gods, that one word undoes me.

Everything changes again, and for the final time, because as we kiss, I feel myself being absorbed, feel my mind and body becoming lost to the wonder and mystery of this man. There's a neediness inside me that wants to crawl inside the prince and never come out. Because he just *feels* right. Like *these* are the lips I'm meant to kiss. Like *this* is the body I'm meant to hold. Like *his* is the heart I'm meant to know better than any other. It's overwhelming and soul-rattling to feel all this for someone whose name I don't even know.

Finally, I free his hands and draw away, groaning as he sucks my lower lip, only letting go when I'm hovered above him.

"Tell me your name." My voice is ragged. Breathy. "Tell me what I can call you. I'll speak it only to you. Only tonight if that's what you wish." I lean down and kiss him again, threading my fingers with his. "I want your name on my tongue."

He stares up at me with those beautiful hazel eyes, but I swear they darken, that a shadow of sudden horror passes over them. He starts to speak but says nothing, as though he can't. He seems confused, gaze darting, like he heard something that shook him, enough that the heat between us grows exquisitely cold.

And just like that, I feel shut out, as though he's emptied his mind of me.

Like a startled animal, he pushes me away and scurries out from beneath me. I watch him half-stumble to the balustrade, catching himself with his hands pressed to the stone railing. His back expands and falls several times with deep breaths, and he rakes those long fingers through that raven hair over and over.

When he finally faces me, his lips are still wet and swollen, his clothes rumpled, his hair tousled, and I just want him to come back to me, to let me take him the way I know he desires. I open my mouth to call to him, but I'm quickly reminded that I still don't have his name.

"This went too far." He scrubs his fingers over his mouth, as if to scrub away our kiss. "I'm sorry, Colden. I shouldn't have—"

"Yes, you fucking well *should* have." I crawl off the lounger and stand on weak legs, my heart still pounding, my cock still hard. "You *know* you should have." He stiffens when I come toward him, so I stop, hating that this is the turn things have taken. "I don't understand. That was nothing short of amazing. What was to come would surely have been even better. Yet you act like I tossed a cold bucket of water in your face, all by simply asking for your name. Is it so terrible, your name? So awful that sharing it with me will make me want you less? Because I can assure you that wouldn't be the case."

He takes another deep breath. Lets it out. "It wasn't that. I simply realized that you are the king of the North, and I am the prince of the East, and the last thing we need to do is…is…"

"Fuck?" I supply, taking a step closer. "Or make love?" I ask in a softer tone.

Because that's where things were headed. I know because I'm quite comfortable with mindless, heartless, passionless *fucking*. And what we were about to do was not that. It was something more. Something special. Something wonderful. I can't believe I can even entertain that idea, that I could make love to a man I hardly know, but it's true.

He holds up a hand. "Stop. Stop everything. I lost my head tonight, that's all. I'm very sorry, but it's best if we just pretend this never happened."

I rest my hands on my hips, incapable of doing anything but staring at him, openly affronted. "It didn't have to end this way. No matter what our titles read. However, if you can walk away from that —" I gesture to the lounger "—so easily, then perhaps it really is for the best that we go our separate ways. Because I deserve better than to be with someone who makes me feel forgettable."

"Colden!" he calls as I turn to go.

But I don't turn around. I keep walking until I'm in the stairwell on my floor.

Then alone in my bedchambers. Only once I'm in seclusion do I let out my frustration, punching the helpless new mattress until my arm muscles burn from the effort.

Finally, I fall back on the bed, despising the way I feel. Rejected. Unwanted. Unloved. It's stupid, really, that a man who hides his identity from the world could make me feel this way after *one* kiss. That he could make me feel anything at all.

I strip off my clothes, scrub the scent of him from my skin and his taste from my mouth, and then I climb into bed and stare at the canopy, one word repeating in my head.

Temporary. This is only *temporary*.

The want. The ache. The hurt.

All of it.

Temporary.

5

COLDEN

"How did it go?" Alexus asks the next morning.

He stands in my room, closing the door behind two of the prince's staff who are currently carrying our bags downstairs to the waiting carriage.

"Did you get the kiss you wanted or not?" He glances over the chambers, looking for evidence of a night that never happened.

I grab my jacket from the bed and stand before the floor-length mirror as I slip into the garment. "I did. And it was enough."

More than enough. Too much. I regret every second of ridiculous yearning I felt on the prince's account.

Eyes narrowing, Alexus leans against the bedpost, watching me straighten the ruffles of my shirt cuffs. "What, it wasn't all you dreamed?"

I glare at him through the mirror and change the subject. "Can we eat now? I'm famished." He smirks as I turn and stalk past him, opening the door. "Stop looking at me like that. Now are you coming, or am I leaving you here?"

He faces me with a look I loathe, the big brute. I hate how easily he reads me. I cannot lie to this man. He *feels* the truth.

That doesn't mean I don't try.

"Are you all right?" he asks tenderly as he stops before me in the doorway. "Because you don't seem all right."

"I'm fine." I lift my chin, my pride getting the best of me. "Just tired, hungry, and ready to be anywhere but here."

"Colden." His voice drops. "If the prince was the man for you, he'd be cradling your heart right now instead of being the one who cracked its fragile layers, which I know is what happened. I heard you come back to your room last night. Sometimes we want things that simply aren't good for us, and we have to love ourselves enough to walk away."

I raise my brows and sweep my arm into the hallway. "I'm *trying* to walk away, and you won't let me. Can we *please* go eat now so we can *leave?*"

It takes a few moments for him to give up, but finally, with a shake of his head, he exits my chambers, and I follow him downstairs. I held no worry that the prince would be waiting. I knew the moment I woke that I'd already seen him for the last time.

Alexus and I dine alone, in fact, save for the staff and one member of the Brotherhood who comes to offer the prince's apologies for his absence. He suddenly isn't feeling well, it seems.

"Do you want to go find him?" Alexus says as we walk to the carriage. "Do you want *me* to go find him? I can absolutely make him regret this."

I stop and face my old friend, a man who cares for me more than probably anyone. "I really don't want to see him. Nothing can fix what happened between us last night, and I don't want to pretend that it can. I just want to go."

He claps me on the shoulder and squeezes. "All right. Let's get the fuck out of here, then."

I hate myself when the carriage finally pulls away, because I look back, only to see the prince bursting out the main doors of the palace. He's still wearing his clothes from last night, his shirt unbuttoned, his feet bare.

Alexus looks at me. "I can tell the driver to turn around."

For a long moment, I watch the prince, his chest heaving as he stands in the middle of the courtyard. I think about what could possibly change if we tried to talk. *Nothing* would change, even if he begged for my forgiveness. I feel something he doesn't, or he feels something which he refuses to acknowledge. We don't have any more time to figure it out.

With one last look at him, I sit back in my seat. "No turning around. It's over."

Alexus nods, squeezes my knee, and settles in for the long trip to Quezira, then Mishan, then the Malorian Sea and Malgros. With every day of travel through the Territories, the stinging emotion that gripped me during my days with the prince lessens, though I can't shake free of him entirely, and at times I wonder if I will ever be free of him at all.

❦

It's nearly three weeks before we reach Mishan's ports. Alexus and I walk toward the ship that will carry us to the Northland Break, its deck alive with busy sailors, their suntanned skin glistening in the summer sun.

Alexus nudges me with his shoulder and eyes the ship. "All of this will pass, my friend. I'd bet a bag of silvers that you'll have forgotten all about the prince with no name by the time we reach Winterhold."

I sense what he's hinting at, that a ship full of rough and rugged men will wipe my mind clear of the lovely face that won't leave my thoughts. But that isn't going to happen. I already know as much. There's a melancholy spirit inside me that I don't care for in the least, but for now, I can do no more than endure it.

Resigned, I watch the Eastland Territories fade from sight as we sail from its royal harbor toward home.

This will *pass,* I remind myself.

It's only temporary.

Because it was just a kiss, one I'm certain I will soon forget.

SOMETHING WONDERFUL
AN ALTERNATE ENDING

Alexus doesn't let me down.

We share an early dinner with the prince and his council in order to allow more time to rest for our coming travels. Afterward, the prince offers a last, short stroll of the gardens, inviting *both* Alexus and I, as he's become accustomed to my friend tagging along.

Thankfully, just as we step onto the veranda that spans the length of the palace, Alexus asks to be excused for the night, stretching the fakest yawn I have ever seen. The prince, of course, dismisses him, wishing him a good night.

Finally, we're alone.

"I'd love to show you the rooftop if you're willing," the prince says. "We've been blessed with such wonderful weather during your stay. It would be a shame to not show you the sunset from the top of Shara."

"I am *more* than willing," I reply with a quirk of my lips. "Lead the way, Your Majesty."

By the time we reach the rooftop, the sun is already halfway set, warming the sky in shades of deep orange, pink, purple, and red. The prince strolls to the balustrade and stares out over the land.

"Beautiful, isn't it?"

"Stunning."

My eyes should be glued to the mesmerizing scene, but I can't help glancing around. The roof is covered with stone pots and trellises overflowing with fragrant roses and lit with ornate metal and glass lanterns. But the most interesting part of the decor is the double loungers lined up side by side. Four, in fact. Covered in soft cushions. For sunset viewing parties, I suppose.

I head to the nearest one, wine glass in hand, and take a seat, propping my feet up, crossing them at the ankles.

The prince turns around, an instant smile lighting his face as I sip my wine. "Can I join you?"

Mmm. His voice. It falls a shade deeper when we're alone. Smoother. Like honeyed whisky.

I pat the cushion beside me. "I would be quite sad if you didn't."

A bolt of excitement races up my spine when he takes his seat next to me, his body mere inches from mine. I can feel his heat, smell the lavender and vanilla on his skin and in his hair.

We stare at the sun-painted sky in silence for a while, and I make myself focus and soak in the warmth. I will ache for this sort of heat soon. I ache for it often, though more so when winter comes.

As the colors fade from the horizon and the sky grows dim, the prince suddenly says, "Does the perfect king have a perfect queen?"

It's such an unexpected question that I blink over at him, sure I heard him wrong. "Pardon?"

He laughs. "Does the perfect *king* have a perfect *queen*? Or *king*? I'm only inquiring, like you did."

"No," I answer, probably far too quickly. "No queen. No king, either. No one."

He bobs his head, as though deep in thought. "Interesting. I found myself wondering. About you and Alexus, mainly."

"Oh, gods, no. We're *very* close." I pause, trying to figure out how to describe what we share. I settle on, "As close as two friends can possibly be. But we're just that. Friends."

"Truly? He's awfully protective of you to only be a friend."

I shrug. "He sees it as his duty, to protect his king." *And to make sure I live so he lives as well.* "He drives me mad sometimes, though his heart is in the right place. But again, no. We aren't lovers if that's what you're asking."

Another topic that's far too complex to truly explain.

With darkness falling around us, I meet his glittering eyes. "I was hoping that would be your answer," he says. His face suddenly morphs, a bit more serious. "I've worried over it all week. From the moment I first saw you step out of the carriage."

My brows rise of their own volition. "Is that so? And here I thought you hardly noticed me, all while I was ogling your ass from every angle."

He laughs, but then he meets my eyes, and everything about his expression sets my blood on fire. "Oh, I noticed you. Surely you could tell? I've hardly looked away from you this entire week." His gaze travels over me, intimate as a touch. "You're quite possibly the most beautiful man I've ever seen. I'd be lying if I said I didn't want to see more."

I swallow hard, my pulse beginning to pound. "Careful, now, Your Majesty. I wouldn't advise flirting with me, unless you like kissing boys, because I've struggled all week as well, and I'm about two seconds away from—"

Before I can register what's happening, the prince leans forward and crushes his mouth to mine. Blindsided, it takes several moments to make my brain work, for my head to tilt the right way, my lips to soften and part for his eager tongue. But then it's over, those first awkward seconds of learning the tempo and shape of our kiss.

And it is divine.

The prince's hand slips into my hair, gripping the roots, and I cup his face, my wine glass forgotten. This kiss is a heady thing, more than I imagined it would be, everything about his mouth tempting me.

We kiss like two starved animals, sucking and biting and licking. I could stay right here, just like this, for eternity. The feel of his plump lips held between mine is that delicious. That perfect.

The wildness between us changes, though. The desperate hunger eases, just enough that our kiss turns softer. Deeper. Slower. An exploration. A tasting. I am utterly lost to it, this divine kiss, a kiss that feels like all that beautiful light earlier, bright and shining and warm, cascading through every part of me.

I turn my body toward his for more contact, and suddenly he presses closer. His hands are everywhere, sliding under my tunic to caress my naked skin, brushing across my nipple, then dragging down, down, down, trailing the length of my thigh before cupping the curve of my ass.

Unable to stop myself, I grip his waist and tug him toward me, gasping into his mouth when I feel the ridge of his thick cock against my hip. It's bold, but I grab his hand and press his palm to my own erection, needing him to feel how much I want this. How much I want *him*.

He traces the outline of my cock, from my throbbing head to my tightening balls, squeezing me through my trousers until I exhale a sob of pleasure. With our mouths still connected, I flip him over, using the weight of my body to press him into the cushions. He spreads his legs to welcome me and whimpers when I rub my cock against his. I swear to the gods, that whimper is the sweetest sound I've ever heard.

I grip his hands and drag them over his head, deepening our kiss. When I pull back a little, he catches my mouth with his, keeping me from getting too far.

"Colden," he whispers, arching his hips toward mine, pressing his hardness against me once again. "Please," he says, grinding. "I'm begging you."

Please. Gods, that one word undoes me.

Everything changes again, because as we kiss, I feel myself being absorbed, feel my mind and body becoming lost to the wonder and mystery of this man. There's a neediness inside me that wants to crawl inside the prince and never come out. Because he just *feels* right. Like *these* are the lips I'm meant to kiss. Like *this* is the body I'm meant to hold. Like *his* is the heart I'm meant to know better than any other. It's overwhelming and soul-rattling to feel all this for someone whose name I don't even know.

Finally, I free his hands and draw away, groaning as he sucks my lower lip, only letting go when I'm hovered above him.

"Tell me your name." My voice is ragged. Breathy. "Tell me what I can call you. I'll speak it only to you. Only tonight if that's what you wish." I lean down and kiss him again, threading my fingers with his. "I want your name on my tongue."

He stares up at me with those beautiful hazel eyes, but I swear they darken, that a shadow passes over them. "I can't give it to you, Colden." His voice sounds sad. Broken. "I can't, because I don't know it."

"What?" I pull back even more, something in his tone tugging at my heart. "You don't know your *name?*"

He shakes his head, his eyes growing glassy. "I've never known it. Not that I can remember."

If he were anyone else, I'd call him a liar. But I sense no untruth in his words. Nothing but honest pain. Pain that he's feeling for *me.*

"Then I'll call you my prince," I whisper, tracing his cheekbone with my fingertip. "And that will be enough."

I feel him relax beneath me, his body welcoming me once more, even more so than before. He slides his hands up my back, feeling the curve of muscle, the divots of my spine, the jut of my shoulder blades.

Then he whispers, "Come here," and draws me down into another kiss.

In moments, all worries about my prince's name are forgotten, and I'm entranced by the inescapable gravity of him. He wraps a leg around mine and buries his hands in my hair, and I melt into him, trailing my kiss to his chiseled jaw, the shell of his ear, the long column of his throat, until he moans and murmurs my name like a prayer.

But it isn't enough. I need his skin on mine.

"Please take your shirt off," I beg him as I strip free of my own. I don't know if anyone will venture this way, and I can't say I care.

He fiddles with the row of endless buttons on his tunic until I reach down and give one side a hearty yank, sending pearls clattering across the rooftop.

"That was my favorite shirt," he says with laughter in his chest, even as he rises on his elbows and hurries out of the garment.

"I'll send you another," I whisper into his neck, pushing him back down, dragging my teeth along the muscle that stretches to his rounded shoulder, just to hear him moan once more.

Gods, if his hands explored me before, it was nothing compared to now. His warm palms smooth over my shoulders and down my arms, squeeze my chest and travel the length of my abdomen. He slides his hands over my ass again, pulling me closer, his strong fingers kneading, making me dizzy with more want than I know what to do with.

"May I put my mouth on you? Please?" I say against his ear as I reach between us and grip his cock. "Right here."

He shivers and drags his thumb across my lips, his voice suddenly ragged. "Yes, Colden. *Yes.*"

I take my time moving down his body, sucking his nipples into my mouth and licking every ridge of muscle along the plane of his stomach. There isn't an inch of him that isn't as beautiful as I knew it would be, including his cock. When I free him from his trousers, he's so hard, his soft skin seemingly straining to impossible lengths to contain his need.

Wanting to remember this—to capture this night in every way I can—I breathe him in, all sweet musk and salty skin. Then I grip him at the base and lower my head to finally taste him.

Just like when our lips first touched, there are moments of acclimation, long seconds when I have to remember what it is to feel a cock, heavy and thick and throbbing, stretching my mouth. But after those few seconds, I settle in, determined to shatter the prince's world with the flick of my tongue.

Hungry, I take him deeper, drawing sweet groans and gasps from his lips. His hands are fisted in the cushions, his chest rising and falling fast, his eyes on every single thing I'm doing. He looks bewildered. Maybe even a little drunk, though I know he had only one glass of wine tonight.

Stroking him, I drag my mouth off him, though not before one last tease of my tongue along the slit at his tip. "Is this all right?"

He blinks and shakes his head around a panted breath. "What?"

I can't help but laugh. "Is this *all right*? You look...rather disoriented."

He smiles. A bliss-drunk smile. "I just can't think when you're touching me. Much less when you're doing *this*. That's all."

"But you want me to continue?"

"Gods, yes," he says in earnest. "If you stop, I might implode and die right here."

So I don't stop. Not when he's begging me for mercy, nor when his fingers tighten in my hair, nor when he warns me that he's going to come. I keep the friction moving, my hand pumping at his base, my mouth sliding up and down the first few inches of his thick length, urging him to just let go.

When he does, he's shockingly quiet, as though all the air has been sucked from his lungs. With his mouth formed around a frozen gasp, he looks down at me with wonder shining in his eyes as I swallow every drop he has to offer. His abdomen is impossibly tight and rippling, his chest glistening with a sheen of sweat and flushing pink as his body convulses from the delicious pleasure coursing through him.

Watching him—tasting him—makes me ache, the heaviness of my own cock suddenly unbearable between my legs. I free myself, and with a wipe of my hand across my mouth, climb back up his suddenly languid body and kiss him as he tries to catch his breath.

There's a crash of heat and want inside me, the feel of him—his hot skin, his strong frame, his softening cock—suddenly too much to stand. He doesn't make me beg for anything, though. As if reading my mind, he turns me over, bearing me into the cushions, and spreads my legs, settling between them.

His mouth is warm and wet and utterly everything I could possibly need in this moment and more. Because the sight of his adoring eyes and that hungry mouth taking me deeper into his throat is like a punch to the chest, a kick straight to my cold heart.

"Oh, my prince," I mutter, my words strangled, my hands guiding his head. "That's it. So good. Gods—"

I hiss and toss my head back as he works his tongue expertly across my tip. What I feel is desire, yes. Aching. Longing. Yearning. But it's also so much more. My prince is on his knees, giving me everything within him, holding back nothing, not even a truth no one else possesses but me.

He wrings more pleasure from my body than I have ever known, teasing me in a place I did not expect him to touch, his finger pressing on that sensitive spot inside that makes every single star in the sky seem like they're falling.

Like him only minutes before, I can't think around what he's doing to me, the liquid heat of my release building and coiling around the base of my spine, tightening in my groin. I feel like I could shout or cry or possibly both, at the same time. The sensations stirring inside me are far too overwhelming to control their outlet.

And he knows exactly the effect he's having on me. I see it in his eyes, in the easy way he tortures me, the satisfaction of an experienced lover who is fully aware they have complete control of the situation.

When I come, he watches. We both do. My head feels so light as each spasm of my orgasm sends a long spurt of cum across my stomach.

I swear to the gods, it's the longest orgasm I've ever had, one that, by the time it's over, feels like it stole my soul.

My prince kisses his way up my body. Deep, sucking kisses, drawing my flesh and my release into his mouth. It turns my bones to water, leaving me a pliant mess beneath him.

"We aren't finished," he whispers against my lips before kissing me. His warm body slides against mine.

"I'm all yours," I reply, threading my fingers with his. "As if that isn't obvious."

I taste his smile.

"Are you sure?" he says, true concern in his voice. "We have the entire night, and if you can, I mean, if you want to, I promise I will make it the most wonderful night of our lives."

I stare up into his hazel eyes, certain that he can do just that, and that I'll be a damned man after this. Damned to want the Prince of the East for the rest of my eternal days.

Then I give the only answer my body and heart will let me give.

"I'm sure. Positively."

With that, he gathers our strewn shirts and leads me downstairs to his chambers. Sometime later, when he lays me naked across his bed and pushes inside me, I know beyond a shadow of a doubt that I've never been more sure of anything in my life than I am of this. Of him.

Of us.

And to think, all I thought I wanted was a kiss.

The End

ACKNOWLEDGEMENTS

First and foremost, I want to send a huge and heartfelt THANK YOU to my Rebel Readers, especially my Patreon members. Without you, this book would not exist. Without you, these stories might have never seen the light of day. They would've stayed inside my head, and that would've been a shame.

My readers have stood by me through so much, and I hope this book shows a tiny sliver of the appreciation I feel for all you've done. The messages, social media posts, book signings, cards, letters, gifts… I love you all to the moon.

I must also give an enormous shout-out to my entertainment attorney, Maggie Marr. Without her wisdom, guidance, and encouragement, I would not be writing this acknowledgement. I also want to thank my assistant, Nicki, for always cheering me on and being so excited for this release. We've come a long way in a short time, and I can't wait to see where we go from here.

For those wondering, I plan to write more bonus scenes and novellas as we move into 2025, and to publish two more volumes like this one between 2025 and 2026. I have stories waiting that my precious Patrons asked for last year. They're coming! I promise!

Thank you again for reading and for loving these characters as much as I do! And thank you for your unfailing support.

ABOUT THE AUTHOR

 CHARISSA WEAKS is an award-winning Amazon Top 100 author of romantic and historical fantasy. She crafts stories with time travel, magick, myth, history, and the occasional apocalyptic quest. Her debut novel The WItch Collector—the first of five books planned in the Witch Walker series—earned a Best of BookTok flag and is published in several languages.

Charissa resides south of Nashville with her family and two English Bulldogs. When she's not writing, you can find her lost in a good book or digging through four-hundred-year-old texts for research.

For updates on Charissa's upcoming book releases and news, including Kingdom of the Forgotten, subscribe to her newsletter, follow her on Instagram, or join her Facebook group, Charissa's Rebel Readers.

Thank you for reading!

Made in United States
North Haven, CT
23 November 2024

60794735R00148